THE ALCHEMIST OF BRUSHSTROKES AND BRIMSTONE

AN ACCIDENTAL ALCHEMIST MYSTERY
BOOK EIGHT

GIGI PANDIAN

GARGOYLE GIRL PRODUCTIONS

The Alchemist of Brushstrokes and Brimstone: An Accidental Alchemist Mystery

© 2024 by Gigi Pandian.

Gargoyle Girl Productions

First edition

Cover design by Gargoyle Girl Productions

Cover gargoyle illustration by Hugh D'Andrade/Jennifer Vaughn Artist Agent

Print ISBN: 978-1-938213-32-8

eBook ISBN: 978-1-938213-31-1

For Julia Motyka, whose audiobook narration brings the Accidental Alchemist Mysteries to life so brilliantly

From the Typewriter of Dorian Robert-Houdin

The Alchemist's Toolbox

The *Tria Prima*

1. Brimstone — also known as sulfur.
   Ruled by the sun. Represents fire.
   Warning: A highly combustible element.

2. Quicksilver — also known as mercury.
   Ruled by the moon. Represents curiosity.
   Warning: A deadly poison.

3. Salt*. No further linguistic clarification is needed.
   From both the earth and sea.
   No warning is necessary when working with salt. Neither flammable nor poisonous.
   *Salt is also an essential ingredient in good cooking. The best of all three essentials.

Dorian pulled the sheet of crisp white paper from his Underwood typewriter. Using a fountain pen from 1908, he scratched out the last line: *The best of all three essentials.*

It would not do to play favorites. It would not do at all. Alchemy was far too powerful a force to be out of alignment.

CHAPTER 1

A haunting shade of white illuminated the faces of the two people in the portrait. It wasn't the usual lead white pigment you'd expect from a painting from 1700. The artist had used quicksilver and brimstone to create this paint, and the color in the oil painting was as vibrant as it had been 300 years ago.

The *Brother and Sister* portrait is the most prized possession I own. That doesn't mean it's worth much, as old paintings go. It's only priceless to me because it's a portrait of me and my brother, Thomas, who died of the plague shortly after it was painted.

As far as the world knows, this humble painting is by an unknown artist. It isn't. I know exactly who painted it. But if I were to reveal the truth, nobody would believe me.

There was no reason for the *Brother and Sister* painting to be of much value to anyone besides me. Why, then, was an art collector desperate to get his hands on it? There was no way for him to know the truth. *Was there?*

The emails began two weeks ago. Friendly, at first. Then more aggressive.

English art collector Arthur Finder contacted my mentor, who had bought the painting for me last year from where it was gathering dust in a dark corner of a small family museum in France. The purchase wasn't a secret, and the painting wasn't famous or worth much. We never thought it would attract attention. Why, then, was a wealthy English lawyer willing to pay far more than the painting was worth, and angry when his offer was refused? Why *now*?

I stepped back and took in the framed work of art, trying to understand why the collector was pursuing this humble painting. Thankfully, he believed the painting was still somewhere in France, not across the world in my house in Portland, Oregon.

I looked more closely at the scene. Thomas and I were bathed in light from a side window of the French farmhouse. I loved the green dress I wore, and Thomas adored his simple wool waistcoat, though I always suspected that was because of the young woman who'd mended it for him. Familiar books and bottles lined a smooth wooden shelf behind us. I didn't recognize a thin parchment notebook that was tucked between thick glass jars of cinnabar and saltpeter. The smaller jar of rough, red cinnabar had a jagged crack from when a raging storm had blown open the window and toppled the inventory logbook from a high shelf, knocking over two hand-blown jars as it fell. Strange, the details one remembered. I wondered why I'd forgotten the beautiful little notebook nestled between those jars.

The portrait was a beautiful work of art. But beauty alone isn't enough to create value.

Perhaps the collector was an art forger. Not that art forgers are nearly as common as pop culture would have you believe. But if an old canvas was his goal, an earlier Renaissance era canvas would be more enticing.

Or maybe it was because the unusual pigments hadn't lost their vibrancy over the centuries. Not even the greens—a color family notorious for turning a muddy brown when exposed to light—had faded. But that couldn't be it. There were plenty of paintings kept out of sunlight that hadn't deteriorated much.

Brother and Sister, artist unknown, France, circa 1700. That's what the small family museum in France had written on a placard, because nobody knew the truth about who painted it.

Well, as I mentioned, I shouldn't say *nobody.*

"Zoe," my boyfriend Max called from upstairs, interrupting my thoughts. "I need some moral support here."

"He is attempting to cheat," a second voice called, this one with a French accent.

"You know that's not true." Max's voice was barely audible now, as he was no longer attempting to be heard halfway across the house.

After one last glance at Thomas's mischievous face, I stepped into the hallway and climbed the stairs to the attic, smiling to myself as I did so.

The art collector didn't know I existed. My mentor was careful not to mention me in his correspondence. I didn't need to worry. I could enjoy this life I'd fought hard to create, surrounded by loved ones. A life I'd never had before. Why did I always try to ruin it by worrying unnecessarily? I knew the answer, of course. I've survived for centuries by being cautious. Alchemists always have to be on guard.

I stepped into my high-ceilinged attic, a fully finished room stuffed to the gills with the antiques I sell to make a modest living.

In the cozy far corner of the attic, Max Liu and a gargoyle stared at each other across a chessboard. The pieces of this antique set were mechanical, so when you pushed a wooden knight's arm, its horse stood on its hind legs. But the queen was my favorite. She tipped her crown when you pressed the stone she stood upon. I didn't think it was just my imagination that the craftsman who'd carved the set had given her a mysterious Mona Lisa smile.

"It is Max's move," the gargoyle said to me in his thick French accent, never lifting his gaze from the board. He gave a salute-like flap of his wings and crossed his gray arms. "He picked up his queen, then claimed it was a mistake."

Max, for his part, was doing rather well for only having learned a few months ago that my friend Dorian is a gargoyle. Dorian tells people he's shy of being seen because of a deformity. But in truth, he was carved in limestone for Notre Dame Cathedral in Paris. That was, of course, before he was accidentally brought to life through alchemy.

The sight of Dorian's wings flapping still startled Max, but I'd say that for a man who'd reached his forties without knowing alchemy was more than a child's fantasy, he was handling the truth about me and Dorian remarkably well.

Max isn't a gargoyle. Or an alchemist. He's sexy, smart, and has exquisite taste in tea. He's a magnificent man all around. I still can't quite believe my luck that he loves me as passionately as I love him.

I'm Zoe Faust. Alchemist, herbalist, and small business owner of Elixir, an online antique shop. I used to run Elixir out of my Airstream trailer, and it's now based in the attic of this fixer-upper in Portland, Oregon's Hawthorne neighborhood that I bought almost two years ago. Even though I'm an alchemist, that doesn't mean I excel at making gold. I'm a plant alchemist, which is great for creating healing tinctures, but not so great for buying a house without a hole in its roof.

I discovered the Elixir of Life in 1704, when I was twenty-eight. Young, for an alchemical discovery, but I was obsessed with saving the life of my younger brother after he'd fallen ill. Desperate to believe my own efforts could save Thomas, I ignored the advice of my mentor who told me the unvarnished truth that I couldn't transfer the Elixir to someone else. Only dangerous backward alchemy could transfer the energy of life to another, but at a cost far too great. The corrupted form of alchemy involved dangerous short-cuts that took the energy of others instead of using their own purity of intent.

Max shook his head, but he was grinning at me as he did so. "You didn't warn me that Dorian was a chess master or that he would insist on the rules of a chess competition."

Dorian wriggled his horns. "I did not create the rules, *Monsieur Liu*. If you lift a piece, it means you have selected—"

"I'm the arbiter," I cut in. "You two are having a cup of tea and breakfast muffins in my attic, so my rules. Until a player sets a piece down in a new square, they can change their mind. Fair?"

"It is my attic as well," Dorian grumbled, "and I baked the carrot muffins." But after an audible sigh and a glance at the chessboard they'd been sitting in front of for half an hour, he gave Max a congenial nod.

Before they could decide what to disagree about next, the landline phone rang. I picked up the hefty black receiver of the antique phone in the attic.

"Good. You're still home."

The voice was that of my mentor, Nicolas Flamel. The man who bought the *Brother and Sister* painting for me. You might have heard of him, though I promise you he's nothing like historical references would have you believe. It's true that he's forgetful when it comes to shaving, but he's never had a long, bushy beard like the dowdy man in the most famous illustration of Nicolas Flamel in recorded history—which, I might add, someone sketched a century after he first faked his death.

"I'll be on my way in a few minutes," I answered. Nicolas and his wife Perenelle were expecting me to stop by with some marigolds harvested from my garden for Perenelle to turn into a natural dye, but I wanted to see how the chess game played out. Max and Dorian needed to wrap up shortly, since Max had to get to his shop, The Alchemy of Tea.

"I'm calling," said Nicolas, "so you *don't* leave."

"If you slept in and haven't eaten," I said, "I have plenty of extra carrot muffins I can bring—"

"No!" He uttered the word so forcefully that I was sure Max and Dorian would hear it.

Dorian's black eyes widened. He jumped up and scampered to my side, where he grabbed the receiver from me with his clawed, gray hand.

"You do me a disservice," Dorian huffed. "If you do not appreciate my muffin recipe, which I do believe is one of my finest creations, you have had ample opportunity to mention it."

I snatched the receiver back. "What's going on?"

"I fear it's best we do not communicate for a while."

I stared at the phone. "I'm coming over."

Nicolas sighed. "Perenelle was right that you'd insist. In that case, I only ask one small favor of you. Whatever you do, *make sure you aren't followed.*"

Of all the things I thought he might say, that wasn't one of them. I grabbed my silver raincoat and headed out the door.

CHAPTER 2

Acting as I imagined a spy would behave, it took me nearly an hour to arrive at the Flamels' house in the West Hills of Portland.

I'd covered my distinctive white hair with a knit cap before taking a bus to the train station, shoved my coat into my shoulder bag while in the middle of a crowd, and caught a taxi from the station.

I thanked the cab driver, who'd humored me about my request to let me know if we were being followed. He'd even stopped halfway up the winding road to the Flamels' house, making sure nobody had followed. They hadn't. I'd let Nicolas's imagination get the better of me.

The monster topiary originally cultivated on the hillside by the Flamels' neighbors now extended even farther down the road. I stepped onto the narrow road near a bush shaped to resemble a dragon. The creature stood as a guardian of the last turn before we reached the isolated house. Pebbles crunched underfoot as I walked the last stretch of the narrow road on my own, breathing in the earthy scent of freshly fallen autumn rain made even stronger by my boots trampling the bright red leaves of the dogwood trees.

As I turned into the private drive flanked by a flower-filled garden, the canopy of trees gave way. Now, the citrusy scent of the freshly harvested orange marigolds in the satchel at my side melded with the fragrant honey scent of the yellow woad flowers I passed.

This pigment garden high in the wind-swept hills boasted madder, woad, and weld, all grown from cuttings I'd taken in my own small garden, plus dozens more plants. The plants had grown strong in my garden, but here, they truly thrived. Soon, these innocuous plants poking out of the rich earth would be transformed into colors including a red as dark as blood, a yellow of unmatched warmth, and a vibrant blue with the intensity of a polished gemstone.

But far more impressive was a different force of nature in that garden. The wind caught hold of her long red curls and swirled the mane around her face. She turned when she heard me approaching. Her taut brow turned to a relaxed smile when she saw it was me.

"Zoe." Perenelle Flamel said my name with love, but also gravity. "You're certain you weren't followed?"

"Nicolas didn't need to be so dramatic." I reached her side, but I knew better than to offer to help her with a basket brimming with freshly picked flowers. "It's a consequence of his spending too much time with Dorian."

She set her basket down and placed her hands on my shoulders. "You need to be prepared. My dear husband *wasn't* being overly dramatic in this case."

I stiffened. "What do you—?"

"Come with me. You'll see." She didn't wait for me to reply, but in one sweeping gesture lifted the basket of flowers and beckoned me to follow her inside. Her long, azure skirt rustled as the hem swished over stone.

If Perenelle Flamel thought something was trouble, it undoubtedly was.

The sun peeked through the clouds above and shone on her strong and confident figure. A few steaks of silver cut through the red waves of her hair, looking more like fierce lightning bolts than a sign of aging. Perenelle appeared to be in her late forties, but I knew better. I first met her over 300 years ago, and she'd already been alive for many more.

I look like a woman in her late twenties who dyes her hair white to be fashionable, but it's really because I didn't get alchemy *quite* right. My hair continued to age beyond the age of twenty-eight. Alchemists who've found the Elixir of Life aren't supposed to age at all, but I've never claimed to be a well-rounded alchemist. I stumbled into alchemy accidentally, at first because of my skill with plants and then because of my love for Thomas.

As for Perenelle? Nothing about her is accidental. She's the sulfurous fire of alchemy embodied. She's left her mark on the world, even if you don't realize it. There's a good chance you might not have heard of her. She's not famous like her husband, the alchemist Nicolas Flamel. *But if the truth got out?* All that would change.

I followed Perenelle down the stone path leading to the house she and Nicolas had recently moved into. Before we reached the house, Nicolas swung open the wood and stained-glass front door. "I wish you hadn't come, but I can't say I'm sorry to see you."

Even though Perenelle had me worried, I couldn't help smiling at the sight of my brilliant mentor. His wild hair, the color of straw and ash, could never be tamed, but today it looked as if he'd walked through a cyclone. There was even a pointed twist on top.

Perenelle leaned against the door as she closed it behind us. "We owe Zoe an explanation."

"Quite," Nicolas said, his face grave. "But first, I need your assistance in finding my spectacles."

"Here they are, dear." Perenelle plucked his glasses from the top of his head, nearly hidden behind the pinnacle.

I'm serious about Nicolas being brilliant. But he's one of those clever people who are so focused on their latest curiosity that they can be absentminded when it comes to anything else.

"It's in here." Perenelle led us to her art and alchemy studio. "We were out at an art gallery reception at Elements Art House last night. When I came into my studio this morning, I found that my paintings had been moved."

"The thief," said Nicolas as he took the two baskets of flowers and set them in a shady corner, "doesn't appear to have taken anything."

"*Thief?*" I repeated as my heart rate skyrocketed. A theft is disturbing for anyone. For an alchemist, it's dangerous in countless ways. That's why Nicolas hadn't wanted to leave me holding anything I would have surely dropped. "Someone broke in?"

I spun around, looking for signs of destruction. No broken glass. No toppled furniture. Nothing that would suggest a random break-in for valuables. The problem was, nobody knew who the Flamels were. At least, nobody *should* have.

"Perenelle's paintings." I stepped to the rack where her newer paintings were drying. Oil paintings that looked so much like the work of artist Philippe Hayden, an artist of note 450 years ago, during the height of the Renaissance. Hayden had never reached the level of fame of Michelangelo or Rembrandt, but rose to prominence under Rudolf II's patronage in Prague, Bohemia, in the late 1500s and early 1600s.

"Nothing else was disturbed," Nicolas said. "*Which is the problem.*"

"You think it was Arthur Finder who did this? That he didn't take no for an answer?"

Nicolas scratched his chin, upon which gray stubble was forming. "I fear I have made a calculated error in replying to his last inquiry. You know I turned down his first two generous offers. To explain why I couldn't accept an offer, no matter how high, I revealed it was no longer mine to sell."

"He must not have believed it," said Perenelle. "He sent someone to check. I don't think they meant to be found out. They were as careful as they could be, but there's fresh sealant on the windowpane they removed to get into this room, and I know exactly where I left my paintings."

"But now they know you don't have the portrait," I said. "Which is why you wanted me to either stay away or to travel here like a spy."

The lines around Nicolas's eyes crinkled as he gave me a sad smile. "I'm so sorry to have put you both in danger through my unthinking reply."

"He's not giving up," said Perenelle. "I don't know why he wants the *Brother and Sister* painting."

"We can't let him have it." Nicolas's voice shook with emotion. He wasn't frightened for himself. I knew him well enough to know that.

"Do you think it's me he's after," Perenelle mused, "or Zoe?"

"This does not bode well for *either* of you."

He was right, of course. The only way for me to have this wonderful life here, surrounded by so many people I love, is because nobody knows who I or the Flamels really are.

"I know," I said, meeting his frightened ice-blue eyes. "Does he suspect the truth about Perenelle?"

The truth is that the artist the world knows as Philippe Hayden is, in reality, Perenelle Flamel, wife of the world-famous alchemist who supposedly died six centuries ago.

CHAPTER 3

"We'll figure it out," said Nicolas, taking Perenelle's hand in his. "Together."

He didn't say he'd protect her, which would have angered her more than the break-in. Perenelle and Nicolas were equal partners, and had been since a time centuries ago when such a thing was virtually unheard-of. Their unique strengths perfectly complemented one another—but in a most unusual way.

In alchemy, the final stage of the long alchemical process of transformation brings together the symbolic Red King and the White Queen, an alchemical marriage representing the dual nature of every step of alchemy that leads opposing forces to perfection. But in alchemy—as with the Flamels—nothing is quite as it seems.

The Red King is associated with a masculine energy, the sun, and the element of sulfur. The White Queen is the feminine principle, associated with the moon and the element of mercury.

Nicolas and Perenelle perfectly represent this duality, but they flipped around expectations. Red-headed Perenelle has a fiery energy that has propelled her around the world as a masterful painter who paints in the sunlight and can harness the elements into her artwork. Fair-haired Nicolas's mercurial curiosity led him to discover alchemy, and he devoured knowledge late into the night, reading by moonlight.

They are one and yet they are two. They are alchemy embodied and yet they are unique.

The third element, beyond sulfur and mercury, that's key to alchemy, is salt. I'm salt. It's the product of an alchemical union. It represents the body, and is made from the calculated ashes of plants. Salt represents me both because I'm a plant alchemist, and also because I'm the alchemical child of the Flamels. I'm not their child in the biological sense, but I'm their offspring in terms of how I came to alchemy.

"I'm not worried," said Perenelle as she picked up a single marigold from the basket at her feet. "Not about myself. I'm *angry*."

She plucked one of the bright petals. "You both know I never cared about receiving credit for my work. I only wanted the freedom of accessing the materials I needed to transform natural colors into pigments. I wanted to have the paintings shown publicly so people ready to understand alchemy could learn about it, not hidden away in a cellar as my first husband's family saw fit for the paintings of a woman."

She continued plucking petals, quicker and more forcefully now. "I don't want the world to know it's *me*, but it's infuriated me to learn that centuries later, while I was imprisoned and unaware of what was going on in the world, women artists were *still* being written out of history. Their work was still being attributed to the men around them—and that was only if they were fortunate enough to have the freedom to paint in the first place. I don't deny I wish it was possible for the world to know that Hayden was a woman, without revealing it's me. But I know that's a fantasy."

She shook her head as she squeezed the barren stem in her hand. She gasped as a fingernail broke the skin of her palm and a drop of blood appeared.

The physical pain shook her out of her revery, and she seemed stunned to be surrounded by a halo of golden marigold petals. I was already at her side with a clean cloth and a healing salve from my bag for the wound.

"I wish the world could know the truth as well," I said as I cleaned the cut. "I wish that was possible."

Perenelle waved aside the assistance for the trivial wound and took my hands in hers. "I shouldn't have worried you with my anger. It's *you* I'm concerned about. If he sees you with the painting..." She trailed off.

"He'll know," I said, "that I'm the woman in the painting."

Were they after Perenelle's secret, or mine? Which one of us was Arthur Finder after?

I groaned as the answer hit me.

"Arthur Finder." I looked from Perenelle to Nicolas. Both of their faces were blank. "Don't you see? Arthur Finder. *Art* Finder. A man who finds art. An *art finder.*"

"An alias!" cried Nicolas as Perenelle cursed under her breath. "How did I not see this before?"

"We *did* look him up," I said. "Whoever he is, he was thorough in setting up a law firm website." Arthur Finder didn't have an online presence beyond the site that oozed respectability. I'd assumed he was a cautious man, which made sense for someone representing the wealthy clients.

"His website must be fraudulent," said Perenelle.

"It's a good fake," I agreed, "just like he is. He's not a rich English lawyer like he claims."

And more importantly, now we had no idea who we were dealing with.

"Why does our fake Arthur Finder, whoever he really is, want the painting at all?" I asked. "It's not valuable monetarily, so does he want to expose us?"

The Flamels' old adversary, infamous alchemist Edward Kelley, was safely out of the way. He couldn't contact anyone from where he was imprisoned, so it couldn't be him seeking revenge.

"The world never believes what it's not ready to believe," Perenelle said. "I don't think this is about exposing us as alchemists. It's something else. Something we're not seeing."

She was right, of course. People only hear the stories they're ready for. Everything else is rationalized away. If I were to tell the people I meet that I'm nearly 350 years old, chances are they wouldn't believe me.

I wish that the world was ready to accept alchemy. Then, I wouldn't have to structure my life around hiding the truth about myself. Things have ended quite badly for alchemists who were believed. Held captive in dungeons to make gold for cruel monarchs or killed painfully for heresy. Most alchemists, however, aren't believed. They're either dismissed as eccentrics or find themselves subjected to psychiatric treatment.

I also occasionally wish that alchemy was truly magic. If that were true, I could simply touch my finger to the painting and hide the fact that I was the subject of a centuries-old painting and hide clues to its origins. Maybe I'd need a touch of brimstone and quicksilver on my fingertip, but sulfur and mercury were easy enough to obtain.

But alchemy *isn't* magic. It's simply a branch of science that's misunderstood: the art of transforming the impure into the pure.

That transformation can apply to the body, as seen in the Elixir of Life that stops the body from aging as well as the subtler transformations that turn plants into healing concoctions. It can also apply to the material world, as alchemy is known for transforming impure metals like lead into pure gold. Lesser-known areas of alchemy include mental and spiritual transformations, which is what most modern-day alchemists focus on.

Whatever the transformation, it takes time, effort, and intent. Years of practice, which can still result in nothing if your intent isn't pure. That's the part that modern science disagrees with: *intent* as an essential ingredient.

But neither of those fantasies is true. In present-day Portland, Oregon, I had to deal with reality. How did we deal with the reality of our disingenuous Arthur Finder? What was he ready to hear?

People only accepting what they're ready to hear is the reason famous Renaissance artist known to the world as Philippe Hayden is an enigma. There's no grand coverup, yet a conspiracy is easier to believe than the truth of alchemy existing.

Many art historians have theorized that Hayden was practicing alchemy, because of the subject matter of his paintings and the fact that he became a painter at the court of Rudolf II in Prague. Those historians have also postulated that Philippe's powerful contemporaries destroyed records of his life to hide his alchemical experiments. They lament that in the process of destroying his records of unsuccessful alchemical science, his unique paint recipes were also lost. Nobody believed that Hayden was a *true* alchemist who'd been alive for centuries. Until recently, people would have been even less likely to believe another truth about Hayden: the Renaissance painter who'd created such masterpieces was actually a woman.

Perenelle Flamel painted the *Brother and Sister* portrait when I was Nicolas's apprentice and Thomas and I lived with the Flamels in the French countryside. That was after she'd given up her public persona of Hayden. She'd realized the power she'd unleashed in the Court of Rudolf II in Bohemia—her ability to paint people themselves into canvas—was far too powerful for anyone to wield. Like the dangers of any combustible element, Perenelle's process of working with alchemical paint had great power, but also great risk. It had led to their imprisonment due to angry alchemist Edward Kelley seeking revenge. Edward was now safely locked away, but he'd escaped justice for centuries before we caught him.

After the Flamels were imprisoned, so much of the artwork at their home had been lost. We didn't know if the paintings had been destroyed or were sitting in dusty attics. But the painting of me and Thomas had ended up with a wealthy family in France who'd opened a small museum after the family fortunes began to fall.

"Maybe the world is ready," I said as my gaze fell to a powerful new painting hanging on the wall. One of Perenelle's new pieces. The still life of flowers was far more than it seemed. If you stood off to one side and looked closely at the petals, you would see arrows pointing to certain parts of the painting that contained alchemical secrets. Brushstrokes that swirled with proper proportions of sulfur and mercury.

"The world *isn't* ready for everyone to know about alchemy," Perenelle insisted. "Only those with purity of intent, and who are ready, will understand how to read my paintings."

"I don't mean the world is ready to know about alchemy." I pried my eyes from the painting. "Or that the artist the world knows as Philippe Hayden is alive today. But people are finally ready to believe that the paintings attributed to Hayden were created by a woman."

"Zoe is right," Nicolas chimed in. "There are now historians and organizations devoted to correctly attributing historical paintings to the women who were written out of history."

He led the way out of Perenelle's studio and back to the living room, to one precarious stack of art history books. With a whip of his wrist, he pulled out a book created for a museum exhibit on the subject of Florentine artwork that had previously been misattributed but was now being properly recognized.

I took the book and put it back on the top of the stack. "We're getting off track. *Why* is our Arthur Finder interested in the portrait of me and Thomas?"

My phone binged. I don't usually have notifications on, but I'd turned it on during my spy-craft today.

It was only a new message for my online shop, Elixir, so I was about to turn off notifications and slip it back into my bag, but before I could do so I glimpsed the subject line.

"There's *another* collector interested in the painting." I looked up from the screen, aware of the quiver in my voice.

There was no way anyone should have known I had the *Brother and Sister* painting. It was hanging on my bedroom wall, because I knew I couldn't display it, no matter how much I wanted to.

"This one," I said, "knows I have the painting."

CHAPTER 4

I read the message aloud to Nicolas and Perenelle.

Please forgive this message about a work of art that might not be in your antique shop's collection. But I'm hopeful that it might be a new piece you have not yet listed.

My name is Gwendolyn Graves. In my official capacity, I'm Dr. Graves, emeritus professor of art history at the University of Washington in Seattle.

I've dedicated my career to studying overlooked artists from history. I believe you might be in possession of a work of art that an unscrupulous art dealer is interested in.

Your website contact form doesn't enable attachments, so I'll describe the painting I'm interested in studying before it's lost to history.

It's an unattributed oil painting from the early eighteenth century, featuring a brother and sister by the hearth, their faces illuminated by sparkling sunlight. It was bought from the private Moreau Museum in France last year. The painting might be valuable, and, more importantly, shed light on a historical mystery.

I'm not interested in purchasing this painting, but in studying it. If I'm right, you can be part of solving a historical mystery—and make a fortune if you ever decide to sell.

"My goodness." Nicolas spun his glasses between his fingers. "Now an academic is involved."

"If this Graves woman is a professor at all." Perenelle snatched her husband's glasses from his hands and bent the wire temple tip back into place. "It's a good thing you know how to make your own gold, my dear. This is the third pair you've ruined this month."

"Spectacles used to be so much heartier!"

"I've heard of her," I said. "She's a well-known art history scholar." I pulled up her faculty webpage on my phone and showed it to them. "I'm emailing her back."

"Are you sure that's wise?" Nicolas asked.

"Someone above suspicion knows something about the painting," I insisted. "I'm not waiting around to see what 'Arthur Finder' is willing to do next."

~

Less an hour later, Professor Graves was on the train from Seattle to Portland.

She hadn't answered my question about why she thought I had the painting she was after, but replied that it was easier to talk in person and that she could be in Portland that afternoon.

That reply set off alarm bells, but surely a scholar with her reputation could be trusted. Right? To be sure, I spent my time before she arrived digging into her background.

Over more than five decades as a professor of art history, she'd built a reputation as a tireless advocate for overlooked artists, which is why I'd heard of her. She championed artists who'd been dismissed as 'serious' artists because of their gender, race, or economic status. Or worse, who'd had their artwork falsely credited to more 'respectable' men. As her career developed, she'd come to focus on Western art, specifically Florence, Prague, and Antwerp during the

20

Renaissance. I knew the work of some of the artists whose work she helped elevate, like Artemisia Gentileschi, who would be as well known today as Caravaggio if not for her gender. Nowhere in Professor Graves's work did she mention Hayden, or any of Perenelle's other paintings that had been misattributed.

My research was only a superficial search, but everything I found online told the story of a respected scholar. Except for one outlier. One odd fact I couldn't verify. Not online. The Internet was an invention I didn't see coming, and as much as it's given us, it's also taken away some of our basic reasoning skills. There was an easy way to find out what I was missing: I could ask a human.

A professor at a local university's art history department who'd referenced her work was holding office hours that afternoon. I grabbed my silver raincoat and set out to see him.

The rail-thin professor didn't look up as I stood in his doorway.

"Knock knock," I said as I looked over the office, filled with books with creased spines and nicknacks. The gilt frames on the walls held his diplomas, dark colored oil paintings, and antique maps.

"You're much more polite than my undergraduate students," he said with a grin as he took off his reading glasses. "Visiting graduate student?"

"Independent researcher," I said. "I hope it's okay that I stopped by."

"Unless a student getting an early start on a paper stops by, I'm all yours for the next half hour."

"I'm researching Gwendolyn Graves."

"You'll need a lot more than half an hour." He gestured to the chair in front of his desk.

I smiled as I sat. "I've got a specific question. There's a gap in what I can find about her on my own. As if something has been removed." I wouldn't call it a *bluff* exactly, but I needed to know what lay beyond the surface. There had to be a reason she was being so cagey with me. I wanted to know what I was getting into.

"Ah." His chair squeaked as he sat back. "You mean the scandal."

Bingo. I gave an understanding nod but didn't speak.

"That happened more than fifty years ago," he continued. "Before she was even a professor. Surely you don't need to bring that into your research, do you?"

"I don't want to ruin her reputation. I'm not publishing anything. I run an antiques business." I handed him a letterpress business card for Elixir. "She's advising me on a painting, and I just wanted to be sure I can trust her."

He chuckled. "You can."

"The scandal you mentioned—"

"I don't know the details. It had happened a few years before I started graduate school. Academic conferences aren't usually filled with scandal—no, that's a lie. But it's usually personal in nature. Gwendolyn Graves got herself involved in an academic scandal. Like I said, it was before my time. All I know is that she presented a paper that she hadn't properly researched. It nearly killed her career before it began. We all make research mistakes when we're young. I hope you won't hold it against her."

"That's all you know?"

"No." He stood. "I also know that if you're looking for a Renaissance painting expert, she's it."

I thanked him for his time.

Part of me thought I should be more cautious and call off the meeting. But I couldn't. Not with so many unanswered questions. So I'd taken precautions. Dr. Graves and I were meeting at Blue Sky Teas, a favorite local gathering spot in my neighborhood, rather than my house.

I was ready for whatever lay ahead. It didn't hurt that The Alchemy of Tea was right next door to Blue's café. Stopping by to see Max was sure to lift my sense of unease.

A new haiku poem stuck out of the red Valentine typewriter in the front window of The Alchemy of Tea:

Tea, an iron pot,
and wind off the high mountains.
A monk blinks and sips.

I imagined the serene scene as I opened the door of the tea shop. The lingering aroma of the fire that had nearly prevented the shop from opening was long gone, and the cozy shop was now filled with the earthy scents of Max's loose leaf tea blends.

As I walked through the door with the soothing bell jingling above me, Max Liu's smile reached every molecule of my body. His presence filled me with a joy I hadn't felt in nearly a century, and a lightness I couldn't ever remember feeling. This shop was an extension of him. Aside from the typewriter Dorian and I had given him, he'd picked out every element, from the tea blends to the elegant wrought iron stands that held books related to tea.

With a line three people deep, Max didn't have time to come out from behind the counter and give me a kiss, but that smile was more than enough.

"Who won the chess game?" I asked when he'd rung up the last of the customers and I reached the counter.

Max gave a chagrinned smile and ran a hand through his black hair, which had recently grown long enough to flop into his eyes. "Do I need to answer that?"

"He doesn't sleep," I pointed out, "so he has far more time than you do to think about chess strategy."

"No time for a break this afternoon," Max said as the chime of the bell over the door sounded once more. He greeted the two smiling women who'd stepped into the shop and asked them to let him know if they needed help.

"I'm not here to tempt you away from the shop," I said as Max turned his attention back to me. "Dinner at my place after you close up?"

Max's harried smile brightened. "Even though it's an autumn sunset and it'll be dark by the time I arrive?"

As a plant alchemist, my body's natural rhythms are tied to the sun, like the plants I work with. I awaken with the sun, and I grow tired when it fades. I can use small amounts of caffeine, *carefully*, to adapt to a modern world not dictated by the cycles of the earth and sun, but it's not a cure. Max loved me enough to put up with my solar challenges.

Even though it had taken him a long time to accept the truth about who I was, in another sense, it was as if he had always been waiting for me. That we'd been waiting for each other.

Max had never fully given up on the magic he'd learned from his grandparents as a child, even when he'd rejected alchemical principles in favor of what he believed to be rationality. Now that he'd met me, he'd embraced what he'd always known to be true. That alchemy was real. His cozy shop, The Alchemy of Tea, was both filled with beauty and entirely practical. The tea didn't simply have nice packaging. It was high quality, with just a touch of alchemical magic.

"I'm guessing that after my day today I'll have a lot to tell you about tonight," I said. "I'll fix us a pot of your gunpowder green tea to be awake this evening."

He raised an eyebrow. "You're purposefully caffeinating? Now you've got me worried."

"No worrying is allowed in this magical shop."

Max gave me a quick kiss before I slipped out of the shop. Before the door closed behind me, I heard the younger woman give a dreamy sigh. Max Liu was as delectable on the outside as he was within. I was a lucky woman.

At least, I was for now. But I had no idea what I was about to learn from a professor who might very well be more than she seemed.

CHAPTER 5

From the Typewriter of Dorian Robert-Houdin

```
The Culinary Alchemist's Toolbox


The tria prima of cooking



1. Fire — the flame of brimstone on the stove,
and the heat of the sun over vegetables, fuels
the transformation of ingredients.
2. Curiosity — Mercurial curiosity, ruled by the
moon, is the element of experimentation that
brings new creations to life.
3. Salt — The element that brings any dish to
life.
```

Dorian sat at his Remington typewriter in the attic. He was at a stand-still on his latest Gothic novel, a tale of a lonely alchemist who was trapped in a tower. Therefore, he had returned to his magnum opus, *Culinary Alchemy: The Art of Transforming Simple Ingredients into a Feast of the Senses.* Each chapter would be prefaced with a few words of wisdom for a culinary alchemist's "toolbox." Advice he could impart with his curious readers for them to keep in mind to think more broadly of the recipes that were to follow.

He sat back and stretched his wings.

Technically, the Gothic novel he had abandoned in favor of his cookbook masterpiece was not his "latest" novel, for he had not completed any of his earlier stories. He had abandoned his drafts after each case he investigated with Zoe was solved. It was only after their last case that he realized the novels were how his subconscious worked through the baffling events that surrounded them. Yet as soon as the baffling was made rational, usually by way of Zoe explaining what had truly transpired, there was nothing left for him to write! No *magic* left in his prose.

Currently, he had a different problem. No crime to solve. No puzzling mystery to delve into. No cryptic enigma to solve.

Yes, it was true that Zoe was wary of the new interest in the portrait of her and her brother. But she was meeting with a scholar this afternoon who would surely put her mind at ease. He could work on his cookbook in peace. Why, then, was it so difficult to turn his thoughts into words? He was a master chef who intimately understood the connection between cooking and alchemy. Perhaps he should try writing in Latin or French, his first two languages. That might—

A door slammed downstairs, breaking his train of thought.

Dorian instantly tucked his wings closely to his side and scurried to the attic door. He cracked the door, yet did not step outside of the room. *Zoe was not supposed to be home.*

"Dorian?" A voice called from downstairs. Not Zoe's voice. The voice of a young man. "I let myself in with my spare key. You got any food?"

Dorian smiled as he swung open the attic door. This was a welcome visit indeed. A friend to feed. He scampered downstairs to meet his young friend.

Brixton Taylor, now sixteen years old, sat sulking at the kitchen table. A pile of mail, which he must have brought in, was strewn messily across the table.

"Veronica bailed on me," the boy said. "Thought you'd be home since it's daytime."

With dark curls and tan skin, on a superficial level, Brixton looked nothing like his fair, blonde mother, Heather. Yet as he matured, his features had begun to look more like hers. The boy was now recognizable as being her son. Dorian had not known any teenagers before accidentally moving to Portland, yet there was something else familiar about Brixton that Dorian had noticed, especially lately. A curiosity in his eyes that was unmistakable. *Oui.* This was what Dorian recognized. His expression that included the mixed emotions of youth was very much like that of Zoe's brother, Thomas, in the *Brother and Sister* portrait Perenelle had painted.

Brixton was not someone to whom Dorian would normally have revealed his identity as a gargoyle, but the boy had accidentally seen Dorian speaking with Zoe. Brixton's curiosity had led him to sneak into the house that was in such a state of disrepair it was thought to be abandoned. There was much drama during those early days, which Dorian was pleased was behind them.

"I was indeed home," Dorian said to his friend. "I was working on my cookbook in the attic."

"I'll go," Brixton mumbled as he stood.

"Nonsense. You will do no such thing. You are hungry. I have much extra food." Dorian had come to learn that referee psychology could be employed to good effect with teenagers. "Feeding you will help me with my cookbook. Sit."

Dorian was an exacting chef and baker. He baked pastries for Blue Sky Teas, and if a pastry did not look as *magnifique* on the outside as it would taste inside, he would not include it in the finished products that would be sold that day at the café. Instead, he brought misshapen pastries home, for Zoe and their friends like Brixton to snack on.

Dorian had learned his craft from a French chef who had lost his sight from injuries sustained in a kitchen fire. It had been the idea of Dorian's father—the man who raised him after accidentally bringing him to life. Close to the end of his own life, his father wished to find an avocation for the gargoyle that would allow him to thrive once he was on his own. Therefore, he introduced Dorian to a blind friend who would not know he was employing a gargoyle.

The chef believed Dorian's reticence in meeting others was due to a deformity that embarrassed him. The chef instructed Dorian as his pupil and live-in cook. Dorian thus began his career as a chef for people who had lost their sight and needed help around the house—and good food.

His skills as a chef were already formidable when he left France, and Zoe's plant-based preferences had stretched his creativity, so he was now one of the greatest chefs on the West Coast of the United States. This was a self-appointed designation, of course. It was not worth the risk of exposure to open his own restaurant.

"Veronica is busy this afternoon?" Dorian asked as he placed a baking tray in the oven to gently reheat two leftover pastries. A pumpkin croissant and a caramel oat bar. When he had baked dozens of pastries for Blue Sky Teas before dawn, these two had been in the far corner of the baking sheet and had charred on the bottom. Blue's old oven in the café kitchen needed servicing.

"Don't ask," Brixton said.

Dorian narrowed his eyes, yet he held his tongue instead of mentioning that the boy was the one who brought up her name in the first place!

The first smile Dorian had seen on Brixton's lips appeared when he bit into the misshapen croissant. The boy did not appear to mind that the monstrosity looked more like an amoeba than a crescent.

"V's taking an art class this semester," Brixton said once he had finished eating a pastry. "She made plans with a friend to do 'plain air' painting after school today. Sounds really boring to paint plain air, but whatever."

"Plein air," said Dorian with a chuckle. "A French phrase for the art of painting outside. They will be painting nature, I imagine. Not the air."

"Oh. I guess that makes—" Brixton broke off as his phone made a pinging noise. He grinned as he read the message. "It's starting to rain, so they gave up." He grabbed the caramel oat bar, lifted the backpack at his feet and stood. "Thanks for the snack and company, D."

With that, the boy left through the back door.

Dorian made sure Brixton had locked the door securely (he had) before returning to his typewriter. He would soon need to figure out who would be his "front." The *Culinary Alchemy* cookbook would surely be a runaway bestseller, and Dorian himself was in no position to give television interviews. Zoe's privacy was important, so she could not be the public face of the cookbook.

Perhaps Nicolas Flamel? He, too, was an alchemist who did not age, yet Nicolas was of an indeterminate age where it was quite possible for him to get away with looking like himself for the next twenty years without raising suspicion. Outwardly, Nicolas appeared to be roughly fifty years old, with salt-and-pepper hair and a scruffy form of dress and mannerism that made it impossible to guess if he was a bedraggled forty or a fit sixty-five. The centuries-old alchemist had boundless curiosity for new experiences. Yes, Nicolas might do quite nicely as the front for *Culinary Alchemy.*

CHAPTER 6

My friend Blue had opened her café, Blue Sky Teas, as a second career. It was an embodiment of her easygoing way of life that was so different from the one she'd abandoned.

A plaque above the door greeted customers with the quote, "There is no trouble so great or grave that cannot be diminished by a nice cup of tea," by Bernard-Paul Heroux. It was the perfect sentiment to greet customers who were about to enter a cozy sanctuary with a living tree growing in the center, local art covering the walls, and lovingly prepared pots of tea.

Three of the works of art on the walls were flower still life paintings by Brixton's artist mom, Heather. She was a bubbly free spirit who was a talented artist, though she was still finding her style. Heather flitted from one new idea to the next, and most recently was excited about a new oil paint color called Renaissance White, which was a modern, lead-free version of the former toxic lead white, which I remembered well for remaining popular with artists long after it was known to be poisonous.

I recognized Gwendolyn Graves from her book jacket photos, despite the decades that had passed. Her long hair was now completely gray, but still piled into a messy bun on top of her head. The vermillion red of the cat-eye glasses from her headshot had been replaced by an equally stylish pair of silver frames that matched her hair.

She'd selected a spot under the weeping fig tree, in the seat facing the door. Presumably the choice was so she'd see me, but she was so absorbed in the book she was reading that she didn't look up when I came in or even as I walked up to the table. I liked this about her immensely. She only noticed me when I sat down.

"Oh!" The sliver glasses slipped down her nose as I startled her. She took them off and folded them, setting them down on top of the book. "Zoe?"

I nodded.

"Thanks for meeting with me." Dr. Gwendolyn Graves was smiling, but there was a worry behind the smile. Whatever it was, it was the reason she wanted to meet in person, rather than simply talking over the phone.

"You have me intrigued, Dr. Graves."

"Please, call me Gwen. And I'm sorry to have been vague in my message and to have insisted on speaking in person. It's rather complicated. Cup of tea before I dive in?"

I breathed in the scent of Blue's herbal blend of peppermint and cloves. A tea with a bright energy without caffeine. I nodded and Gwen poured from the tea pot in the center of the tree ring table.

As I took a sip of tea, Gwen stared intently at me, making me feel as if I had broccoli in my teeth, which I was only reasonably certain wasn't the case.

"I study Renaissance art," she began. "I'm mostly retired now, but I still can't resist a historical mystery from that fascinating time."

I nodded. "I'm familiar with your work."

"So you must know," she said, "that I've always been interested in art that was misattributed or forgotten."

"You didn't want to meet me in person simply to tell me that," I said. "It was a long trip for you. You don't even know if I have the specific painting you contacted me about."

"I described the painting and its provenance well enough for you to reply. I enjoy trains. But you're right. I didn't simply want an excuse to come to Portland." She took a breath and lowered her voice. "I believe this painting might be a lost masterpiece."

My eyes grew wide. She leaned back and took in my surprise as if she'd expected it. It was, after all, a natural reaction to being told one might have been in possession of a lost masterpiece.

I wasn't faking my surprise. *How could she know?* How could anyone? No, she couldn't know *who* painted it. The dates were all wrong. She suspected something else.

"A masterpiece by which artist?" I asked, forcing myself to stay calm.

She shook her head. "I can't be certain without studying it. That's why I want to study it. An art dealer has been asking questions of people I know in the art world, and he traced this painting to Portland. I'm so angry about what he does, so I've been contacting collectors and antique shops who might not know what they purchased. Is this your painting?" She put her glasses back on, retrieved her phone from her purse, and left it face-up on the table for me to see the tiny photograph of my painting.

I hesitated before answering. "You said an untrustworthy art dealer is interested in it as well."

"I understand your reticence to tell me anything if you've already been contacted. And I know it's a lot to take in that you truly bought a lost masterpiece. But I'd hate to have it lost to history."

"Who is it that I should watch out for? Who's this art dealer you keep mentioning?"

She didn't answer right away, and I couldn't read her face. Was she frightened?

"Might he be an art *finder*," I said, "rather than a dealer?"

Gwen put her head in her hands and shook her head for a few moments before looking back up at me. "Is it too late? Has Arthur Finder already gotten to you?"

"Do you know who he really is?" I asked.

Gwen leaned forward across the circular table, her elbows touching two different lines of the tree ring table that showed decades of time. "He's not someone you want to get involved with. Unfortunately, one of the realities of working in art is crossing paths with people I wish I didn't have to associate with."

"You've met him?"

"Not in person. He's too clever for that. All I know is his 'Art Finder' alias that he thinks is so clever—and his reputation."

"He's a criminal?"

"Not proven." She sighed. "A tip for your antiques business, since you're young enough I can tell you're just starting out. If anyone ever offers you an awful lot of money that seems more than you thought your antique is worth, go to a museum or research institution to find out what you've really got."

"This is more than I expected for a Monday afternoon," I said.

"Zoe." She gripped my hand as I made a move to stand. "You can drop the pretense."

"I don't know what you—"

"I've *seen the painting*." Professor Graves pointed to the image on her phone. "The similarity is obvious. Are you going to tell me how you ended up in a painting from 300 years ago?"

She leaned back in the mismatched café chair and crossed her arms.

Breathe, Zoe. I reminded myself yet again that people only believe what they're ready to believe. I didn't advertise how long I'd been alive, but the clues were there. People simply rationalized it away. The problem was, if anyone dug too deeply, they'd find things that could only be explained by thinking I'd changed my identity to hide from the authorities. It was far better to stay under the radar. Which was becoming increasingly difficult to do in the modern world. Even though I didn't post photos of myself online, and asked my friends not to do so, I couldn't avoid security cameras or the high-end cameras that everyone walked around with in their pockets.

"Tell me," she continued. "Is it an old family resemblance? Is that why you bought it but it's not listed on your Elixir website for sale? Do you know who the woman in the painting is? That would go a long way in helping scholars put together the missing pieces of history."

I seized the opening. "I *know about* the painting, which is why I replied to you. I've visited that museum, when I was in France visiting family. I don't know its history, but my grandmother was French. I assume it's a distant relative. What else could it be?"

I expected her to make a joke about me being a vampire, or reference a meme from several years ago about museum doppelgängers, but she did neither. "Zoe, you do realize how close the resemblance is, don't you?"

"It's not that similar. Her hair—"

"Obviously, I know it's not really you. But it explains why you bought the painting even though you didn't think it was worth much."

"I've *visited* the painting," I clarified. "I didn't say—"

"I can make some calls. If I can authenticate it, a museum would protect it from con men like Arthur."

"I need to go." I stood up abruptly. A museum getting their hands on my painting was nearly as bad as a con man getting it. "I'm sorry you came all this way when I don't have what you're after."

"Sleep on it," Gwen said. "But I hope you're ready to call me in the morning to tell me the truth. I got myself a room at the Phoenix, on the waterfront. Be careful. If Arthur Finder sees you—"

"I know," I said. "He'll see the resemblance and think I'm the one who has the painting he's after."

That was the real danger. I didn't care that Gwen didn't believe my lie. But the art dealer willing to resort to theft now knew the Flamels didn't have the painting. If he learned who I was, he'd know I had the painting. I'd never sell it—but how far would he go to get it?

CHAPTER 7

From the Typewriter of Dorian Robert-Houdin

```
The Culinary Alchemist's Toolbox

The alchemical transformations of food will be
strongest if you have considered fire, curiosity,
and salt.

Fire: Care for your stovetop, and learn the heat
levels it gives you. Allums (onions, shallots,
and garlic) are perhaps the easiest food to
transform into something entirely new with fire.
Caramelizing allums requires only one skill: the
patience of time.

Curiosity: What are your favorite flavors? Exper-
iment with dried herbs and whole spices to
discover which will be in your alchemical
signature.

Salt: All salts are not created equal. Do not
accept salt with added preservatives. Be sure to
```

have on hand, at the very least, sea salt for
cooking and flaked salt for finishing dishes with
added flavor and texture.

Though Dorian had believed he was only humoring Brixton, the boy's visit had indeed helped with his cookbook. In Brixton's selection of the caramelized oat bar with flaked finishing salt, Dorian was reminded that his best executed recipes were those that included complex flavors, not seasonal gimmicks. Pumpkin croissants were the type of recipe people *believed* they wanted when the seasons changed from summer to autumn, yet in truth, they were more interested in the novelty of the Halloween-associated squash.

Dorian reminded himself he should stick to his strengths. Complex flavors that danced on the tongue. Not flashy eye candy that fell flat as soon as they were experienced. Pumpkins could be elevated in many ways, yet neither coffee nor flaky pastries were where the nuances of the autumnal squash could shine.

The telephone rang before Dorian could continue his thoughts on whether his croissant recipe was salvageable. Yes, yes, he knew he had dismissed the idea already. Yet the great Dorian Robert-Houdin was never one to shrink from a challenge.

As always, he did not answer the phone right away. Zoe and the Flamels had a special pattern of rings so that he would know it was safe for him to answer.

"I need you to make sure the house is locked up," Zoe said once he answered, "then get the painting of me and Thomas and hide it in the attic."

"*Hide* it?"

"Slip it in between other paintings in the crate of artwork so it's out of sight."

Why was such a course of action necessary? Zoe failed to explain more, only saying that she would return home shortly before signing off. Rather rudely, at that.

Dorian hurried to check each lock in the house, including the windows, then climbed the stairs to retrieve the portrait from Zoe's bedroom wall and bring it to the attic.

Before placing the painting into its crate, he propped it against a shelf. Perenelle Flamel was indeed a talented artist. Zoe was most taken with the life-like representation of her brother, yet Dorian was far more interested in the ingredients used to create her oil paints. The pigments were not like modern recipes. As an alchemist, he could detect the subtleties of ingredients. As a gourmand, he was most attuned to *edible* ingredients, yet he was coming to realize that the recipes for pigments were not so different than the preparations he followed meticulously to craft exquisite feasts.

This, he mused, explained why Perenelle Flamel was most enamored by Dorian's culinary creations. Zoe appreciated good food, but it was Perenelle who truly looked as if she was in ecstasy when she tasted a spoonful of his cashew cream and mixed mushroom risotto, or crunched on one of his herb-infused fresh croutons. Because she could taste every element.

Perenelle Flamel was a woman with such command of the raw materials of both paint and the living world, coupled with the intent of alchemy, that she had discovered how to transfer real objects into paintings through alchemical intent. But she had given up experimenting with that process, because she wisely concluded that nobody should wield that much power. Instead, Perenelle focused on subtle alchemical hints in her artwork, for all to see and learn from—if they were ready and willing to put in the time and effort for transformation.

The visual elements of this *Brother and Sister* painting contained very little alchemy, yet Dorian sensed the *tria prima* ingredients: sulfur, mercury, and salt.

At the sound of the front door unlatching, Dorian slipped the painting into the crate with a dozen other paintings, then placed the wooden cover on top.

"Dorian?" Zoe's voice echoed through the house as the stairs beneath him creaked.

Bon. It was only Zoe. Not whomever she worried sought her painting.

As Zoe breathlessly explained what had transpired, all thoughts of his sure-to-be-award-winning cookbook fell from his mind.

CHAPTER 8

I felt a little bit better after telling Dorian what was going on, but I'd feel even better once Max and the Flamels arrived for dinner.

I didn't like the fact that Perenelle's painting was generating such interest. I wished I'd taken better care to set up the Flamels' identities after rescuing them. Their papers were superb and would hold up to scrutiny, but they didn't have a history that could be traced if anyone tried digging into their pasts. In the twenty-first century, ID documents no longer told enough of one's story. There was a void where their pasts should be.

When creating a fake identity, it's always best to stay as close to the truth as possible. For the Flamels, that meant their current identities were that of a French married couple who'd emigrated to the United States long ago, changed their names to reflect people they believed to be a distant relative of Perenelle, and become naturalized citizens several years ago. Which is why they only had US IDs and passports, but no birth certificates.

In my case, to explain why I looked similar to women who lived decades ago, I made up a mother and grandmother who did not exist. That was the easiest way to deal with encountering living people who might remember me from another time. I was named after both my mother and grandmother, of course. Zoe III.

Zoe wasn't a common name in the English-speaking world

when I was born in the late 1600s, but it's the name I was born with in Salem Village in the Massachusetts Bay Colony. I changed my surname to Faust after I discovered the Elixir of Life in 1704. I was seeking the Elixir for Thomas, hoping I could transfer it to my brother. When I realized I'd wasted Thomas's last weeks on earth in isolation in my lab, I felt as though I'd made a foolish deal with a devious Devil who'd tempted me with a reward Nicolas warned me was impossible. I'd sacrificed weeks that would have meant the world to me, in exchange for an eternal life I hadn't wanted.

Before Goethe wrote his tragic play about Faust selling his soul to the Devil in the early 1800s, Johann Georg Faust was a German alchemist who truly lived the 1500s. A chapbook that combined fact and fiction about Faust told of his alchemical research, framing it as a cautionary tale about selling one's soul to the Devil for knowledge. The legend has been retold so many times, because it continues to speak to modern struggles. Even though I've come to love my life, I still find it's an appropriate name.

Perenelle's *Brother and Sister* painting was one of the reasons I was able to let go of most of the guilt I felt for letting Thomas down. It reminded me of the good times we'd had after we fled Salem Village. We'd had more than a decade of adventures, five of them with the Flamels.

I wished they'd hurry up and arrive. When my phone rang, for a fraction of a second I thought it was the doorbell.

"Nicolas isn't up for leaving the house, I'm afraid," Perenelle said when I picked up the phone. "There was nothing we could find in the news about why the *Brother and Sister* painting might be of interest after all this time, so we spent the afternoon looking for art history clues in bookshops and libraries."

"He overdid it?" I asked. Nicolas's health hadn't been the same since his near-fatal encounter with Edward Kelley.

"He'll be fine," Perenelle said, her voice betraying her words. "He's on his way to bed now."

"Give him a hug for me."

"Should I still come over after getting Nicolas to bed? If you learned anything in your meeting with Dr. Graves—"

"Nothing that can't wait until morning," I said. "Look after Nicolas. That's the most important thing."

I hung up the phone, more worried about Nicolas than I admitted to Perenelle. Even under the medical care of Max's medical doctor sister Mina, Nicolas hadn't fully recovered. Edward Kelley had failed to kill him, in spite of his best intentions, but the alchemist had caused Nicolas and Perenelle's imprisonment until I found them a year ago. Dorian had been plying Nicolas with healing food, and I'd been administering homemade herbal teas and tinctures to help his recovery.

Alchemists aren't immortal. We can die through mortal means. We've simply transformed our aging cells so we can continue to live at our present age when we found the Elixir of Life. Or, in my case as an accidental alchemist, I was foolishly seeking the Elixir for Thomas when he fell ill. I didn't realize what I'd discovered until it was too late for him to live and too late for me to die. I remained physically unchanged, except that every hair on my body turned white as the years passed.

I pushed through the swinging kitchen door and found Dorian standing on the stepping stool he needed to work comfortably at the kitchen counter.

"The Flamels won't be coming to dinner," I told him. "Nicolas isn't up for it."

Dorian placed the garlic he was dicing into a small bowl next to a larger bowl of diced onions. He believed in *mise en place*, the concept of preparing all of your ingredients and having them in one easy-to-reach place before diving into cooking.

"He is unwell?" Dorian hopped off his stepping stool and dried his hands on a kitchen towel.

"Just tired." I hoped.

"This is unfortunate. My charred cauliflower steaks with romesco sauce do not save well. I will not be able to send leftovers to him."

"He'll be fine with some sleep." I took an almond from the glass bowl sitting on the counter.

"Do not touch the ingredients!" Dorian admonished as he brandished his rolling pin like a cudgel. "The almonds for the sauce have been weighed precisely," he grumbled.

I lifted my hands in the air. "No more snacking," I agreed.

"It is lamentable that the Flamels cannot join us for our evening discussion of the mystery of Perenelle's painting," Dorian said as he prepared cauliflower steaks for the oven. "And your beau is more than fashionably late. "

Before I had time to worry, the doorbell rang.

"Sorry I'm late." Max held a bouquet from the flower shop not far from The Alchemy of Tea. He used to pick flowers from his own cutting garden to bring me flowers, but now that he was a small business owner, he wanted to support other local small businesses owners he was getting to know. I smiled at the sweet scent of honeysuckle.

"I thought for sure Nicolas and Perenelle would have beaten me here."

"The Flamels will be absent this eve," said Dorian.

"Nicolas spent the day roaming the aisles of bookshops and libraries in search of helpful research," I explained, "so he wore himself out and needs to recharge tonight. We'll regroup tomorrow."

While Dorian put the finishing touches on dinner, I got Max up to speed on what I'd realized about Arthur Finder and learned from Professor Graves about the painting.

"It's clearly *you* in the portrait," Max said. "That's what I'm most worried about. I don't like this."

"One cannot live life worrying about what *might* happen," said Dorian as he served his feast. "It is impossible to know what foul events fate might toss onto the road of life."

I eyed Dorian. "Are you working on your Gothic novel again?"

Max laughed. "Even I can tell you don't usually talk like that. You're working on a novel? I didn't know that."

Max and Dorian's initial meeting this past summer hadn't gone as smoothly as I'd hoped, and had necessitated smelling salts, administered by our friend Tobias, a fellow alchemist I first met over a century ago. Now that Max and Dorian were friends, they were learning more about each other, but there were still some gaps.

Dorian pursed his lips and gave his wings a solitary flap before folding them tightly against his back. "I have set aside my previous story. Once I solved our last case, I no longer had the desire to write *Le Chat et le Monstre*. I have begun working on a new cookbook."

Max caught my eye and only partially succeeded at concealing a smile. Dorian had indeed been pivotal in catching someone who was about to escape during the last murder we investigated, but solving the case had been a group effort.

"My cookbook will be the definitive cookery guide for chefs and bakers who wish to truly understand food transformation," Dorian continued.

He was well aware that there were many excellent cookbooks on the science of cooking, like *Salt, Fat, Acid, Heat* and *The Flavor Equation*, both of which he owned. He used the vast majority of his modest income from his Blue Sky Teas baking on cookbooks, culinary tools, and contributing to our grocery budget. I decided not to point out that he knew these other cookbooks existed. The digression would take us into the wee hours of the night.

Instead, I yawned. It wasn't a statement, but an involuntary reflex. The sun was down, so my energy was quickly depleting.

"You're really not worried?" Max asked me.

"It is the sun making her yawn boorishly," Dorian stated as he pushed my plate towards me.

"Dorian is right," I said. "Both that I can't sit around worrying about what might happen, and that I'm mostly just tired since it's so far into the evening. What else can I do? I've hidden the painting away, and I'll talk with Perenelle in the morning before deciding whether or not to work with Professor Graves. Tonight, it's more important to take time to appreciate the small things in life," I said, "like spending time with those I care about."

"With good food." Dorian wriggled his horns before taking a bite.

By the time the meal was over, I wasn't nearly as worried about the art collector. Whatever the future held, I'd face it with people who cared for me.

Dorian had prepared the perfect dessert for the evening. A bite-size biscuit with salted caramel on top, which included just enough sugar to wake me up for a short time before bed. After Max and I had properly praised the meal, Dorian insisted on cleaning up. One benefit of having him be so particular about "his" kitchen was that he both cooked *and* cleaned.

"I'll be over at Max's," I told him before grabbing a small overnight bag and my silver raincoat.

My arm shot out for my ringing phone, my heart racing.

I had no idea how much time had passed, only that I'd been in a deep stage of sleep. It took me a moment to remember I was at Max's house.

"Ignore the phone," Max murmured into my ear, pulling me back to him.

"I can't," I insisted. "It's set to silent for everyone besides you, Dorian, and Tobias. It's too late for it to be anything besides an emergency." I shook off Max's arm and looked at the screen. The number on the screen was my own house. *Dorian.* I answered the call.

"The thief! The thief!" Dorian cried into the receiver, nearly splitting my eardrum. "I could not stop them!"

"A thief?" I repeated. "Are you all right?"

"I am unharmed, but a burglar has broken in."

"Are they still there?" Max asked. "Get out of—"

"The burglar has gone."

"I'm calling the police." Max already had his phone in his hands. "We'll be right there."

"There is no use," Dorian said. "The thief has fled with their quarry."

"What did they steal?" I asked. Even though I already knew the answer.

"The painting," Dorian wailed. "The painting of you and your brother is gone."

CHAPTER 9

Max and I hurried back to my house. I couldn't let myself believe I'd never see my brother's angelic face again. Thomas was far from an angel, but he was my baby brother who'd abandoned his life to save mine. Perenelle's painting couldn't bring him back to life, but it was the closest I'd ever get. A photo of the painting wasn't the same.

I fumbled with my key so badly that Max took it from me to open my front door. Since the burglar had already fled, I'd convinced Max to hold off on calling the police before we got the full story from Dorian.

"Je suis profondément désolé," Dorian cried as we burst inside. "I have failed you."

"It's not your fault," I insisted, locking the door behind me, though I no longer felt I had anything of value.

"It happened in the attic?" Max asked.

Dorian led the way upstairs as he explained he was in the kitchen when the thief broke in.

"At first," Dorian said, "I believed the noise to be the nocturnal cat who lives next door. He enjoys our backyard. I regret that I wasted a precious few minutes under this misguided belief." We reached the attic and Dorian pointed at the opened crate.

"And the burglar?" Max held me back from trampling evidence.

He tapped his foot anxiously, as if it was difficult for him to stay back as well.

"I did not hear the miscreant until glass broke from above me. From here in the attic." Dorian pointed toward a pile of broken crystal glassware. The thief must have dislodged the set in their search for the painting.

"I took the sturdiest weapon I could find," Dorian continued. "My rolling pin. Then, I wrapped a tablecloth around me like a cape—for my proper cape was in the attic with the thief—and approached with trepidation and fortitude."

I imagined Dorian brandishing the rolling pin over his head.

"That was very brave," said Max. "But we should probably leave that out when we talk to the police, so it doesn't confuse—"

"*Je suis une gargoyle*," Dorian stated matter-of-factly. "It does you service that you have forgotten this quandary for revealing my visage to others, yet I cannot speak with *les flics*."

"It's you and me," I said to Max. "We need to get our story straight for the police."

"Right." Max blinked rapidly and shook his head, as if the full gravity of a gargoyle as a witness sunk in. "Did the thief see you?"

"Only what he could see of my cloak around me. Which is to say that no, he would not have realized I am a gargoyle." Dorian blinked his liquidy black eyes innocently up at Max. "May I continue my story?"

"There has to be a way Zoe and I can safely tell the story to the police." Max began to pace.

"There is," I said. "But we can't tell them the whole truth."

Max nodded, but his jaw was clenched, and he looked at the broken glass instead of meeting my gaze. It was still hard for him to reconcile the way things had to be.

"The thief was surprised to see me appear in the attic doorway," Dorian said. "He was kneeling over Zoe's painting—"

"He'd already found it when you got here?" I asked.

"You saw his face?" Max added.

"Yes, to Zoe's query," said Dorian. "Alas, I did not see the burglar's visage, for in addition to black clothing and gloves, he wore a ski cap. Though I will remember his eyes for eternity. Bright, haunting eyes that grew wide with confusion. I am certain he did not expect anyone to be in the house."

I groaned. "He must have followed Gwen to find me. I walked straight back to the house after meeting with her at Blue Sky Teas, leading him right to the house. Right to the portrait."

"And he saw you leave with me," Max agreed. "So he thought the house was deserted."

"He waited a short time longer until the neighborhood would be asleep," I theorized, "then broke in." I turned to Dorian. "You heard nothing until the glass breaking in the attic?"

"That is correct. The thief quickly recovered after his surprise from being discovered. I was worried at first that he would use the knife in his hand upon me—"

"He was armed?" Max cut in.

"It was a… how do you say? An exacting razor blade knife?"

"An Exacto knife," I said. "Like to cut a painting out of a frame." My heart sank at the thought of the painting of Thomas being damaged.

"Upon seeing me, the man was not so evil as to be past redemption. He returned the knife to his pocket, rather than launching at me, and tucked the framed art underneath his arm. He kicked the rolling pin from my hand, and alas, I was less dexterous because of the tablecloth wrapped around me. He was able to use the heavy frame to shove me aside, then ran down the stairs."

"I'm so sorry my first concern wasn't asking if you'd been hurt." I knelt next to Dorian and inspected what I now saw was a gray lump forming on his temple.

"There was no real harm done to me," said Dorian, brushing away my hand. "Only my pride."

"It's got to be Arthur Finder," I said. "Or someone he sent on his behalf. When I call the police, I'll tell them about the emails he sent, and get them from Nicolas. The thief wore gloves, but maybe they can trace him that way."

"You can't tell them you were the one the thief knocked down," Max said.

"We weren't at home when the burglary happened," I said. "I'm simply going to say we came back to the house and found broken glass."

"You mean both lie and leave out the details?" Max shook his head. "I don't like it."

"It is the only way," Dorian said.

"And it *is* true," I insisted. "We did come back to the house and find broken glass, which we then investigated."

"We ate dinner at your house," Max said, "so why conveniently go out while the thief came and stole this painting, then happen to come back after such a short time? Do you have insurance for the painting, Ms. Faust? These are the questions we'll be asked."

"I don't have insurance for it," I answered calmly, as if Max was the investigating officer, "because its main worth to me is its sentimental value. And my boyfriend keeps his house about five degrees colder than mine. I wanted to come home, so he came with me."

Max's eyes creased with concern. "You think my house is too cold? You should have said something. I have central air—"

I stopped him with a finger to his lips. "Your house is perfect, Max. I'm telling you my very plausible answers to the questions we might be asked."

Max raised an eyebrow. "Since when did you get good at lying?"

"I'm not. If you listen to what I said, you'll notice I *didn't* lie. You're the one who made assumptions. You *do* keep your house cooler than I keep mine. Many women get cold easily, so when I said, 'I wanted to come home,' you assumed it was because I was cold. But really, it was because Dorian called us."

Max groaned.

"She is a wise one, our Zoe," Dorian said with a chuckle. "We alchemists must use the assumptions of others to keep ourselves safe."

"Security cameras," Max said. "Your neighbors—"

"No cameras in our immediate neighborhood," I said. "Which is good for Dorian. Even though he's disguised in his hooded cape when he leaves the house at night, it's best for him to avoid as many cameras as possible."

Dorian's cape wasn't an affectation. It was a child's costume that he wore when he was out in public. Even though he only left the house on his own during the quietest hours of night, people were occasionally about, and security cameras were becoming more common. With his cape, it was impossible to tell he was a gargoyle, though occasionally a concerned parent thought a child had snuck out of bed and tried to apprehend him.

Before we called the police, Max had one last idea—one I should have thought of myself. He opened a photograph of my paintings of Thomas in a photo editing program and added a brushstroke over my face. It was just enough to obscure my features in a way that looked like the painting had been damaged. It was a smart idea. The fewer people who thought I looked like the young woman in the painting, the better.

Once we'd saved the image file, Max called the police.

The theft was a low-level property crime that didn't involve anyone being harmed, so the police didn't call for the team of specialists that had descended when my handyman was murdered on my porch. The responding officers were polite and capable, but I wasn't confident they'd do much, even with Max being a former detective.

After filing a police report, I was so exhausted my body was screaming at me to sleep, but my mind wouldn't listen. I knew that if I wanted my painting back, I needed to take action myself.

CHAPTER 10

Since Nicolas had gone to sleep before seven that evening, I hoped he'd rested enough for us to be waking him up at three o'clock in the morning. I knew that Perenelle would have wanted me to wake her, and I was right. She insisted we come right over.

Max drove, since I didn't trust myself to drive at this time of night. At three in the morning, I barely trusted myself to walk and talk at the same time. Dorian accompanied us on our drive across town, hidden safely away from the prying eyes of any night owls or cameras.

As we approached the Flamels' house, the moonlight danced off the leaves of the topiary bushes shaped into the alchemical symbols of a serpent eating its own tail and a phoenix rising from the earth.

Nicolas looked refreshed when he opened the grand wooden front door for his weary guests.

In this secluded spot, Dorian didn't need to transform to stone to be carried into the house in secrecy, so he walked beside me and Max.

"I'm sorry for your dreadful ordeal," Nicolas said. "After finding the *Brother and Sister* portrait after 300 years, only to lose it once more—"

"We're not giving up getting it back," said Max. "The police are looking into the theft."

"*Les flics* are not taking this horrible turn of events seriously at all."

Dorian paced around the stacks of books in the Flamels' living room. "Are we not a group of accomplished detectives ourselves?"

Max gave the gargoyle a doubtful look.

Dorian jabbed his clawed index finger into the air. "It is time for me to put my little gray cells to use! It is up to us to solve the dastardly crime!"

Dorian, being carved of gray limestone, had latched onto the notion that he possessed "little gray cells" far more literally than Agatha Christie's famous detective Hercule Poirot. The Belgian detective Poirot used the phrase to refer to his brain function as he solved baffling cases. Because Dorian had helped me solve several puzzling crimes here in Portland as well as in Paris, the idea of his own little gray cells had gone to his head.

I didn't mind his ego. I was just happy he was thriving. When I first met Dorian, he had sought me out to help him decipher an ancient book of alchemy called *Non Degenera Alchemia*, which was partly responsible for bringing him to life from stone. After 150 years of life, Dorian had been slowly reverting to stone. He was in danger of being trapped in stone while conscious, for eternity. He believed the secret to saving his life lay within the pages of the strange book written in Latin and filled with woodcut illustrations of birds with twisted necks, bees circling counterclockwise, and knots of toads. Dorian was partly correct. We discovered *Non Degenera Alchemia's* connection to monstrous backward alchemy and were able to sever the ties to its power, but the book was now lost. It was only through Dorian's personal discovery of the Elixir of Life that he was alive today.

Max held up his hands in defeat. "For once, I agree with you. This painting means a lot to Zoe, and a low value property crime isn't going to get many resources elsewhere."

Dorian narrowed his eyes. "You do not wish to leave this to your former colleagues?"

"I drove us here at three in the morning, didn't I? This isn't the time to leave things to the authorities. We need to figure out what's going on with this painting. It was of no interest to *anyone* for hundreds of years, yet all of a sudden, a whole year after Nicolas bought it for Zoe, it's attracting unwanted attention. I want to know *why*."

"Nothing happened immediately after I purchased the painting," said Nicolas. "Something else must have triggered this new chain of events. What is it that the thief is *truly* after?"

"Hang on," I said, looking around. "Where's Perenelle?"

"She was most distressed when you called," said Nicolas. "She retreated into her art and alchemy studio, but she promised to return shortly."

"This is too important for her not to be here." I left the group and walked to Perenelle's sanctuary. The door was shut, so I gave a soft knock before entering.

The high-ceilinged room was dark. Perenelle stood at the windows that stretched from floor to ceiling, facing the moonlight.

"I'm so sorry," she said, not turning to face me.

"It's just a painting," I said. "Nobody got hurt. Besides, I'm not giving up getting it back."

She turned, and the remnants of tears on her cheeks caught the faint light of the moonlight.

I crossed the room quickly. "I get it. It means a lot to me as well. Thomas—"

"It's not just Thomas," she whispered. "There's a great deal of knowledge in the painting."

"I know. A piece of the story of alchemy. For those who want to learn. But after your 'Hayden' years with Rudolf II, your paintings haven't gotten the attention they deserve."

She grasped my hands. "It's so much more than that, Zoe."

For a moment, I could have sworn that her eyes blazed with a sulfurous dark red, but the illusion was gone in the blink of an eye. A trick of the light or not, the furious intensity of her gaze was unmistakable.

"What aren't you saying?" I asked.

"I'm worried about why a thief cares so much about *this* painting. There are others that have information about alchemy—ones that have so much more. Some that are in museums, for all the world to see, if they wish. Yet this one? It has barely a whisper of alchemy. It was all about you and our dearest Thomas. Well, *mostly*."

I broke away from her. "There's something else about it?"

Perenelle walked back to the window. I hadn't turned on the light when I entered the room, but my eyes had adjusted, so I could now see more of what she was looking at. The waxing gibbous moon, only a few days from being full, illuminated a section of her pigment garden.

"I knew I'd never part with this painting," she said. "Not if it was within my control. That's why I put it there."

"*The notebook*," I said, my mind flashing back to the notebook in the painting that I'd never remembered from life. Because I'd never seen it when she painted in secrecy.

She spun around, and this time there was a quicksilver sparkle in her eye and a broad smile spread across her lips. "You spotted it. My notebook."

"*That's* why someone wants the painting. You used alchemical paint to hide your notebook on the shelves in the painting."

"Nobody else knows," she insisted.

I hesitated before asking my next question, almost dreading the answer. "What exactly did you write in that little book?"

"That's what doesn't make sense." Perenelle picked up one of her sable brushes. Though the brush was only a few months old, the birch wood handle was dented and stained. Well loved. "It's similar to a ledger, I suppose. Details about my paintings, and the dates they were created, so I could keep a record of what I created. It doesn't contain the secrets of alchemy. No shortcuts, since those don't exist. My paints on the canvases themselves have far more information about the secrets of alchemy."

"But nobody else knows that," I said. "If the thief knows who you really are, they might think it holds the secrets of making gold and of eternal life."

Secrets people had killed for. What would happen when the thief didn't find what they were after?

A sharp rap sounded at the door to the studio. Max burst inside, not waiting for an answer.

"Your phone," said Max. "Someone just called you."

"In the middle of the night?"

"That's why you'd better see who it was." He handed me the phone. "It only rang once."

I looked at the missed call. "Professor Graves's cell phone."

Dorian peeked around Max. "Elderly people are known for waking up quite early."

"Four o'clock is too early for her to call," I said. "That must have been why she hung up, after she realized the time."

But when I dialed Gwen's number to return the call, it went straight to voicemail. As I tried again, Perenelle explained to Nicolas, Max, and Dorian that a journal with notes about her paintings was hidden in the *Brother and Sister* painting.

I shook my head at my third failed attempt to reach Gwen.

"Something's wrong," said Max.

"Or maybe she simply turned off her phone to get some sleep." But I didn't believe my words as soon as I'd spoken them. "I know what we can do. Gwen told me the hotel where she's staying. Let's swing by and find out why she called."

If the art thief had followed me back to my house from my meeting with Gwendolyn Graves, that meant they knew who she was, too.

CHAPTER 11

It wouldn't do to have a gargoyle come with me and Max when we went to check on Professor Graves. Blue Sky Teas was on our way to the hotel, so we could drop Dorian off at the café's back door that led to the kitchen, then stop by the hotel without the gargoyle in tow.

"I am prepared to tell Blue I am ill and cannot bake today," said Dorian from his hiding spot under a blanket in the car's back seat. "If there is anything I can do to help track down the miscreant who stole your beloved painting, I wish to help."

"There's nothing you can do while we talk to Professor Graves," I said, "except bring people joy through your pastries."

Dorian preferred cooking to baking. It was a distinction I'd never thought about before meeting Dorian. But he was nearly as talented a baker as he was a chef. He enjoyed experimenting in the kitchen, and I felt a pang of regret that he never got to see the joyous reactions customers had when they sank their teeth into one of his croissants.

"I have not forgotten it is my responsibility to get your lost painting back. I will never forgive myself—"

"You should never blame yourself for being a victim of a crime," Max cut in as we pulled into the alley that stretched behind Blue Sky Teas, The Alchemy of Tea, and other neighborhood shops. I caught Max steal a fond glance at the back door to his new shop. He reddened as he saw me looking.

"And you," I said to Max, "shouldn't feel guilty about having a new shop you love, even if you're worried about me and my lost painting. We're here, Dorian. You can come out."

Dorian emerged from the blanket and scowled at us both. "It is a good thing we arrived when we did, or I may have been smothered by both of your attempts at psychoanalysis. It *is* my fault Zoe's painting was stolen. And Max, you *should* feel guilty for placing your commercial desires above that of Zoe's revered painting."

"Ignore him," I said to Max. "He's cranky because Blue's customers haven't given the best reviews to his pumpkin croissants, so Blue won't order more pumpkin for him to experiment."

"I nearly had the recipe figured out!" Dorian cried. "And you are incorrect, Zoe. I am displeased that I cannot do more to assist in your quest at this juncture. Never fear. I will be using my little gray cells as I bake!"

With that, he donned his hooded cape and leaped out of the car.

"Leave him," I said as Max started to go after Dorian. "He enjoys being a martyr. And he really does have good ideas while he's baking."

Gwendolyn's hotel was only a few minutes farther at this deserted time of night.

The parking lot was illuminated by the soft light of six Victorian-style streetlamps. This was the type of boutique hotel for which charm was as important as convenience. It was a motel style layout, with two stories of rooms with doors facing the parking lot. It probably had been an inexpensive motel in the past, before being upscaled because the other side of the rooms had stunning views of the Willamette River.

I swore as Max parked.

"This is it, isn't it?"

"She didn't tell me her *room number*. How are we going to—"

"I don't like this." Max stiffened. He'd spotted something.

"What is it?" I followed his gaze.

"One of the doors is ajar."

"At four o'clock in the morning?"

"Exactly. Stay here."

"I'm not staying in the car."

Before Max could object, I leaped out. My long silver raincoat caught in the wind as I hurried to the door where I could see a sliver of light. Max caught up with me as I reached it.

I should have stayed in the car.

Gwendolyn's body lay on the bed, fully dressed on top of the covers. She lay face-up, and her eyes were wide open. *Unmoving.* There was no mistaking it. Gwendolyn Graves was dead.

CHAPTER 12

Max ushered us out of the room as he called 911.

Why would someone kill Professor Graves? What did she know? Had she been trying to call me when the killer stopped her? Was there anything I could have done?

As I sat in Max's car while we waited for help to arrive, I tried to breathe. For a woman who'd spent her life advocating on behalf of forgotten women to be killed in the middle of the night in a hotel room was too much of a tragedy for me to bear. I lowered my head into my hands, but my hands were shaking so it only made me feel worse. I tried closing my eyes, but I only saw the face of the not-quite-retired professor.

"It'll be all right," Max whispered as he reached over and held my hand. He was still on the phone with emergency services, and he'd locked us in the car to avoid both contaminating the crime scene and the possibility of danger. We didn't have to wait long. First responders arrived quickly.

I answered questions from the police first in the hotel parking lot, then at the station. I'd met the detective assigned to the case before, which put my mind slightly more at ease. Detective Vega was smart and open to ideas. Up to a point. She didn't know about alchemy or Dorian's existence, but I trusted her integrity and her willingness to listen.

I went over what I knew multiple times, explaining that I didn't know why the *Brother and Sister* painting would be valuable for any other reason than the sentimental value it had for me. The only lie I told was Dorian's role in discovering the break-in that I was sure was related. It was true that Max and I had found the broken glass and painting gone. It was also true that as soon as we each mentioned that we'd been fooling around, the questions moved on to what we found when we arrived in the attic.

Max couldn't bring himself to lie to his former colleagues any more than was necessary, so when asked if anyone else was with the two of us when we looked around the attic, Max had said, "Just me and Zoe and her gargoyle statue."

Since I'd been with Max the entire evening, I wasn't treated as a suspect in the professor's murder—which, frustratingly, they told us very little about. Detective Vega had met Nicolas and Perenelle before, but now she asked more questions about Nicolas since he'd bought the painting for me. As we were wrapping up, she let me know she'd need to follow up with the Flamels. The Flamels would also need to tell the police about their suspected burglary.

I vowed to get better backstories set up for Nicolas and Perenelle, starting today. My friend Tobias Freeman had already recommended someone more thorough in setting up backgrounds. Someone Tobias had trusted with his life for over forty years. I should have taken him up on it, but I hadn't imagined a murder-level degree of scrutiny. Luckily, Detective Vega seemed most focused on why a thief might be interested in the painting, not treating the Flamels as suspects. At least for now.

By the time Max and I were done answering Detective Vega's questions, I felt like a zombie. If I could only make it to sunrise, which wasn't far away at this point, the energy of the sun would sustain me. I had to last just a little while longer. Now that my burglary was related to a murder, a crime scene crew was sent to my house. I needed to show them where the painting had been stolen.

I called Dorian from the car to warn him the attic was about to become a crime scene. We'd been gone for so long that he was back home already. Otherwise, I wouldn't have been able to reach him. He didn't use a cell phone because his clawed fingers didn't work on the screen. He was careful to always return to the house under cover of darkness in his cape, so I knew he'd be there as it was approaching dawn.

I used the special sequence of rings so he'd know it was me calling.

"Murdered?" Dorian repeated after I hastily explained what had happened. *"Mon dieu."*

"The police know it's related to the theft of the artwork," I added, "so they're heading over to the house to gather evidence from the attic."

"Do not worry yourself. I will hide."

When we arrived at the house a few minutes later, a car and a van were pulling up as well. The detective, along with a crime scene team of two. This wasn't like the crowded hotel, because a murder hadn't taken place here. Not this time.

I opened the door for them and led them to the attic. Dorian hadn't fled to another part of the house. He was here in the attic—in stone form.

I sighed. It was a perfect way for Dorian to eavesdrop, and he was perfectly safe, but he was going to *hate it* when the police dusted him for fingerprints.

Max and I showed Detective Vega where the painting had been hidden, and yet again went over what we knew about the painting and theft, hoping being in the attic would help our memories return.

After looking over the scene, the detective left the crime scene techs to do their thing. She needed to begin investigating the murder. Max left with her. Did he think she'd tell him more without me there?

As the crime scene team took fingerprints, I explained that in addition to my and Max's fingerprints, they'd find fingerprints of Brixton, Veronica, and their friend Ethan.

"You invite teenagers up to your attic?" One of the techs blinked at me.

Yet again I was relieved I had a good relationship with Max and was known to be trustworthy to Portland PD. Otherwise, that fact could have sounded much creepier than it was.

"Brixton has a part-time job working in my garden," I said, "and the attic is a cozy spot surrounded by antiques that's nice for a snack break for him and his friends."

"This place has an aesthetic between dark academia and romantasy," a younger tech dusting for fingerprints cut in. "I can see why teenagers would like it." She smiled wistfully at the row of thick blown-glass jars on a low shelf next to the sloping ceiling. The impure glass of the mismatched pieces held a green tint and rough sheen that did indeed make me think it likely that a movie studio prop designer would snatch up these antique jars for the backdrop of a secret society's lair. I wondered what the wide-eyed young woman did when she wasn't working at crime scenes.

"I feel like I've seen this statue before." The crime scene tech pointed at Dorian. "Is it mass produced?"

I could have sworn I saw Dorian's nostril's flare.

"It's based on one of the gargoyles of Notre Dame in Paris," I told her.

"Right!" She grinned. "I visited before the fire that almost destroyed the cathedral. It looks like the *Thinker* gargoyle, but the pose of this one is different. Plus he's got legs. Who ever thought of a gargoyle having legs?"

"Millie," the other tech said sharply.

She didn't look as if the admonition phased her one bit. She simply gave a shrug and said to me, "The only way it works to stay in a job involving crime scenes, or anything related to crime, is to remember what we're fighting for in life. Those unexpected moments of wonder. Otherwise, why does it even matter?"

I smiled at her as I walked in the opposite direction to where Dorian was hiding in plain sight. "I agree. I'd be happy to answer any questions you have about the items here. I could use the distraction."

"You don't mind if I ask you about these hideous things?" She pointed at a collection of white porcelain figurines on the shelf next to where I'd led her eye. I'd almost passed on them at an estate sale because the trinkets were both ugly and reminded me how it had been painted by poor children in the mid-1800s. However, these ones were genuine, rather than the knockoffs that flooded the market in the 1970s. The descriptions I wrote for the Elixir website always included the historical significance of the objects I sold.

"Staffordshire porcelain," I said, "are a great reminder of history. Especially the centerpiece here. It's a mantelpiece pocketwatch holder. For working men in the mid-1800s who were successful enough for small amenities like a pocket-watch, but *not* wealthy enough to own a clock for their home, this decorative figurine was made with a circular slot where a pocket watch could rest. Turning the working-class man's pocket watch into a clock for his family home."

"Then why are the people in the figures so scary? These could be a prop in a horror movie. Did people in the past really want little cherubs with messy lipstick and insane hair in their homes?"

"Each figurine is different. The color on each one was painted by hand—by small children."

She gasped. "No."

"Sad, but true."

My phone rang before I could tell her more history she probably regretted asking about.

"Was anything else stolen from your inventory?" It was Detective Vega's voice.

"Just the painting. Why?"

"It wasn't the only painting stolen during the night," the detective said. "It's a good thing you weren't at home. There's another person whose painting was stolen tonight. He was attacked."

"Is he—"

"He survived the attack," she said. "But he's in the hospital. His wife gave me permission to share his name with you. Does the name Adam White mean anything to you?"

Adam White… It was vaguely familiar, but I couldn't place the name. "Should it?"

"He's the owner of a local company. Renaissance White."

The name clicked. "The new company that's making high end paints for artists."

"I'm sending you a photograph of Adam's stolen painting," the detective added. "It looks a bit like yours. It's called *The Apothecary's Cabinet.*"

I was glad she couldn't see my face as I looked at the photo of the painting. *The Apothecary's Cabinet* was more than "a bit" like my

Brother and Sister painting. Rows of glass jars, large and small, bursting with dried flowers, ground roots, and colorful pigments lined smooth wooden shelves. A ray of sunlight filtered in from either a door or a window, casting light on the vermillion. A long-stemmed, narrow jar was on its side, black salt pouring from the lip and strange shapes in the granules. Grains of salt that I was sure held subtle secrets of alchemy.

I had no doubt that I was looking at one of Perenelle Flamel's paintings. It wasn't just the style, or even the energy. I recognized the scene. It was a detail of one corner of the Flamels' French farmhouse.

There was no longer any doubt. It wasn't me the thief was after. *It was Perenelle.*

CHAPTER 13

From the Typewriter of Dorian Robert-Houdin

The Culinary Alchemist's Toolbox

What makes a work of art valuable?

A work of art can refer to a delicious meal as much as a painting. Both expressions of art are more than the sum of their parts. Cooking and traditional expressions of art both involve alchemical transformation.

Alchemy is the process of using your intent to transform imperfect raw elements into something greater than the ingredients you begin with.

The intentional selection of materials and a good recipe can result in a transformative feast. This is the same process that gives an artist pure pigments (though, of course, with different ingredients).

Similar to a meal that is elevated to a gourmet experience that results in you being called upon to be the primary chef for your social circle, some works of art become masterpieces that generate far more interest than the artist intended.

When you begin your journey, be clear in your intent. Stated more plainly, so there can be no mistake: Be careful what you wish for.

Before turning to his stone form, Dorian had forgotten to remove the typewritten words he had left in his typewriter, so now that he had the attic to himself once more, he was relieved to discover it was only inconsequential musings.

He was also thankful that modern fingerprinting was not as invasive as in the past. The indignity of being fingerprinted was well worth it, for he was able to hear firsthand what the detective thought about the two interwoven cases. And Zoe, to her credit, had led the crime scene technician away from Dorian's stone form when she lingered there for too long.

Dorian had hoped he would get additional details from Zoe after *les flics* had departed, yet Zoe did not have time to remain at home for a proper breakfast. She felt it urgent to meet with the other person who had been burgled, Adam White of Renaissance White. Zoe believed the cases to be connected because both stolen paintings had been created by Perenelle Flamel. But why was a thief after these paintings that would not be appraised for much money at all?

He could not speak more with her until she returned. For the moment, Dorian was left to his own devices. Yet Dorian Robert-Houdin was not one to wait for others to act. He was a self-reliant gargoyle.

The sun had risen, and Brixton and his other young friends would be getting ready for school. Dorian opened Zoe's computer and considered how to convince Brixton, Veronica, and Ethan to pay him a visit. Mentioning a burglary might be enough to entice them, yet *peer pressure* of messaging all three was sure to do the trick. This was key in convincing them to visit him before school, when time was short. He used a program that allowed him to text them simultaneously.

A burglary??? It was Veronica who was the first to respond, mere seconds after Dorian had sent the message.

!!!??? Ethan texted next.

On our way. Brixton wrote.

Dorian left the laptop open in case they wrote more, but turned his attention elsewhere while he waited. The device was an eye-sore, yet a necessary one.

Dorian had recently fixed three old typewriters that had not functioned properly when he bought them. He preferred the solid metal keys of a typewriter to the plastic buttons of Zoe's laptop.

There was *some* value to be had, he grudgingly admitted, from saving words in an electronic document, which could then be edited. Yet it did not make up for the clickity-clack of the typewriter keys that reminded him of the sound of rain falling on stone.

Screens of modern devices did not respond to Dorian's fingertips, and he did not enjoy the use of a magic pen that allowed him to fumble on such screens. He could use computer keyboards and was indeed a fast typist, yet he still felt awkward using them. It did not feel *natural.* And it would not do for the great Dorian Robert-Houdin to feel awkward!

He was, at heart, a creature made of stone. Though alchemy had given him life beyond stone, he felt at peace with the heavy, natural elements that constituted his typewriters.

Or, if he were being truly honest with himself—he was a self-aware gargoyle, after all—he might admit that the typewriters gave him a better excuse to abandon his works in progress. Each page was a fleeting expression, not easily revised or shared with others.

He had begun writing two Gothic novels in the past year, both of which he had abandoned. One about the Witch's Castle, a crumble of stone ruins near a Portland wildlife trail. The other about a Frankenstein's monster who befriended a cat. The beginnings, those were easy. Yet how did one stay motivated? It was *très difficile!* Now that there was another mystery afoot, in addition to his cookbook musings, he could begin another Gothic novel based on an art thief. Surely this would help his subconscious work through the mystery.

Bof! He should not be thinking of a Gothic tale at this moment.

What kind of host was he to have neglected to think of his guests who would be there in ten minutes or less?

He scampered to the kitchen and put together a platter of the misshapen pastries he had brought back from Blue Sky Teas before dawn this morning. He was still selecting the least misshapen of the lot when he heard an engine.

He carefully peered through the front curtains. It was the three teenagers, in Ethan's shiny white car. Ethan's parents had bought him the new car for his sixteenth birthday. The boy was far wealthier than either Veronica or Brixton, and until meeting his boyfriend Harry, far unhappier as well. Ethan's miserable parents were acrimoniously divorcing, so they thought a new car would cheer their boy. Dorian wondered how so many of the people who were the most successful with money could be so idiotic in other realms of their lives.

"My parents will kill me if I'm late to school," Veronica said as she dumped a huge backpack onto the floor. "Be quick."

Veronica Chen-Mendoza was now several inches taller than either boy, though Brixton had also grown in the time since Dorian had met him two years prior. This height differential had once bothered Veronica, but since this new school year had begun, she held herself more confidently. With her tall frame and effortless style—for she wore no discernible makeup and had repaired a red vintage coat she'd discovered at a local thrift store—he believed she would fit in very well in Paris, if she were to visit.

Dorian sniffed the air and frowned. "Did one of you step in what our neighbors euphemistically call 'doggie doo-doo'?"

They inspected their shoes and shook their heads.

"I don't smell anything," Brixton said.

"Me neither," Ethan said. "Only a good smell—these muffins you baked. And you know I wouldn't have let them in the car with dog—"

"I'll clean it up after school if anyone brought anything gross into Ethan's new car," Veronica interrupted. "We only have five minutes until we need to leave."

"At least eight," Ethan said, taking a cran-apple muffin.

"Ignore them." Brixton was the only one not to have sat down. "What was stolen?"

Dorian sniffed once more. "Do none of you smell that strange scent? It is quite metallic."

Brixton and Ethan shook their heads, but Veronica's eyes grew wide. "Are you having a stroke? My grandmother smelled burnt toast that wasn't there when she started having a stroke."

Dorian gasped and flapped his wings. Every part of his body reacted as it should. He did not feel as if he was falling ill. "*Non.* I am certain there is an odd aroma."

"Was your grandma okay?" Ethan asked Veronica.

"My mom knew what to do right away, so she was fine."

"I am glad for this," Dorian said with a smile. He was both pleased for the girl's *grand-mère*, and for having located the aroma. "The scent is from your backpack." He pointed at Veronica's overly stuffed backpack.

"My lunch?" Veronica reddened.

"That's messed up," Brixton said to Dorian. "You shouldn't criticize people's food."

He glowered at the boy. "I am not referring to her lunch, which has no scent at all." He presumed it was in a sealed lunch case. "There is something else."

Veronica grinned. "Must be my paints, then. I've got a couple of tubes in my bag. They're strong, I know."

"She's taking an art class," Ethan explained. "She's really good."

"The class is *amazing*," Veronica gushed. "My parents say art can't be a career, but I have a free elective, so I can do what I want with it. Do you want to see what we're studying?"

"Um, didn't you say we needed to leave soon?" Brixton asked.

Veronica's eyes grew wide. "Sorry! What happened with the burglary? What was stolen? Zoe found something valuable for Elixir?"

"Zoe's most beloved painting was taken." Dorian paused and drummed his clawed fingertips together. "The portrait of her and her brother."

Veronica gasped. "That's horrible!"

"What can we do to help?" Brixton asked.

Zoe did not like it when Dorian enlisted the help of the teenagers. She said they were children, which was quite insulting. They were sixteen now, which was as old as Zoe when she was forced to flee Salem Village for being suspected of witchcraft. Perhaps Veronica was only fifteen, but no matter. His young friends had proved both trustworthy and resourceful.

"I wish to utilize your social media talents to search for anyone who mentions a person carrying a large, framed artwork through Portland last night," Dorian explained. "Since I was unable to stop the intruder who stole Zoe's painting—"

"You were *here* when it was stolen?" Veronica gaped at him.

"I attempted to stop the thief, but I was kicked aside—"

"Are you okay?" Brixton asked, his gaze searching for injuries.

Dorian pointed at the small dark gray lump that had formed on his temple. "Only a minor inconvenience. I am physically well, but emotionally bereft. I have failed Zoe. I cannot go in search of the painting, and the police are not treating the theft as a priority because they are more concerned with the murder—"

"Murder?" The three young people said as one.

"Is this always what it's like being friends with a gargoyle?" Ethan asked his friends. The boy looked pale.

"Pretty much," Brixton answered.

Ethan and Veronica had learned the secret of Dorian's existence more recently than Brixton's accidental sighting of Dorian in Zoe's house. Veronica had adapted much more quickly. Ethan was indebted to Dorian for a courageous act which Dorian was quite proud to have performed, but the boy was going through a challenging time of life, with his parents flinging cruel accusations at each other as they divorced. He understood this to be challenging for children. If he could give the boy something productive to do, this would surely help his self-esteem.

"Who was murdered?" Veronica asked.

"The thief who stole the artwork," Dorian explained, "may also be the killer of another person interested in the artwork."

"He murdered someone?" Ethan said. "Truly?"

"An art historian is now dead." Dorian attempted to remove all emotion from his voice. It would not do to dwell on the tragedy. They could not save the woman, but they could avenge her. "It is possible that the thief saw her as a rival, as she was also interested in the painting. A second painting was stolen during the night, yet the recovery of the paintings are secondary to the police. They will only pursue the artwork as far as it leads them to their murderer. I, however, care most for my friend."

"That's beautiful." Veronica smiled at him.

Brixton rolled his eyes. "He also cares about solving a mystery."

Dorian clicked his tongue. "I have information that will help Zoe, which we are unable to tell the police, for they do not know I exist. This is why I need your assistance."

"What do you know?" Veronica asked.

"I did not hear the sound of a car. I believe the thief was on foot. *Alors,* someone may have seen the thief with Zoe's painting. Will you help?"

"Of course," Brixton said. "What else can you tell us—"

"We can't be late to school." Veronica scrambled up. "We already know what Zoe's painting looks like. I have photos as well. We'll figure it out. Ethan, come on."

She pulled the stunned boy from his seat.

Brixton grabbed another muffin as they hurried out. He paused in the attic door.

"Dorian." Brixton leaned in the doorway. With the hesitancy in his voice and naked concern on his face, he looked more boy than man. "If the thief killed a historian for being interested in the painting, doesn't that mean Zoe is in trouble as well?"

"She could be," Dorian said. "She very well could be."

CHAPTER 14

It had been a long time since plague doctors stuffed beaked masks with myrrh and rose petals to protect from the miasma that they believed surrounded illness, poking and prodding their patients from a distance with canes, offering little that could truly help their desperate patients. As much as medicine has progressed, hospitals still make me uneasy.

But it was worth it to be here this morning. A thief was after paintings Perenelle Flamel had painted. The police were intrigued by the connection of two paintings in a similar style being stolen, but I couldn't tell them that Perenelle was the artist. I needed to understand what the thief was truly after. What was so important that he was willing to kill a professor? Did Gwendolyn Graves know something? Had she lied to me about not knowing the true identity of Arthur Finder?

The other victim was my best lead, so after talking with Nicolas and Perenelle about what had happened, I was here at the hospital, waiting to see Adam White. Max had wanted to come with me, but I insisted he open his shop on time. He was the only employee for now, so it wouldn't open without him. I also expected it would be easier to see Adam White on my own.

As I waited on a pink chair in the cold waiting room, I yet again kicked myself for not getting better backstories for Nicolas and Perenelle. What if the police dug deeper than their IDs and superficial stories? I was thankful that at least I had someone to contact.

Theo—an alias and only known by his first name—was a former FBI agent turned identity forger. He'd left the bureau after an unjust tragedy, vowing to help worthy people in need through backchannel means. Though Theo wasn't his real name, Tobias swore that he was trustworthy. Tobias told me he'd become disillusioned with the system when he was unable to protect a woman who was testifying against her abusive boyfriend. The FBI had pressured her to take the stand in a larger criminal trial against the man, promising protection. But the man on trial had her killed. After that, Theo decided to help good people who needed to disappear, but who had to do it on their own.

Theo knew I'd be contacting him, thanks to a note from Tobias, so I hoped the former agent would help us. Even if he agreed to help, *would we have enough time*? As far as I knew, they weren't suspects, so they wouldn't be under too much scrutiny. But I had a bad feeling about where the investigation would lead.

He didn't help everybody. He ran whatever kind of background check a former FBI agent turned criminal knew how to do, judged whether someone was worthy of his assistance, then created meticulous documents and fully developed backstories. When possible for the circumstances, Theo recommended people take one of the identities of people who didn't exist that he'd created over time. The Flamels already had names and IDs. What we needed was for Nicolas and Perenelle to have backgrounds built out that fit their names and lives.

The Flamels were born three hundred years before me. They had so much history behind them, but were also skilled at adapting. We'd settled on a story that was close to the truth: Perenelle had been previously married, and she feared for her life from the man's family. That's the story we needed help with. The idea was for Theo to plant the breadcrumbs that anyone who dug deeply would follow.

Though the story bent the truth, it was easy to remember because at its core, it was true. Perenelle's first husband had been a good man

—she would never have married him if this had not been true—yet his family was horrid to Perenelle after his death. They refused to display her portraits of him. It crushed her spirit when her brother-in-law hid the paintings instead of celebrating the life of the man she'd loved. Perenelle fled this constrictive life to Paris, where she met Nicolas. It was a sad truth that it was all too believable for a woman to be forced to flee a powerful, vindictive man. It was also a story Theo was predisposed to believe.

From the hospital waiting room, I wrote a message explaining to Theo as much as I safely could reveal about the Flamels, then held my breath as I hit *send*.

I wasn't asking for help for myself today. My backstory was something I always kept in mind. It's why I'd spent so many decades living out of my Airstream trailer without a permanent address. An itinerant young woman following in the footsteps of her mother and grandmother might solicit shaking heads from well-meaning people who wished she'd settle down, but it hardly raised suspicion.

"Zoe?"

I stood hastily as a dark-haired woman with a slight frame and large, stylish glasses said my name. She wasn't dressed like a doctor or nurse, and she wore slippers. She winced when she saw me glancing at her feet.

"It didn't even occur to me I was in slippers when I left the house," she said.

"I'm pro foot comfort," I assured her. "You know who I am, but I didn't catch your—"

"Oh! Sorry. I'm Willow Matsumoto. Adam's wife. When the police banged on my front door in the middle of the night to tell me Adam had been attacked, I wasn't thinking straight. That's how I ended up here in slippers."

I'd read their bios on the Renaissance White website, so I knew the couple had met in graduate school for chemistry a decade ago. Adam and Willow, along with Oberon and April Salazar, had founded the company three years ago. I didn't recognize her because there were no photos with their bios. Instead, each of them had a photo of a glass jar of pigment next to their bio. Adam's jar held bright white granules, Willow's a golden yellow and orange powder, Oberon's a charcoal as black as night, and April's an assortment of green crystals.

"How's Adam?" I asked.

"Awake, but he got a nasty bump on the head, so I'll be on concussion watch—once they let me take him out of here. Thanks for coming. You were robbed by the same thief last night?"

"I got off lucky."

Willow nodded. "I was just talking with a detective. She told me a woman had been murdered and that it might be connected. They said you weren't under suspicion, so I told the detective it was all right to tell you about Adam. I thought maybe we could figure out why both our paintings were targeted."

"My thoughts exactly," I said, relieved I wouldn't have to make up an excuse for why I was asking questions. "My painting wasn't close to being the most expensive they could have taken, but it's in the same style as yours."

"A killer who cares more about beauty than money? I don't know if that's reassuring or not."

"What worries me most," I said, "is that my painting wasn't even listed online. I don't know how they knew about it."

"Ours wasn't a secret." Willow looked up at the ceiling, as if caught up in a memory. "It used to hang in the lobby outside our lab, but Adam worried it might be mistaken for something more valuable than it is, since it's so old."

"Is Adam up for talking about what happened last night?"

"Of course. He's desperate for answers about—" Willow broke off. "There's something you should know about my husband before you meet him."

I waited for her to continue.

"The way his mind works," she began, her voice still hesitant. "He cares so much about both art and science. Those thoughts are always at the forefront of his thoughts. He was devastated about the theft of *The Apothecary's Cabinet*."

"You mean," I said, "that I shouldn't expect him to shed a tear for Gwendolyn Graves, the woman who was murdered?"

Willow pursed her lips. "Not exactly... Since the murder

happened after he was attacked and both of your paintings stolen, the police had already taken his statement. He was with the doctors when they followed up with me just now to tell me about that…"

"You mean," I said, "Adam doesn't yet know there's been a murder."

CHAPTER 15

Adam White's face was pale, but perhaps it always was, if he spent all his time in a chemistry lab. He smiled as I entered the room and Willow introduced us.

"You," he said, "look like an artist."

"Is it the hair or the coat?" I asked. I'd agreed not to tell him about the murder yet. He'd find out soon enough, and up close, I could tell his sickly pallor was due to his injuries. Bandages were visible on both his head and right hand.

He laughed, then immediately winced and touched the back of his head. Willow stepped to his side and took his hands so he'd stop fussing with the bandages.

"That's where the thief hit you?"

He began to nod, then groaned again. "I hope you got off better than I did. And to answer your question, it's your boots."

I didn't need to look down at my feet to know which boots I was wearing. Chestnut brown ankle boots with pewter buckles I'd taken care of and resoled for decades. They were simple enough, but a closer look would confirm that they weren't anything you could buy in a store.

"I wasn't at home when it happened," I said. "I was at my boyfriend's house when the painting was stolen from the attic where I store all of the merchandise for my online antique shop."

"Lucky." He gave me a sharp look. I couldn't tell if it was suspicion, or simply the pain of being bashed on the head.

"You were working late last night at your chemistry lab when the thief broke in?" I asked.

"I often work late, but not *that* late. At about two o'clock in the morning, I got a call that our alarm at the lab had gone off. The police were dispatched but didn't see anything wrong, so they left. I was worried, though, since Renaissance White is my life. Our life." He squeezed Willow's hand.

"I'd taken a sleeping pill," Willow said, "so I was too groggy to come with Adam to check it out."

"Which I'm glad for," Adam picked up, "because when I showed up, I learned that the thief had played me."

"They were waiting for you."

"It was stupid of me to go. I played right into his hands. Once I unlocked the front door—which needs a code—the thief forced his way inside behind me. I tried to run farther inside to lock myself in the lab, and that's when he hit me. It was something hard, but I don't know what. I tried to fight back—a self-preservation instinct, I guess, but in retrospect was the stupidest thing I could have done. When I was on the floor, feeling sick from the pain, he whispered in my ear that I'd be opening up the safe for him."

"Whispered?" That was curious. "Like he was someone you knew who was disguising his voice?"

"All I can tell you was that it was creepy. I had no desire to be a hero after that knock on the head and that whispering voice right out of a horror movie. I opened the safe for him without him having to ask again. I did my best to also not look his way, even though he was in a ski mask already. I wasn't going to give him another reason to hurt me."

"You said you fought back. Did you manage to hurt him?"

"I honestly don't remember. I was terrified and pretty sure I was begging for mercy at that point. Please don't repeat that to the press." He laughed nervously.

"Bad for our image right when we're getting off the ground," Willow explained. "Our new line of oil and acrylic paints is launching soon. The first color that's rolling out this fall is Renaissance White."

"I won't be talking to the press," I assured them. "I just don't understand why the thief took our paintings. My painting is old, but it's unknown."

I held up my phone and showed them the image of the *Brother and Sister* painting where Max had obscured my face.

"Similar style," said Willow, "but the subject matter is different. A portrait compared to an interior detail. Are those apothecary jars in the background of your portrait?"

"They are," I confirmed, and pinched the screen to make the background larger, taking the focus away from my blurred-out image.

"I can't tell in the photograph," said Adam, "but the colors look like they might be the same vibrancy as ours. And those jars are similar to the ones in ours. We used our painting, which we started calling *The Apothecary's Cabinet* for obvious reasons, as a reference as we replicated colors. We knew if we were able to get colors as vibrant as the ones in that old painting, we'd be onto something great."

"That's what Renaissance White does," Willow explained. "We use modern scientific methods to recreate lost colors from the past."

"*The Apothecary's Cabinet* had an amazing shade of white in it," Adam said, "so it was helpful to have around as inspiration as we created Renaissance White."

"My *Brother and Sister* painting was most recently in a small family museum in France," I said. "Where did you find *The Apothecary's Cabinet?*"

"Oberon found it at a flea market on the outskirts of Paris," Willow said. "The one in the suburb of Saint-Ouen. No provenance. Just a beautiful hidden gem."

The Marché aux Puces de Saint-Ouen was filled with high end antiques, but still, I hated to think of Perenelle's works of art ending up in flea markets. But what had I expected would happen after they'd abandoned their home abruptly?

"Did you test the composition of the paint?" I asked. If they had, they wouldn't have liked what they found. Perenelle was skilled enough to use ingredients such as mercury, which were both dangerous and banned in modern products.

"Of course." Willow grinned. "We're scientists. We tested samples from hundreds of paintings. Modern methods don't require taking more than a microscopic fragment of a painting to test, and some x-ray techniques don't remove anything at all."

"Anything interesting?" I prompted.

Adam's face lit up. "*Everything* about color is interesting. Old paintings are filled with poisonous materials we can't use in our paint, and this one was no exception. Testing doesn't tell us what materials to use, but it sheds light on history and inspires us to do better. This was one of the paintings that inspired us to create the most beautiful white the world has ever seen."

"So you've captured the spirit of lead white?" I asked.

They both grinned like giddy children.

I knew the color well. It was one of the many highly toxic paints that used to reign supreme. Some toxic colors from the past now had replacements. Scheele's Green was a luscious green that had the side effect of poisoning people with deadly arsenic. It was so prized that people continued to use it long after they realized how poisonous it was. Luckily, similar colors could now be reproduced synthetically. But lead white, an ethereal white that slowly poisoned anyone who used it, hadn't yet been adequately replaced.

Adam and Willow shared a smile that made it clear their marriage partnership was as strong as their scientific one. Their radiant smiles as they gazed into each other's eyes reminded me of the Chemical Wedding in alchemy. The Chemical Wedding stage of alchemy brings together the complementary opposites of the sun and moon, sulfur and mercury, at the near-final phase of alchemical transformation.

"Our paint," said Adam, "produces the brilliant white *without* the toxic lead that makes lead white a banned substance. We're giving it back to artists who haven't been able to work with it like their forbears who paid the price for gorgeous colors by poisoning themselves."

"We think of ourselves as modern alchemists," Willow said, giving me a start.

"Present-day chemists who were inspired by the ingenious chemists of the past," Adam added. "Those early scientists didn't have everything right. They weren't even close."

"But," said Willow, "they had a commitment to rigorous experimentation and high-quality ingredients."

"Which they sourced themselves," Adam said. "A painter from a few hundred years ago wouldn't have been able to buy a tube of paint at their local art store. They had to make colors themselves, mixing pigments and using binders to bring colors to life. Before artists became so separated from their materials, they knew how to make their pigments from scratch. Or at the very least they understood how the process worked, if it was a color like Tyrian Purple or Cochineal Red that was too labor intensive for them to make themselves."

I smiled to myself as the couple seamlessly picked up the threads of each other's thoughts and excitedly told me about the history of color. I had many fond memories of my apothecary shop in Paris, where I sold ingredients that could be used for remedies as well as paint. Many artists bought their raw materials from me. I was their neighborhood art store.

Willow was the first to notice my knowing smile. "Adam." She playfully poked his side. "I believe Zoe knows everything we're telling her."

Adam reddened. "Was I mansplaining? Willow, please kill me now."

"I'm as guilty as you," she said.

"Don't worry about it," I assured them. "You're both scientists who clearly love your work. And you're inquisitive people. Do you have theories about *why* the thief would want both of our paintings?"

Adam shook his head and immediately regretted it. "The police asked us that already. They—" He cried out in pain as he broke off. His face contorted in agony as he clutched his head.

Willow rushed to the door to call for a doctor, but someone had already heard. A nurse ushered both Willow and me out of the room, and when a doctor appeared a moment later, they shut the door, leaving us in the sterile hallway.

Everything looked worse under fluorescent lighting, but that's not why Willow's face appeared twisted in grief.

"I can't lose him," she whispered. "Not after everything else. Not after—"

A medical assistant interrupted her to usher us to the waiting room. The attempt to cheer the sterile room with a bland painting of the seaside only made it worse.

I was about to ask Willow what she meant about *everything else,* when the nurse who'd come to check on Adam told Willow that he was asking for her.

"Only his wife," the nurse said to me when I stepped forward to follow.

As Willow hurried after the nurse, one of her slippers fell off. When she stopped to grab it, I caught a glimpse of her face. Tears streamed down her cheeks.

Head injuries could be worse than they first appeared. I hoped a second victim wouldn't be dead before the day was out.

CHAPTER 16

I left the hospital, wondering what Adam had wanted to say about what he'd told the police and what Willow meant by *everything else.*

Everything that was happening centered around Perenelle. Was it her paintings? Her notebook? Her identity? I needed to see her. Dorian would never forgive me if I left him out, so I stopped home to get him. I told him what I'd learned as I bundled him into my truck and drove us to the Flamels' house.

"I am displeased with this situation," Dorian said from where he was tucked under a green wool blanket on the floor of the front passenger seat.

I glanced at the bundle. "You know it's not safe for you to sit on the seat."

"This is not of which I speak. You are refusing to tell me what you learned until we reach the Flamels."

I scowled at the hidden lump of gargoyle. "I *did* tell you everything I learned."

"*Pfft.* Then you have learned nothing! You spent too much time with pleasantries before the killer thief's second victim slipped into oblivion. Your desire to be friendly has cost you our only opportunity to question the victim—"

"He's not dead." I braked harder than was necessary at a stop sign, causing Dorian to bump into the glove compartment. "Sorry. Adam wasn't even unconscious. He'd taken a turn for the worse, but that's to be expected with a traumatic head injury."

"I will refrain from mentioning your driving skills," Dorian grumbled, "for I am aware you came of age long before the invention of the automobile. But I must point out that you are a bad, bad detective, Zoe."

"Because I'm *not* a detective." I scowled more deeply at the lumpy blanket before setting off again. "I still managed to learn a lot." Well, perhaps it wasn't *a lot*. But it was a start. "You know they found the painting in a flea market in Paris."

"*Le Marché aux Puces de Saint-Ouen* is a respectable market that has existed for 150 years," Dorian said. "This makes sense."

"And I told you we were talking about the history of pigments. That's relevant, too, because they're color scientists who tested Perenelle's painting for its chemical makeup. They know she used dangerous materials, but also that it was the norm at the time. They recreate historical colors without dangerous toxins."

"That is barely enough information to form a theory," Dorian stated.

"That's why we're going to see Perenelle and Nicolas. Someone after Perenelle's paintings is willing to resort to murder, so none of us is safe until we figure out what's going on."

There was no need for Dorian to hide once we reached the secluded hillside sanctuary in the West Hills, so Dorian stepped out of the truck once I pulled my 1942 Chevy pickup truck into the Flamels' driveway.

We walked through the rock and flower gardens. Unlike in my backyard garden, where the few flowers I grew were well taken care of, here in Perenelle's garden it was as if the flowers felt valued. As if they sensed they were about to be harvested to create a masterpiece.

The autumn garden was bursting with dozens more varieties of plants with elements that could be coaxed into colorful dyes across the spectrum of the rainbow, and could be transformed into paint. The surrounding earth held ochre clay and an assortment of mineral-rich rocks that could be ground into complementary pigments. But Perenelle wasn't in her garden today.

"No Maximillian?" Nicolas asked as he ushered us inside. Only Nicolas could get away with calling Max by his given name.

"He wanted to close his shop for the day to help," I said, "but I didn't want him hurting a business that's just getting off the ground."

"She has been sending him text messages to assure him she is staying safe," Dorian added. "An uncivilized form of conversing, yet I understand its practicality."

"Are you and Perenelle okay?" I asked Nicolas. "Was Detective Vega telling me the truth that you aren't suspects?"

"It appears that way," Nicolas said. "She was most interested in my correspondence with Arthur Finder, to investigate whether he's tied to the murder. A tragic affair."

"It is," I agreed. Also one that didn't make sense. Why had the thief needed to kill Gwendolyn Graves? Why was she a threat?

"One cannot trust *les flics*," Dorian said. "You must always be on guard."

Dorian was distrustful of the police, but to be fair, he was distrustful of anyone outside of our small circle of friends.

We located Perenelle in her art and alchemy studio. She faced the floor-to-ceiling window, looking out over the overcast sky. In profile, her expression held a look of longing. As if she sought something in the distance she couldn't quite grasp.

Even though she claimed she hadn't felt the passage of time when she'd been imprisoned, I knew she'd experienced it on some elemental level. Because now, she longed for freedom as if gasping for air itself. I wondered how long this mansion, with its expansive art and alchemy studio and its sprawling gardens, could contain her.

Or perhaps it was only my imagination. She'd always sought more than this world would allow her. Those choices so long ago were what had nearly killed her and her beloved Nicolas.

"It's really true?" she said without turning. "It's another one of my paintings that was stolen?"

I pulled up the image Detective Vega had sent me. "There's no provenance for it, but I recognize the scene. It's being called *The Apothecary's Cabinet*."

"*The Apothecary's Cabinet*," Perenelle repeated as she zoomed in on one of the glass jars. The one containing dried golden roses, which had alchemical symbols subtly visible in the veins of the petals. She smiled. "That's a good name for it. Where did it end up?"

"A flea market in Paris. They were drawn to it because of the colors. They don't suspect it of being a Hayden or about the alchemical subject matter. Replicating lost colors is what Renaissance White's business does."

"You have no proof that they are not interested in the alchemical subject matter." Dorian stood on his tiptoes to see the portion of the painting Perenelle was looking at. "Alchemical secrets are hidden in these rose petals. This fact is clearly the most important of them all. We all know alchemists are not immortal. Adam White's head injury may yet kill him. We must question him once more before it is too late!"

"I'll talk with him and his wife again if I can," I said. "Not because I think he's an alchemist, but because our conversation was interrupted. They might know something that can help us."

"You must ask about the secrets hidden in *The Apothecary's Cabinet*," Dorian insisted.

"The alchemical symbols for sulfur and mercury are in the rose petals," said Perenelle, "to show the symbolism of the king and queen, a marriage of opposites that culminates in the Great Work. Nothing in that imagery is a secret. Nothing worth killing for."

Red roses would have symbolized sulfur and the sun, and white roses mercury and the moon. But here, she'd used gold to represent the Golden Child. The final stage of alchemical transformation.

"Is there anything else hidden in this painting?" I asked. "Anything that someone would need to possess it to learn?"

Perenelle scanned the image before handing the phone back to me. "My pigments themselves might be of interest to modern chemists."

I nodded. "They tested the painting and know the materials you used. Which they also know are substances that are banned today, so they can't use them, even if they could replicate your recipes—which they can't. We need to take a few steps back. We don't know who Arthur Finder is. We don't know if he's the one who stole the paintings and killed the professor. We don't know if the thief and murderer are the same person. And we don't know why Gwendolyn Graves was a threat. Did I forget anything?"

"We do not know if the thief meant to kill Adam White," Dorian added.

I shook my head. "We do know the answer there. Adam wasn't even unconscious when the thief left him. He didn't see the thief's face and can't identify him, so maybe the thief didn't consider him a threat."

"Or perhaps the thief and the killer are two separate people," Nicolas said.

I groaned. He was right. "There's so much we don't know. Which is what worries me."

"Quite," said Nicolas.

Dorian scowled at us. "Detectives must consider all the possibilities. It is my curse that I can see several steps into the future. This is why I also excel at the strategies of chess. Perhaps if we—"

Nicolas sneezed.

Perenelle handed him a cloth tissue. "He claims it was only dust made him feel poorly yesterday afternoon."

"Nonsense." He accepted the handkerchief. "I merely said it was the straw that broke the water buffalo's back."

"I believe it is the camel's back," Dorian said.

"Thank you, good man." Nicolas picked up a pocket-size commonplace notebook where he catalogued interesting expressions. He flipped through the pages. "Ah, yes! I had camel here already." He shut the notebook. "As I was saying, my coughing fit was precipitated not only by dust, but by my day-long bookstore treasure hunt yesterday. I'm afraid I forgot to eat."

Dorian gasped. Forgetting to eat was nearly as shocking to him as murder.

"I had to make sure he got both food and rest," Perenelle said, "which is why we could not attend dinner last night."

Now that the issue of food had come up, and it was nearly lunchtime, Dorian insisted on cooking so we could feed our minds.

Using only items from the pantry, he fixed a warming stew of caramelized onions, scarlet runner beans, sun-dried tomatoes, and dried chilies, which he sprinkled with Himalayan black salt, a unique salt that's cooked in a kiln with spices that give it a smoky, sulfurous flavor.

Once satiated with the hearty food, our minds were ready to focus on the task at hand.

We divided up the research between the four of us. Nicolas and Perenelle tackled the stacks of obscure art history books they'd acquired, looking for Hayden's surviving art, artwork in the style of Hayden that might have been Perenelle's unattributed work, and alchemy in art.

Dorian and I were the online researchers. He used the Flamels' desktop computer to search online sources for any other news of art thefts that might give us clues about what the thief was after. My task was to delve deeper into Gwendolyn Graves's research, to see if I could figure out how her path had crossed with that of Arthur Finder. I was at a disadvantage that I didn't know who he really was, but there had to be clues out there. Her death, which had been preceded by an attempt to call me and ended with her hotel room door left ajar, was far from a perfect crime. While the police were tracing down evidence from the crime scene, we could approach the mystery by finding out the true motive.

"*The Red Queen!*" Perenelle cried. She pointed to a hefty book on Rudolf II's Court in Prague, open on the dining table in front of her. It was open to a page towards the back.

We gathered around her as she pointed to a black-and-white photograph of an oil painting with a woman in a crown in the center, a king and a child at her side. The small image was one of many on the page that looked like an inventory.

"I didn't think this one would have survived," she said as I leaned forward to get a better look at the two-inch reproduction. "It's buried in this list of *hundreds* of paintings from Rudolfine Prague. This book catalogues an exhibition from the 1990s."

Nicolas grinned. "*The Red Queen* survived. You told me about it, but now I get to see it for the first time. Um, if someone might help me locate my spectacles? This image is quite small."

Perenelle lifted his reading glasses from the top of his head.

"This is a most unflattering photograph." Dorian tapped his

pointer claw on the black-and-white photograph. "There is a smudge in the lower section."

Perenelle grinned as she shook her head. "That's not a smudge. It's a brushstroke and the alchemical symbol for brimstone." She clasped her hands together. "I'd forgotten about Anne."

"The wife of the dull English merchant you befriended?" Nicolas asked.

"Yes, the wife of a wealthy boor," said Perenelle. "Adding one last element of whimsy to the painting was her idea."

Perenelle turned to me and Dorian to explain what Nicolas presumably already knew. "Anne was the one person in Prague I told that I was a woman. She sat for a painting, but that quickly became a cover story so we could converse. She was the one who pushed me to make my most daring painting, showing the true power of women in alchemy. Showing—" She broke off and squinted at the image. "It's too small to see it here. I wonder if we might find a copy of the painting online?"

We searched for *The Red Queen,* but it didn't appear to be a famous enough painting to be found in a museum, at least not one big enough to have catalogued it online. Even though the painting was noted as being part of Rudolf II's Court, where Philippe Hayden had been a patron, *The Red Queen* was unattributed here in this volume cataloguing the exhibit that had been shown in Prague decades ago. It wasn't listed prominently, only hidden here in this two-inch reproduction that sat alongside hundreds of other paintings and sketches. Odd, since "Philippe Hayden" had been an official court painter.

"Why isn't this signed with your signature 'P' that would have made sure this was attributed to Philippe Hayden?" I asked.

"I did many foolish things when I was in Prague," she said. "One of them was thinking this would be the painting that proved Philippe Hayden was a woman. There are many hidden symbols inside it that I hoped one day it would have been discovered."

"You recorded *The Red Queen* details in your stolen notebook?"

"I did."

If the thief was tracking down Perenelle's artwork, what was he really after?

CHAPTER 17

We'd spent all afternoon at the Flamels' house, and I was due to meet
Max at his shop at closing time.

Max didn't usually have a five o'clock shadow, but when I spotted
dark circles under his eyes along with the stubble, I remembered he
hadn't had a chance to shave this morning. We'd only slept two hours
last night, so my eyes must have looked equally haggard, but sunlight
and adrenaline had kept me going.

"Busy day?" I asked as I surveyed the disheveled shop. Strands of
loose-leaf black tea were visible in two separate corners of the hardwood floor, as if they'd been hastily swept up. I spotted the broom
leaning against the wall behind the counter.

"Much busier than expected," he said as he locked the door behind
me and turned the OPEN sign on the door to CLOSED. "Still, I
should have been helping you—"

"Ruining your new business wouldn't have helped." I breathed in
the intermingled scents of the dozens of tea varieties that filled the
shop, catching hints of cocoa, tobacco, and toasted rice. "I can fill you
in over dinner, but I'd understand if you want to go home and get
some sleep."

"Before you catch me up? Not a chance." As he swept me into his
arms, the warmth of his body and strength of his gentle hands made
me feel as if the last two days had never happened.

Before his lips met mine, a sharp knock rapped on the glass door, making us jump apart.

Detective Vega's face was visible through the glass. "We need to talk."

"You caught the perp?" Max asked her as he unlocked the door.

"Not exactly," Vega said.

Not *exactly*?

A strangely familiar woman stood behind the detective. Did I know her? A frail, older woman, she gripped a hand-carved wooden cane in her left hand. The joints of her fingers were ravaged by arthritis, but she walked nearly as briskly as the detective as Max let them both inside and locked up once more. She wasn't as delicate as she looked at first glance.

"Do you recognize this woman?" Detective Vega looked from Max to me.

"What are you doing, Vega?" Max took hold of my shoulders and turned me around. "You know you need a proper lineup if you think we saw someone involved. You can't show a suspect to us like this."

"It's all right," I said as the truth hit me. My pulse quickened. *I knew who this was.* I broke free of Max's grasp.

I hadn't recognized her at first, but it was her. Gwendolyn Graves. She wasn't dead—and, more surprisingly, *I'd never met her.*

"Professor Graves," I said. "We haven't met, but I've been learning all about you." I turned to Detective Vega. "This *isn't* the woman I met with yesterday at Blue Sky Teas. That's why you brought her over, isn't it? To make sure I'd never seen her before? That it was someone else I met yesterday?"

This Gwendolyn Graves—the authentic one—looked *less* like herself than the imposter. At least, she looked less like the headshot that was more than two decades old. The real semi-retired professor's wavy gray hair wasn't pulled into a bun like it was in her headshot, but had been cut shorter and rested on her shoulders. Her frame was also quite slim, almost gaunt, and of course there was the cane. She'd aged in a less glamorous way than the fake Gwendolyn, but the curiosity on the true Gwendolyn's face made her look far more youthful.

"Thank you," said the detective. "I can confirm this is the real Dr. Graves. I had to be sure this wasn't the woman you met yesterday."

"Zoe's meeting yesterday," said Max. "That woman was an *imposter*?"

The detective nodded.

"But why—" I began, but stopped myself. I knew why. "She was the thief who stole my paintings?"

"Looks like it," Detective Vega said.

I groaned. "She impersonated Professor Graves so she could follow me home and steal a painting that everyone is after. And I fell for it."

"It's not your fault," said Max.

"He's right," Vega added.

"I should have been more careful," I insisted. I knew why I'd slipped. It was exhausting to always be so careful. To always be pretending. Max squeezed my hand and my apprehension immediately faded. I didn't have to be careful with Max. I could be myself completely.

"You thinking the dead woman's partner double-crossed her?" Max asked Detective Vega. "Who—"

"We're still putting the pieces together," the detective said. She didn't volunteer more information.

"You haven't found the paintings, have you?" I asked.

"They won't show me the paintings this is about," the real Professor Graves cut in. "Could I see—"

"I need to get a statement from you," Detective Vega said as she steered the real professor out the door. "Thanks for your help, Zoe. Max."

"How long will you two be?" I asked. "I'd like to talk with—"

"You don't need to speak with Dr. Graves. We've got it covered."

Behind her, Dr. Graves caught my eye.

"You're in good hands with Detective Vega," I said to her, reaching forward to shake her hand—and to slip my business card into her palm. Now she could contact me directly.

Max leaned against the door after he let them out. "I wasn't expecting that turn of events."

"No." I also wasn't expecting such a big setback.

It was *the thief* who was killed, leaving me even further away from the truth. It was up to me to get my painting and Perenelle's irreplaceable notebook back, but my best lead was dead.

It was a good thing I had a secret weapon. Or rather, a secret gargoyle.

CHAPTER 18

"Betty Kubiak?" Dorian repeated the name I'd spoken.

I was at home in the attic with Dorian, explaining what I'd learned about how the person killed at the hotel wasn't Gwendolyn Graves. After getting a quick update from me about the events of the day, Max had gone after Detective Vega in hopes of getting more information out of her. He'd called me with the information that the dead woman had been identified as local resident Betty Kubiak.

"She was both an actress and an artist in addition to being a thief." I swept my gaze across the wares once owned by people across centuries and continents. So many lives and stories.

"An actress." Dorian steepled his fingers together. "She used her skills for the nefarious purpose of assuming the role of a professor."

"So she could gain my confidence and steal the *Brother and Sister* painting."

Dorian unclasped his hands and ran to my laptop. He tapped the password and his search so quickly that his claws tapping sounded like a woodpecker.

"The detective is fairly certain she was the thief," I said as Dorian typed. "But the two stolen paintings still haven't been recovered."

Dorian sat back on his heels. "*Mon dieu,*" he whispered.

"What is it?" I ran to his side.

There she was. Betty Kubiak in the playbill for a musical that ran in Portland a decade ago. *It was her.* The woman I'd met as Gwendolyn Graves, looking a few years younger and with much different hair.

"Those eyes," Dorian said. "They are the eyes of the burglar I swore I would never forget. The detective is correct. She was indeed the thief."

I closed my eyes and thought back on how she'd tricked me every step of the way. "And I led her straight to us. Straight to my painting of Thomas."

Shouldn't I have been smarter than this by now? Part of me wished I was more skeptical of people. The positive side of this deficiency meant I'd retained my humanity. It's a danger for alchemists who live too long to lose their compassion and connection to others. It's easy for heartbreak to become numbness when you watch loved ones die and see the human race repeat the mistakes of history again and again. Even though I've seen wars and starvation, I've also seen generosity and love. I don't spend my time looking for deception. I expect people to be good, because most of them are.

"I can confirm with certainty that she was the thief," Dorian said. "After following you home from Blue Sky Teas, she waited until you left with Max and Brixton, then broke in to steal the painting. Are you going to tell the detective?" Dorian blinked up at me.

"Max and I didn't see the burglar, so I can't say I suddenly remembered that I recognized her eyes." I shook my head. "The police already suspect that she was the thief. I confirmed she impersonated Professor Graves, and they must have other evidence from the crime scene they aren't telling us."

I opened a new tab and searched once more for Professor Gwendolyn Graves and up popped the headshot she used on her books. There was definitely a resemblance, but now that I looked more closely, it was entirely superficial. They were white women of approximately the same age and build, with similar blue eyes. Beyond that, Betty had mimicked the professor's distinctive hair, which was enough to distract from the other differences.

"She's not the only villain, though," I added. "Someone killed her."

"Perhaps she was betrayed by an untrustworthy partner," Dorian suggested. "Arthur Finder, whoever he really is. This is why a life of crime does not pay. One cannot trust one's accomplices."

The doorbell rang at the same time as a text arrived from Max, letting me know it was him at the door. Now that he'd met Dorian, he was much more understanding of my privacy at the house. I went down to let him in.

"Dorian confirmed Betty was the thief he saw," I told Max as we climbed the stairs. "He recognized her eyes."

"I'm glad Vega already figured that out." Max rubbed his tired eyes. "I don't know how we could have arranged for a gargoyle to give evidence."

"It pains me," Dorian said from the door of the attic, "that I will never find myself in a position of giving testimony. I would be a most excellent witness." He looked up at Max. "Has Zoe informed you that I have excellent night vision?"

Max blinked at the gargoyle. "I can't say that she has."

"And my little gray cells possess a superb ability to recall scenes I have witnessed."

"It's hardly a fair chess match if you're a savant." The hint of a smile flickered on Max's lips.

"He doesn't have perfect recall," I said as I pushed them both into the attic. "He looks for any opportunity to point out his similarities to Poirot."

Dorian puffed up his chest. "This is a most relevant fact for the solving of a mystery."

"You're incredibly observant," I assured him. "But right now, I'm glad you won't have to tell Detective Vega what you saw." I turned to Max, who'd plunked himself down into one of the wooden chairs at the chess board. "Learn anything more from Vega?"

"A lot. Vega already found evidence that the thief—the Betty Kubiak woman—was hired to play a part to figure out where the painting was. Kubiak emailed dozens of people who might have had it, based on whatever intel she and her partner had on Nicolas. Which, thankfully, didn't appear to be much. So it's not just you who was targeted. She assumed the role of this professor to add an air of legitimacy to her cold emails. That way people would get back to her and she could con whoever had the painting."

"What a loathsome creature." Dorian scrunched his snout in disgust.

"I wish that were true." Max rubbed his eyes again. "She looked after her dead sister's adult son with a disability. The cost of the assisted living institution where her nephew lived had gotten expensive—"

"So Betty was desperate," I finished. What a terrible situation to find herself in.

I'd immediately liked Betty when I met her, so it was good to see I hadn't made a complete mess of judging her character, even though she'd been conning me at the time. I'd had the feeling she was conflicted about how much to tell me about what she knew—and I'd been right. But I'd been wrong about what it was she was holding back.

Max stretched his neck from side to side and stifled a yawn. "I could use a coffee. Could I trouble you, Dorian?"

Dorian walked to the attic door before noticing we weren't following. He narrowed his black eyes. "I am a partner in this investigation. I will not be relegated to the kitchen while the 'adults' talk. I am far older than you, Max."

Max held up his hands. "I promise we'll follow in just a minute. It's not, um, information sharing that I had in mind."

Dorian grumbled about love birds taking over his attic as he slunk out of the room.

Max's face was scratchy with stubble, but I didn't care as he kissed me with more vigor than I imagined possible for someone who'd gotten a grand total of two hours' sleep in the last forty-eight hours. He tasted of spearmint, tangerine, and most of all, like *home*.

"Better than a double espresso for energy," he said when he leaned back. I agreed.

Downstairs in the kitchen a minute later, Dorian handed Max not only a double espresso, but served it on a tray with chia pudding cups with dollops of cashew cream and a sprinkle of finishing salt on top.

I wouldn't sleep if I ate a whole pudding cup so late at night, but

Max offered me a small spoonful of his for a taste. The sweet and salty flavors danced on my tongue, and I savored the heavenly bite.

"Back to the matter at hand," Dorian said. "The thief, Betty Kubiak, was in over her head."

"And someone killed her," I said, "for her part in the deception."

CHAPTER 19

From the Typewriter of Dorian Robert-Houdin

```
The Culinary Alchemist's Toolbox

     It  is  essential  to  set  up  a  sacred  space
devoted  to  your  craft.  An  aspiring  culinary
alchemist  might  not  have  a  room  of  their  own,  but
a  cubby  of  one's  own  will  suffice.  The  two  most
important  elements  are  to  have  selected  your
ingredients  carefully  and  prepared  your  space
with  intention.
     Warning:  If  you  share  a  home  with  someone,  be
very  clear  about  what  you  expect  of  them  in  the
kitchen.  If  not,  you  will  be  sorely  disappointed
when  your  carefully  considered  ingredients
disappear.
```

Dorian stepped out of the pantry of the kitchen. Zoe needed rest and had gone to sleep, and Dorian needed to clear his mind so he could best determine next steps. Therefore, he had spent the last hour organizing the pantry. This would help him with his cookbook as well as reset his cluttered mind.

Using a green marker from the squeaky junk drawer in the kitchen, he wrote "CAUTION: Do Not Enter!" on a piece of stationery and taped it to the pantry door. He would have preferred black ink to convey the severity of the message, but most things Zoe bought were green, as it was her favorite color.

Dorian did not feel bad for banning her from the pantry. Zoe did a small amount of cooking in their shared kitchen, but she cared more for *growing* vegetables, fruits, and culinary herbs. She did much in the garden but required very little in the kitchen. He left a dish of sea salt on the counter next to jars of garlic-infused olive oil and apple cider vinegar. A wicker basket of lemons, apples, and avocados was also on the countertop. She kept almonds and sunflower seeds in the freezer, so Zoe did not need anything else from the pantry.

Satisfied with his sign, he climbed the stairs to the attic. With a clear mind, he began work on his biggest project of the night: a murder board.

Dorian had learned of the concept when reading a novel about a true crime podcaster. He had implemented the idea on a previous case, to good effect. They knew so little about this baffling case that a murder board was a good place to start.

He retrieved his stack of notecards and fountain pen.

On the first notecard he wrote *Arthur Finder — Alias*.

He opened Zoe's laptop and looked for the two pieces of information they had about the man, which were the email messages exchanged with Nicolas and the website he had set up pretending to be a solicitor in England. The police would be conducting digital forensics with these bits of information, which Dorian had to admit was beyond his own skillset.

He frowned at the card. How else could he find information about this "art finder"? Was he an art collector seeking Perenelle's artwork for himself? An art dealer working on behalf of an unscrupulous client? Was he Betty Kubiak's killer? Was he even a *he*?

Perhaps it was best to begin with the person for whom they had a name.

On the second notecard he wrote *Betty Kubiak — Impersonator of Dr. Gwendolyn Graves, Actress, Artist.*

Here was someone with a true online presence. In her younger days, she had acted in many plays in various cities along the West Coast of the United States. Her photograph was occasionally on the poster advertising a production, but more frequently she was a supporting actress. Betty Kubiak was no twin of Dr. Graves, yet they were not dissimilar. They might have been sisters, yet after more digging online, he decided this was not the case.

In recent years, the roles were less frequent, but her artwork became a greater part of her life. Her work had been featured in a smattering of gallery shows, but her medium was watercolor, not oil paintings like Perenelle Flamel's. She could have been interested in other forms of art, of course, but he had the strongest suspicion it was Arthur Finder—a man who did not exist—who was pulling the strings. Deviously manipulating the poor woman, taking advantage of a fading career with promises of riches to save her impoverished nephew…

Zut alors! He had not meant for his imagination to take over the investigation. Surely this story would make an incredible Gothic novel. An innocent young man imprisoned in a crumbling tower, his desperate relation willing to do anything to help him even if it corrupted her soul. This was an inversion of the gender roles so frequently seen in Gothic fiction, but for this reason it was imperative that he write the story.

Non! He must not get distracted. He had a cookbook to write and a murder to solve. Alas, he was not making as much progress as he had hoped in the most pressing task at hand: solving the murder and getting Zoe's painting back. There was much more to be discovered about Betty Kubiak's past. But first, perhaps it was time for a midnight snack.

Before heading downstairs, he checked his email. There were not many people with whom he emailed, so he was not in the habit of checking it.

"*C'est magnifique,*" he whispered. Ethan had emailed earlier this evening with information. Dorian knew the teenagers would come through. Dorian had assumed it would be Brixton who would follow up with him, for it was Brixton with whom he was closest, but it made sense that Ethan was the social media expert. As Ethan's parents fought, he had retreated into the online world.

Dorian opened Ethan's message.

Social media sightings in the neighborhood didn't find a thief carrying a painting, but these are the weirdest sightings in your neighborhood last night:

Hawthorne at SE 40th: Man with a beard carrying the top half of a mannequin. Close to the theater, so probably easily explained.

Hawthorne at SE 33rd: 2 people with 10 boxes of Voodoo Doughnuts. Where were they going with so many donuts at midnight?

Lone Fir Cemetery: 6 Senior Serenaders singing and holding candles at a grave. (Harry told me the alliteration of that line was distracting, but it really was 6 of them, so it stays.)

Under Hawthorne Bridge: 3 figures wearing capes with hoods. Too early in October for a Halloween party, right?

That last group wasn't nearby your house, but still in East Portland, so I couldn't resist including it. Hooded figures at midnight sounds like a secret society.

A secret society, indeed. This was most interesting.

CHAPTER 20

I awoke at sunrise to find a gargoyle standing over me. This used to be disconcerting, but I was used to it now. I wasn't *always* greeted to the start of a new day by a smiling gargoyle. But since my internal clock was attuned to the sun, Dorian could guess down to the minute when I'd wake up.

"You learned something," I said as I sat up.

"*Oui.* Get dressed and I will tell you what I have discovered in the night!"

Three minutes later, I was climbing the stairs to the attic, my morning glass of lemon water in my hand. Normally I liked to step out onto the back porch for a few minutes of sunlight as an invigorating start to the day, but this wasn't a normal morning.

"Why is there a warning sign taped to my pantry?" I asked as Dorian met me in the attic doorway.

He drew his brow together, causing his horns to tilt inward. "*Your* pantry? Have we not agreed that the kitchen is my domain? Do not answer. We have more important things to discuss at present. I have learned many things during the night. Shall we begin with my murder board?"

I blinked at the gargoyle. "Your murder board?"

"I was busy preparing it during the night."

Because of course the gargoyle had created a murder board.

"The board is in its infancy," Dorian said once we'd reached the attic. He led me to the cork board he'd used before. "I have not yet connected the dots... or, to be truthful, discovered many dots to connect, but I believe it will prove useful."

Most of the large cork board was half empty, but Dorian had sections on Arthur Finder and Betty Kubiak. Arthur's section only had questions underneath it, since we knew nothing about him, not even whether he was the killer and thief. Betty's section was far more developed.

I unpinned the top printout. "She acted in Marlowe's *The Tragical History of the Life and Death of Doctor Faustus*?"

"*Oui!* This is the most promising lead I discovered. She played the devil, a role not usually performed by a woman in the play."

I eyed Dorian. "I don't think the fact that she played the role of the devil means she was actually evil."

"Of course not." Dorian gave a single flap of his wings. "But it does suggest a connection to alchemy. The character of Faust, also known as Doctor Faustus in Marlowe's imagining of the Faust legend, *was an alchemist*. One who sought shortcuts, similar to *backward alchemists*. She had a leading role in a play about a corrupted alchemist who sold his soul to the devil."

I opened my mouth to reply, but Dorian continued on before I could do so.

"Betty Kubiak is interested in both art and alchemy," he said. "Her watercolor still life paintings are mediocre, at best. Someone who takes *shortcuts*. You realize what this means, do you not?"

I did not.

He was staring at me with unblinking eyes, waiting for my reply, so I said, "You think because she acted in a play about a man selling his soul to the devil that she did the same to become a better artist?"

"Do not mock me, Zoe. You know as well as I that one cannot do such things."

I fought the urge to roll my eyes. "I have no idea the connection you're trying to make."

"She has a connection to both art and alchemy. Just as our Perenelle does. Perenelle also wields a power that would be dangerous in the wrong hands."

"You mean her ability to paint people and objects into canvases."

"*Oui.* I understand she cannot transfer this skill to others. Yet the stolen paintings she created include alchemical elements, including a hidden notebook. An interest in alchemy indicates a possible line of investigation."

I sighed. "How many plays did Betty act in over her career?"

Dorian snatched the printout from me. "So be it. We will set aside this clue. Perhaps you would rather discuss the secret society taking over Portland?"

"I'd hardly consider the Freemasons to be taking over Portland." I finished my glass of water and looked more closely at the murder board, wondering how my life had changed so drastically that this wasn't the first time I'd had a "murder board" constructed in my attic.

"*Pfft.* Not the Freemasons. Their existence can hardly be considered a secret."

"Who are you talking about then?"

"I have not yet discerned the identity of the hooded individuals seen at midnight the night before last."

"The night the paintings were stolen?" Now he had my full attention. "*Hooded individuals?* Was Betty—"

"I do not yet know the identity of the three figures seen near Hawthorne Bridge."

The doorbell rang. It was too early for a casual visit from anyone. Dorian met my gaze. He nodded silently, then crept upstairs to hide.

The doorbell rang once more.

With Dorian out of sight, I peeked through the window curtains in the living room. A woman gripping an oak cane stood at the door.

The real Gwendolyn Graves.

CHAPTER 21

I swung open the front door.

"I hope I didn't wake you," she said. "I've been wide awake since before five o'clock this morning, eager for answers."

"You didn't wake me. I was about to have breakfast. Would you like to join me, Dr. Graves?"

"Please, call me Gwendolyn."

"I feel as if history is repeating itself."

"She said that to you?" the real Gwendolyn asked as I welcomed her inside.

"Exact words."

She cringed. "It's a surreal experience, being impersonated."

"Actually, wait. She said to call her—you—Gwen."

"That's even worse than being impersonated! Please. Stick to Gwendolyn."

"You should be flattered to be impersonated. You're so well-respected that she used your name to get me to trust her."

"The dead woman."

We both fell silent for a moment.

"Let me get you a cup of tea," I offered. "I have a mint from my own garden. Unless you'd prefer something caffeinated."

She smiled. "Already had coffee. Mint tea would be perfect."

"Come through to the kitchen. It's cozy in there." It was also where Dorian could eavesdrop through the pipes.

Gwendolyn took a deep breath as we entered the kitchen. "It smells like sourdough bread in here. I love that scent. Wherever I am, it always smells like home."

I opened the bread box. "You've got a good sense of smell. This loaf is from yesterday. I'm going to have some for breakfast. I'll make extra for us both. We have a lot to talk about."

"That we do." She took a seat at the small kitchen table. "When the police called me and told me about someone impersonating me, they wanted to know why the thief chose me as their fake identity. I didn't know the answer, so I jumped in my car to talk with Detective Vega in person."

I looked up from the kettle. "From Seattle?"

She nodded. "I no longer teach, aside from an occasional guest lecture, but I've still got my office at the university and advise students. It's only three hours away, and the detective wouldn't tell me much over the phone."

"Did she tell you more when you arrived?"

"She showed me the dead woman's photograph," Gwendolyn said. "I can't say I saw the resemblance."

"She was an actress. She shared your eye color and was around your age, but the rest was a disguise."

"I still don't understand exactly what had happened. The police told me she claimed to be warning you against a criminal art dealer who wanted to buy a painting you acquired last year, but that was a lie to meet up so she could follow you home and steal the painting herself. And another painting that same night! Why even meet with you at all? That sounds so risky."

"Because that's not exactly how it happened." As I poured hot water in the teapot and placed two thick slices of sourdough bread onto the cast iron skillet, I realized I hadn't figured out what exactly I should say to Professor Graves when I had a chance to talk with her. I'd been woken by a rascally gargoyle, after all. "I have two old friends who recently moved to Portland. They're the closest thing to parents I have. Nicolas bought the painting for me last year."

"Because the woman looks like you?"

The kettle in my hand faltered and a splash of hot water splashed onto the kitchen counter. "You noticed?"

Max had the foresight to digitally smudge my face, so how could she know?

"It's unfortunate that your version of *Brother and Sister* has a smudge over the woman's face," Gwendolyn said, "but I've seen a better reproduction of the painting. I have it in my research notes. It's a black and white photo, but there's no damage. I presume that in the larger painting itself, you can see the face better than in the low resolution image the detective has?"

"I can." As I set the kettle back onto the stovetop, I considered how forthcoming I should be with Gwendolyn. Since she had a better photo of the painting, there was no point denying my resemblance, and the police knew everything else about the theft.

"The painting has great sentimental value to me," I said, "both because Nicolas bought it for me, and also, as you guessed, because the brother and sister in the painting resemble me and my brother. My brother passed away many years ago."

"I'm so sorry. It really is a remarkable resemblance for a painting from 1700."

"It is. It's mainly the mischievous expression that reminds me of Thomas," I added, even though that was only partly true. "My grandmother was French, so as for me looking like this woman, it's one of those familial connection coincidences you see sometimes."

"I'm sorry I got us off track," she continued. "You were telling me how you came to have the painting that was previously in a small French museum."

"It's by an unknown painter, and the private family museum attracted fewer and fewer visitors over the years. It takes a lot of money to keep up a chateau. Nicolas knew the painting would mean a lot to me, so he made a generous offer. They accepted, and he surprised me with it. It's been hanging in my house, my prized possession, for the past year. Until a few weeks ago. That's when Nicolas started receiving email messages from an art collector offering to buy it, which he turned down."

"The detective already asked me if the name Arthur Finder meant anything to me."

"Does it?"

She shook her head. "Only that I can't decide if it's clever or stupid to use a name that can easily be seen to mean 'art finder.'"

"He's clever enough. We're pretty sure that he's behind a break-in at the house of Nicolas and his wife while they were out at an event."

"In search of the *Brother and Sister* painting?"

"Nothing was taken, so they couldn't be certain. But that's how Arthur Finder knew they didn't have it. That's when I heard from the woman claiming to be you, who was contacting people she suspected might be the current owners of the painting, warning me about the unscrupulous art collector. Because they knew Nicolas was telling the truth about not having the painting, they cast a wide net to find who did. Since I own an online antiques business and my inventory includes some old paintings, she reached out to me. I can see now that every bit of information she gave me was a con." I felt myself reddening at my foolishness. I should have known better.

"The detective wouldn't tell me if she thinks the thief, this Betty Kubiak woman, was working for him."

"Or her," I said. "We don't yet know who Arthur Finder is. It was a well-done con. Sprinkling details so enticing that whoever had the painting now couldn't say no."

Gwendolyn smiled. "Because who wouldn't want to believe that a dusty old painting turns out to be a lost masterpiece?"

"Exactly." I shook my head, berating myself once again, but also remembering the difficult position she'd been in. "She tried to convince me I'd be *saving it* from the very unscrupulous collector she was really—"

"I hate to interrupt your worthy tirade, but you're clutching your silk shawl within an inch of its life."

I looked down at my white knuckles. I hadn't realized I'd been twisting the smooth, emerald green shawl in my hands. I brought the teapot and two handmade mugs to the table, followed by plates of crisped toast and a jar of homemade huckleberry preserves.

"These mugs are beautiful," Gwendolyn said as she accepted a ceramic mug painted with a deep orange ochre and vibrant vermillion red.

"Handmade by a woman in New Mexico." I smiled at the memory, feeling a piece of my stress lift as I breathed in the steam from the mint tea and held the handcrafted mug in my hand. The artist had put a loving energy into her mugs that I could still feel more than fifty years after I bought them.

"I understand your frustration. I'm frustrated even though I'm barely involved. The detective said a *second* painting was stolen as well. That one she didn't show me."

"*The Apothecary's Cabinet.*" I held up a photo of the painting.

She gasped, but covered it with a cough. "The same artist. *I knew it.*"

"You did?"

"I—" She broke off and looked at her hands that encircled the mug. "This is going to sound terrible, but I didn't come here to help find out who killed the woman impersonating me."

"I know," I said. "You want to find out what's so special about the paintings."

"Is it that obvious that I'm so terrible?"

"That's not terrible of you. That's human."

"Humans are terrible!" Gwendolyn laughed.

"And phenomenal. Plus everything in between."

"Zoe Faust," she leaned in close with a wicked smile on her lips, "I do believe you're an old soul."

"I've been told that before." I tucked a lock of white hair behind my ear. The tips were still black from when I'd dyed it over the summer as part of an investigation. "I believe we can learn from the past. That's what drew me to both herbalism and antiques."

"And art."

I shook my head. "I appreciate art very much, but I'm not an expert. I have no idea why my painting enticed you enough to drop everything, hop in your car, and drive more than three hours."

"My research, all my professional life for over fifty years, has been devoted to righting wrongs in the art world. In particular, finding details about women artists whose work was attributed to men."

"Your imposter told me that much. Plus I looked up your work. You specialize in the forgotten women artists from the Renaissance era. That's long before the year my stolen painting was made."

"Your painting is reminiscent of a famous Renaissance painter."

108

"It's in the style of Hayden," I said. There was no reason to hide this obvious truth.

"I can't believe I'm going to say what I'm about to, but now that I've seen the second painting, I have nothing left to lose."

It was a strange turn of phrase to use in this situation, but I waited for her to continue.

"I believe Philippe Hayden isn't who the world thinks he was." Gwendolyn took a breath. "I believe he was actually a woman."

I froze. She couldn't know.

"I know it goes against what you might have learned about Hayden if you ever took a Western Art History class," Gwendolyn continued in a rush, misinterpreting my expression. "And my theory goes even further—which is where your painting comes in. Why it's so crucial you get it back. It's one of several paintings that resemble Hayden's work that couldn't possibly have been painted by him. That's why I remembered it and have it in my notes."

Her hands shook, and when she continued her words flowed out of her in even more of a rush. "Nobody can deny that works of art in a similar style continued to be created for a century after Hayden's death, many of them using the same paint recipes. And now that a *second* similar painting was stolen? It can't be a coincidence. Not a chance. I'm *not* going to let this history be lost just because I'm a coward."

A coward?

Gwendolyn took a deep breath and met my gaze. "I believe *Philippa* Hayden had a secret pupil who passed along Hayden's secrets —*her* secrets."

I stared across the table at her. She'd told me far more than she realized. *This was it.* A believable story, so close to the truth, that the world was finally ready to hear. It was time for a leap of faith.

"What if I told you," I said, "I know someone who has the same theory?"

Gwendolyn's eyes lit up. "Truly?"

"There's someone you need to meet."

CHAPTER 22

Gwendolyn and I drove together in my truck. Before stepping into my green 1942 Chevy, I sent a text message to Perenelle, letting her know I was bringing the real Gwendolyn Graves to see her.

"Are you going to tell me who this mysterious person is who you're taking me to meet?" she asked.

"It'll be easiest to explain once we're there. You'll see why." I winced. "That sounds sketchy, but really—"

"I trust you. I asked Detective Vega all about you and that handsome former detective. I know you've helped solve a couple of mysteries."

"She told you that?"

"There are *some* benefits of being a little old lady. People do open up to you more."

"The Miss Marple effect."

"Which happens to be very true, though you have a way to go before you'll experience it. I'm honestly surprised you're taking my theory seriously at all."

"Why didn't you ever publish your theory?"

"It's complicated… I did so much research. And there are so many clues. Philippe Hayden didn't join any Artist Guilds, and only worked secretively in Rudolf II's Court in Prague. If she was a woman who'd disguised herself as a man, that would explain a lot. And because so many masterpieces that appear to be Hayden's span a period of time over 150 years, it only makes sense if she trained an apprentice in her style and with her recipe of mixing paint—again, needing to be done more privately than if she'd been a man. Hayden produced paint recipes that nobody else has managed to reproduce since the 1700s."

"Countless historical recipes for paints have been lost over the years," I said, feeling almost physical pain as I said so. So many recipes for healing have been lost as well. "Back when knowledge was handed down through apprenticeships."

Gwendolyn was looking out the car window at the evergreen trees—Douglas Fir and Yellow Cedar in this stretch—but turned back to look at me.

"The established experts don't want anything to change about our understanding of history," she said. "When I was young, I was egotistical enough to think I could make big changes. Instead, I've settled for moderate ones. But Hayden… Hayden was the one that got away."

"You still have your research?"

"Of course. But I wasn't foolish enough to publish anything before I could prove it."

"That's why you mentioned being a coward?"

She scoffed. "Academia is difficult enough without making baseless claims. I was afraid when I was young, but what are they going to do to me now? Although… of course I still can't publish anything without *proof.* I don't know why I'm even going with you on this mysterious visit! I suppose it'll be nice to talk with someone who has a similar idea, even if I can't publish my findings."

I glanced away from the road for a moment to study her face. Optimism was trying to poke through, but losing.

"What if you could get proof?" I asked.

"It's what I've been seeking for fifty years."

"The world," I said, "wasn't ready fifty years ago."

"You think it is now?"

Was it?

"People *are* beginning to question art connoisseurs now," she admitted. "Now that less invasive techniques to test paintings are available, they can't argue as loudly against scientific testing that challenges their assessments."

I turned off the road onto the narrow road leading to the Flamels' house.

"This woman you're taking me to meet," she said. "She's an artist?"

"How can you tell?"

"Even I as a dusty old academic can see the beauty of the light through the trees here. It's the perfect spot for an artist."

"Nearly there." I turned off the road onto the private drive leading to the Flamels' house.

"Stop the car!" she cried.

I slammed on the brakes and came to a stop next to the start of the pigment garden.

"I'm sorry. That was overly dramatic, wasn't it? But I need to see this." She stumbled out of the car and stepped toward the edge of the garden. She turned to me. "These plants… I swear I've only seen some of these in books before. Never planted in real life. This is a pigment garden, isn't it?"

"It is."

She gasped. "Even the rocks. All the minerals right here…. Where did this artist find these rocks?"

"I don't know," I said honestly.

Using her cane to steady herself, Gwendolyn knelt. She let go of the cane and pressed both palms to the rocks. "Before we go any further, I need to say something."

I waited, not wanting to break the magical spell Perenelle's garden had cast.

"Regardless of who this is that I'm about to meet, this whole experience since yesterday has made me realize something. That's why I'm telling you this dream I haven't spoken aloud for decades. I always thought that one day I might be able to convince the world that Philippe Hayden was a woman, but 'one day' never came. And here I am, eighty years old, scared that I might be embarrassed by my colleagues like I was more than half a century ago. What am I so afraid of?" She laughed at herself. "I can't believe I'm the same woman who once thought I would change the world. I won't let a thief steal away the evidence that I'm right that Philippe Hayden was Philippa Hayden. I can't believe it took a murdered woman impersonating me and two stolen paintings to get me off my duff!" She chuckled again. "Speaking of which, could you help me up?"

I offered her my arm, and with the help of me and her cane, she hoisted herself from the ground. She brushed the traces of rock dust off her slacks. "I know it sounds foolish that I could finally prove the truth—"

"It doesn't sound foolish," I said. "But it's not my decision to make."

"What do you mean?"

"It's mine," another voice said.

Perenelle strode up the path from the house, her emerald-green skirts billowing behind her, her copper hair swirling in the wind.

"I hear you're a Philippe Hayden expert." Perenelle's eyes shone with a wicked glint. "We have much to talk about."

CHAPTER 23

The three of us sat around a wrought iron table in the garden, a pot of untouched peppermint tea between us. Autumn clouds were blowing in above, but rain had held off so far.

"Tell me," said Perenelle, "what do you know about Hayden?"

"It's only a theory," Gwendolyn hedged.

"Women have been selling themselves short for far too long," said Perenelle. "Your modesty does all of us at this table a disservice."

Gwendolyn didn't answer. Instead, she held a plain rock between her thumb and index finger before placing it next to the teapot. She must have picked it up in the pigment garden.

"Hayden," she said, "would have turned this into a red ochre, and used it to paint the flames under a glass vessel."

"More of a yellow," Perenelle murmured. Her eyes held a far-away look, as if she was already imagining the universe of the painting the rock would fit into.

"But Hayden used more reds than yellows," Gwendolyn insisted.

"Those reds," said Perenelle, "were vermillion."

Gwendolyn lifted a well-worn journal from the slim bag at her side and scribbled a note.

I gasped. "You haven't only saved your old research. You've *still been researching* your theory."

She met my gaze. "Never with enough proof."

"That's where I might be able to help." Perenelle gave her a Cheshire Cat smile. "But first, I need to know what you've already found out."

"Where to begin?" Gwendolyn slipped the journal back into her bag. "Hayden would have had access to a garden like yours."

"I love it out here." The wind whipped Perenelle's hair around her face, but she didn't make a move to tame it.

"Hayden painted in the late 1500s, the end of the Renaissance. He—and yes, I'll use the male pronoun for the official part of his biography—was beginning to gain prestige before he joined Rudolf II's court in Prague, Bohemia. In the historical record, Hayden is a curious figure, wanting fame and fortune, yet eschewing the center of the art world in Italy."

Perenelle squeaked as Gwendolyn said the words "fame and fortune." She cared nothing for fame and fortune, but she couldn't very well correct Gwendolyn.

"Apologies," Perenelle said stiffly. "Allergies. Please continue."

"Hayden was French, and the French weren't seen as being nearly as sophisticated as the Italians at the time."

Another squeak from Perenelle. She covered her face with a handkerchief.

"Would you prefer we go inside, away from the pollen the wind is whipping up?" Gwendolyn asked her.

Perenelle shook her head. "Ignore me. I'm indubitably well."

Gwendolyn gave her a skeptical glance, which could have been due to Perenelle's strange word choice or her contorted, red face. Probably both.

"Hayden," she continued, "didn't train at any of the known guilds. You both know about the guild system?"

"I don't know as much as Perenelle," I said.

"It was the precursor to academies. The guild system had control of who could run a professional art studio, in different disciplines. For painters, this meant a master painter, approved by the guild system, running a studio and taking on apprentices. Artists had to apply to be accepted, and of course it was only men who were accepted."

"The Guild of Saint Luke," Perenelle said, "since Luke was the patron saint of painters."

"One reason for excluding women was because so many of the artists lived on site, so the only women trained in the guild system were relatives of the artists who ran the studios. Artemisia Gentileschi is one of the rare examples of a woman recognized for her work in Baroque era Italy. She had talent that was fostered only because her father was an accomplished artist with a studio. Even so, scholars later dismissed work that was originally credited to her. She should be at least as famous as her peers, but she's not. Not only that, but so many male artists were explicitly credited with work that's been proven to be hers. That's one of the reasons I speculated Hayden would have wished to be known as a man. If she saw things like that happening all around her—but I'm digressing. Back to what the world knows about Hayden. There are three things that stand out about the artist that are a mystery."

As she folded her hands on the table and looked intently at the two of us, I could tell she'd imagined how she'd present her theory countless times.

"First," she began, "even though he was a master painter who, like Artemisia, should be seen as an equal to the Old Masters everybody knows, *something* about his life prevented Hayden from being adequately recognized. It's not enough to say he was a jerk. Caravaggio was a murderer, and nobody seemed to care. *Why* was Hayden on the outside of success?

"Second, alchemy was the subject of his artwork. That's why he became a patron of Rudolf II, known as the 'mad alchemist.' Hayden hid messages in his paintings using perspectival techniques like anamorphosis, and if you stand at the right angle to view the artwork from different perspectives, you see different alchemical messages. Why that subject matter? Was it for his patron, or did he really believe in alchemy?

"Third, he used a unique recipe for his pigments. One that's been lost to time. That in and of itself isn't unique. So many paint recipes have been lost to time, because the intentionally vague written recipes don't replace the knowledge of being taught complex processes by someone doing it themselves. Like vermillion and Egyptian Blue."

"Those are lost?" Perenelle blinked at her in surprise.

Gwendolyn smiled. "I can tell you're an artist who mixes her own paints, but I take it you ignore historical research?"

Perenelle smiled enigmatically. "What do *you* think is the answer to those historical mysteries you presented about Hayden?"

Gwendolyn took a deep breath. "I believe that scholars have it all wrong about Hayden. Yes, Hayden was the artist who we know as having been a court painter for Rudolf II in Prague and who was a genius for both pigments and finished paintings. But I believe he was secretly a woman, and that *she* was a master at creating paint recipes that she passed down to an apprentice outside of the official guild system. That apprentice taught another apprentice, and this passing of the torch happened *for generations*. But in the mid 1750s, the line died out. My working theory is the next apprentice died in childbirth, as was sadly the case with many of the few women artists of the time, so there wasn't time to train an heir. Whatever stopped the women passing on their secrets, the line died out after 150 years."

"That's too long for one person to be active as a painter," I said. "Your theory is a plausible explanation how it looks like Hayden produced work across 150 years."

"Many scholars thought those later paintings were meant to be forgeries, since Hayden was a relatively famous painter," Gwendolyn said. "But they *weren't*. The artists didn't try to cover up their use of modern canvases or ingredients, as a forger would have done even back then. Those paintings were simply the artwork of her apprentices who continued in her tradition. Unrecognized."

A light rain began to fall, but none of us made a move to stand up. The light brown rock turned to a deep, burnt sienna as splashes of water seeped into its surface.

"Perenelle," I said, "wouldn't you like to share your thoughts on Dr. Graves's theory? Your *additional* information?"

"I wouldn't know, Zoe," Perenelle said sharply.

"It's up to you," I said, holding her gaze, "but I think the world is ready to know."

Gwendolyn leaned forward. "Have you really uncovered something?"

"I wouldn't put it like that." Perenelle looked out over her pigment garden, and I could see the conflict weighing upon her.

"I knew it was too much to hope for." Gwendolyn sat back with slumped shoulders. "Even if we share the theory, how could we prove it, even if we're right? The lineage died out centuries ago."

The sky opened up above us. Perenelle stood and faced us with a wicked smile as the rain streamed over her face. "You're wrong about that last part of your theory, Dr. Graves. You see, I'm one of the apprentices who was trained in her tradition."

With great effort, Gwendolyn pushed herself up from her seat. She stared at Perenelle with a wide-eyed look of wonder like a child meeting Santa Claus. "You're joking… Wait… You're *not* joking? You're really—" She broke off, her voice thick with emotion.

Perenelle turned to me. "You're thinking my notebook is the proof?"

"The notebook *passed down to you*," I said, holding her gaze.

If we got that notebook out of the *Brother and Sister* painting, the world wouldn't know it was Perenelle herself who'd created it, but it was the next best thing: that she was one of the women it had been passed down to.

"What notebook?" Gwendolyn's voice shook as she looked from me to Perenelle. Her hopeful expression nearly broke my heart. She'd waited over half a century to prove what she hoped to be true. What *was* true.

"A small, handwritten journal exists," Perenelle told her. "It has Hayden's true name, and it lists the paintings by her and her apprentices."

"A notebook with paper and ink that can surely be dated by conservators," I added. I could imagine scholars arguing over why the handwriting remained the same, but it would never enter their minds that it could be the same person. They'd most likely come up with theories about how copying a handwriting style was an important art lesson.

"You have it?" Gwendolyn asked, oblivious to the rain drenching us all. The rain I barely felt myself. "You have the notebook?"

"We did," Perenelle said. "It was stolen. It was hidden with the *Brother and Sister* painting that was taken."

"By the thief who impersonated me." Gwendolyn's face fell. "Is that what Betty Kubiak was after?"

"I don't think so," I said. "Perenelle hid it there for safe keeping after Nicolas bought the painting."

As angry as I was, I also knew that Betty Kubiak was in an impossible situation, desperate for money to help the nephew she loved. She was hired to play a role, but she was killed for her part in the deception. A deception I also needed to solve if I was going to get my painting back. It was all connected. I might just be able to bring justice to Betty if I also brought justice to Perenelle's legacy.

"It's time," I said as a powerful clap of thunder crashed overhead. "The three of us are going to set the historical record straight. To do that, we're going to get the stolen painting back."

CHAPTER 24

From the Typewriter of Dorian Robert-Houdin

The Culinary Alchemist's Toolbox

Sourdough bread is an alchemical transformation.

There is no "speeding up" the process of
fermentation that raises the dough. A small nudge
of fire may slightly reduce the time, but alchemy
cannot be rushed. Natural yeasts, flour, and
water work together with the elements of air and
time. Salt must be added, but only at the right
time.

When you begin your journey into sourdough
bread baking, there is no need to buy a sourdough
starter. All you need is flour, water, and air.
And, of course, patience. Patience is key to any
alchemical transformation.

After Zoe and the professor left the house, Dorian had begun
preparations for his next loaf of sourdough by feeding the starter.

"Feeding" in this case meant adding flour and water to the already existing concoction of flour, water, and natural yeast from the air. He set aside the glass mason jar in a warm spot in the kitchen near the stove, giving it the time it needed to transform.

Rain pelted the skylight atop the attic, where he now contemplated his next steps in the investigation into the stolen paintings. Though the rainfall was torrential, the thick glass held fast.

When Zoe had first bought the home she had called a "fixer-upper," the roof was half gone, as if ripped apart by a giant who took issue with the craftsman style of architecture's gabled roofline. The gaping hole in the attic was covered only with a tarp. An escape route that was practical for a gargoyle who could not be seen, yet a crater in one's roof was impractical in the Pacific Northwest. They had since found funds to repair the roof and had installed a proper skylight that opened when Dorian needed to creep out of the house.

This was perfect weather for crafting a Gothic novel, yet Dorian did not have time for such frivolous pursuits today. He did not even have time to continue work on his cookbook.

Zoe had telephoned to tell him about her plan to correct the historical record about Philippe Hayden while getting justice for the murdered thief who was sympathetic in Zoe's eyes. This would also result in Zoe's beloved painting being returned to her.

This plan would, of course, require catching a murderer—and it was in this regard that Dorian excelled. Thus, while Zoe conferred with Perenelle and Professor Graves, Dorian hatched a plan for how to help.

Zoe's plan to right a historical wrong involved the work of both Professor Graves and Perenelle Flamel. Dorian understood Zoe's desire to work closely with the two women, yet he could not help but feel slightly rebuffed that he could not be part of the conversation. There was, of course, no way for him to be physically present in person. He had listened in on their discussion in the kitchen that morning, yet this was not a scalable solution. Calling in via speaker phone was a more realistic possibility, and something that had worked on occasion in the past. He would propose this to Zoe. He also hoped to entice Dr. Graves back to the house with freshly baked sourdough bread.

In the kitchen that morning, Dr. Graves had spoken of overlooked and forgotten women artists. This was well-documented in her work. Her research was most focused on the Renaissance, so she had not written about one artist Dorian had come across in Paris: Rosa Bonheur. He felt an affinity for the nineteenth century French artist who did not conform to societal norms. She had been forced to petition the police for permission to dress as a man, which is the only way she was permitted to visit the horse market to study the horses she wished to paint. A special dispensation to dress in trousers! *C'est intolérable!* At least the artist had been recognized in her lifetime and was awarded the Legion of Honor Grand Cross. The honor was bestowed five years after Dorian was brought to life, in 1865. He remembered his father speaking of it.

There was indeed much interesting history of the art world, yet there was one word Gwendolyn Graves had uttered in his kitchen that spoke to him: *recipes*. She was speaking, of course, of recipes to create vibrant pigments and paints.

Although Dorian strongly identified with his important role of detective, he felt, at the very core of his being, that he was a chef. As such, he was attuned to the ingredients he used. Recipes were another way in which he could assist the investigation!

There was a signature style of recipes that Perenelle used in the paintings she created. Pigments and paints went hand in hand, with pigments being granules of color and paint having binders and solvents added so that a paintbrush could be used to apply the color. Pigments and paints made by hand were like a fingerprint. Could this fact help them find the missing paintings?

He scampered down the stairs to his kitchen. This was the most conducive atmosphere in which to think about alchemical transformations of all kinds.

As he browned onions on the cast iron skillet, with heat from the flames creating a reaction that fundamentally changed the chemical makeup of the onion, he thought about the process of transforming raw materials to pigment, and then on to paint that could be applied to a canvas.

Dorian knew from Zoe how artists had lost touch with their roots as the creators of their own paints. Modern artists were many steps removed, and had been since the Renaissance. Apothecaries, such as Zoe herself, had sourced minerals that were then sold to both artists and "colormen," who turned pigments into paint.

When investigating an art forgery case with Zoe the previous year, he had learned that the famous forger Van Meegeren, who had forged many Vermeers, had created paintings indistinguishable from Vermeer's in terms of scientific analysis, except for an adulterated pigment he bought. Van Meegeren believed himself to be buying genuine ultramarine, a pigment that was authentic to the historical period of time in which Vermeer painted, yet it had been adulterated by a cheaper cobalt blue. The forger was exacting in his choice of materials and techniques, yet a dishonest dealer had duped him. Ironically, it was this deception that backed up his claim that he had not sold genuine Vermeers, a national treasure, to the Nazis. Art forgery was a lesser crime to confess to than selling national treasures to Nazis.

Dorian sniffed. *Zut alors!* While he was lost in thought, his onions had transformed beyond sweet caramelization to a charred mess with a sulfurous scent. He turned off the flame.

He allowed himself a frustrated flap of his wings. Perhaps theorizing about paint recipes was not a viable course of action.… But some form of skullduggery was afoot. Dorian was nothing if not an industrious researcher. He hurried upstairs to use Zoe's computer.

Modern scientific analysis would prevent the more recent works of *Brother and Sister* and *The Apothecary's Cabinet* from being recognized as Haydens. Thus, profit from selling the stolen paintings was unlikely.

What of Perenelle's recipes? Here, too, he was stymied. One could not simply reproduce an archaic pigment recipe, even with present-day methods. Especially not one that involved alchemical processes. It was like recreating a recipe of a dish one had eaten. One might be able to detect different flavors, but knowing the list of ingredients and the method of preparation was essential. Each step could easily go off course, and there was a narrow window between a caramelized and ruined ingredient, as his charred onions reminded him.

Many artists today were returning to the old methods of creating their own pigments. There were many online resources to do this. As well as many, many resources that discussed historical paints, pigments, and dyes.

This would not do! Rather than casting a wide net that would lead nowhere, he should begin with what they knew. He returned to his sparsely filled murder board.

He had already gathered information about artist, actress, and thief Betty Kubiak. Zoe was correct that simply playing the role of a devil who tempted an alchemist did not give them answers about the world off the stage. As much as he hated to admit it, the police were best equipped to find the connections of this thief to their mysterious Arthur Finder.

Armchair detecting was most frustrating today.

What about Dr. Gwendolyn Graves herself? The professor's theory was so close to the truth that Zoe wished to reveal to the world. Had she come to her conclusions as innocently as she claimed?

Zoe had already looked into the research of Dr. Graves. Though Dorian did not take pleasure in pointing out Zoe's weaknesses, it was only the truth that Dorian's little gray cells gave him an advantage when it came to detective work. As an outsider with a talent for noticing details, he could see things that others could not. Zoe could not possibly have read the entirety of Dr. Graves's publications. With his keen eye for detection, Dorian would delve deeper.

He quickly located many publications by Dr. Graves. There were also photographs of her, all from decades ago, when she had traveled to Italy, France, and the Netherlands, searching through forgotten archives and dusty storage facilities. He was most intrigued by one publication that was referenced in multiple places, yet he could not find the paper, or even its title. When Dr. Graves was a graduate student, she presented a paper at a symposium, which he found referenced with different descriptions and titles. It was as if the paper was a chimera that had changed forms before vanishing from history.

What was Dr. Graves concealing about the start of her career? The woman was hiding something.

"Gwendolyn Graves," he murmured to himself, "is not what she seems."

CHAPTER 25

I'd been on the go from the moment I'd woken up that morning, so I returned home to have a moment to shower, think, and eat.

The first two were not to be. Dorian was waiting for me at the dining table, a sour expression on his face.

"You have not revealed too much about yourself to Dr. Graves, have you?"

"Of course not," I assured him. "As I told you, the closest we can get to the whole truth is that Philippe Hayden was actually a woman who'd disguised herself as a man, and that Perenelle is part of a long line of women who learned from Hayden to mix paint recipes inspired by the techniques of early chemistry—"

"Alchemy," Dorian corrected.

I smiled. "The world is ready to accept that many artists previously thought to be men were actually women, but I don't know if they're ready to hear the word 'alchemy,' even when it doesn't mean the Elixir of Life or transmuting lead into gold."

He agreed and went on to tell me about the missing publication of Dr. Graves.

"I came across something similar when I looked into her," I said.

Dorian blinked at me. "You did? You did not tell me of this subterfuge!"

"Because it wasn't a deception. It was a presentation more than fifty years ago, and my guess is that she was asserting her theories about Hayden being a woman before she had enough proof."

Dorian scowled. "You cannot trust her, Zoe."

"She can help right a historical wrong," I said, "and get my painting back in the process. There's a killer out there, and we don't know why they're after Perenelle's paintings."

"You also rightly care about helping Perenelle," said Dorian. "And it is a worthy cause to seek justice for the murdered woman, who was desperate to help her family."

"But you're right," I admitted. "What I think about when I close my eyes is the lovingly created portrait I've lost. Of Thomas."

Dorian told me lunch would be ready in half an hour. I had time to take a quick shower and fix myself a mug of sage tea that I took to the backyard porch.

Standing on the small wooden porch and breathing in the earthy scent made stronger by the rain, I looked out over the sprawling garden. It wasn't what modern sensibilities would consider desirable. My garden would never be featured in one of those home tours Brixton's best friend Veronica loved to watch, even when it wasn't bedraggled from the wind and rain.

To those who weren't looking closely, the garden might appear unkempt. But in truth, it was carefully cultivated. A balance of nature and nurture. I listened to the earth and the sky, and to the plants already growing in the soil, to determine how best to cut back undesirable plants in favor of the delicious herbs and vegetables I wanted to grow for both good health and flavorful cooking.

I'd planted an assortment of healing herbs and desirable vegetables. I cultivated plants that would thrive and that I knew I'd use in abundance for meals and for herbal preparations. I prioritized varieties that were out of fashion and thus hard to find, plants that were tastiest when harvested an hour before eating them, and also flowers that attracted bees and fostered a healthy ecosystem.

Blackberry brambles wended their way through cucumber vines. Collard trees grew spindly yet hearty as they surpassed my height and produced hearty greens. Nettles were as contained as they could be in wine barrel planter boxes, though I feared they'd soon be leaning so far over the sorrel that the stinging leaves would make it tricky to harvest the spinach-like green below. A good problem to have.

I listened to my instincts with the plants. A cultivated knowledge learned from experience. To me, it was a near perfect garden. What it *wasn't* was neat and tidy.

With so many people practicing herbalism once again, and selling local produce from organic gardens, it might have appeared that it wasn't essential to grow my own food. But at its core, alchemy is about transformation, and the heart of its transformations are about intent, so growing food with my own hands added that necessary element.

I shivered as a gust of wind blew rain sideways onto the porch. My sweater kept me warm enough if I was dry, but I should have taken a coat.

"You have missed another message." Dorian pointed at a blinking notification on my phone.

It was an encrypted message from Theo, the former FBI-agent-turned-ID-forger. He'd agreed to help, but he needed a few more details. I had expected him to question why they chose names of famous people from history for their fake identities, but that wasn't his concern. He needed to know where exactly they'd lived at different points before a year ago, so he could build this into a believable backstory.

"I'll be a few minutes," I said to Dorian as I took my laptop to the living room and stretched out on my green velvet couch, thinking about how best to answer.

The truth was that Perenelle had used her powerful and unique skill of creating and using alchemical paint to save the life of Nicolas and herself. Imprisoning the two of them inside a painting was the only way to suspend their grave injuries caused by alchemist Edward Kelley until they could get medical help. Things hadn't gone to plan, and they'd been trapped far longer than intended. Edward Kelley had finally been held accountable for attempted murder. Perenelle had made a full recovery from being forced to swallow toxic paint, but Nicolas's head injury still sapped his energy.

They were adjusting to life in the twenty-first century quite well. I expected nothing less from the couple who'd lived through centuries that saw worldwide upheaval, colonialism, the invention of the movable type printing press, the Renaissance, and the Scientific Revolution before their imprisonment that began shortly before the Industrial Revolution. They clung to a few remnants of the past—Perenelle refused to wear trousers, Nicolas wouldn't entertain the idea of reading eBooks no matter how crowded their home became, and they both still preferred spoons and knives to forks—but they greeted the twenty-first century with a fierce curiosity.

When I'd first met them, I was enamored with the fact that they'd tailored their clothing to enable their curiosity. Nicolas customized his jackets with extra interior pockets for both paper notebooks and glass vials that allowed him to take samples wherever he went, and Perenelle added numerous pockets to her billowing skirts to hold her art supplies as well as any ingredients in the world around her that caught her attention.

They paid attention to the world around them, so they had a deep understanding of the dangers that came with alchemy. Would-be alchemists who failed in their experiments could be tempted to abandon true alchemy and seek out dangerous shortcuts. Backward alchemy grew out of this temptation, which is why the Flamels had always warned against it and tried to stop it for good.

But I couldn't tell Theo *any* of that. Instead, I wrote back to him with the explanation that the Flamels had lived off the grid in various parts of France, hoping it would be enough.

I closed my laptop to find Dorian looming at the foot of the couch. I clutched my locket and caught my breath.

"Je suis désolé," Dorian said. "I did not mean to startle you."

"I was lost in my thoughts and didn't hear you come out of the kitchen."

"Do not fault your senses. I am practicing walking silently. Now that we have another case, it may prove useful."

"No creeping," I said as I tossed the laptop onto the coffee table. "Nothing we're doing requires creeping."

Dorian eyed me from head to toe. "Camouflage? This is how you plan to sneak around?"

I looked down at my clothes. I was dressed in an emerald green knitted sweater, dark gray slacks, and olive green woolen socks.

While sitting on my green velvet couch. It was fair to say I blended into my surroundings.

"Green suits me." I tucked my feet under me. Green is my favorite color, because it makes me feel like I'm outside in a garden, even when I'm not. I get complimented when I wear green, but I'm honestly not sure if it's because it suits my skin tone or whether I'm happier in green and that's what comes through.

"If you are done working with a criminal," said Dorian, "lunch is served."

<h1 style="text-align:center">CHAPTER 26</h1>

My conversation with Adam and Willow about our related thefts had been cut short yesterday when Adam had taken a turn for the worse. They must have felt similarly, because after lunch I found that Willow had sent me a message through the Elixir website. She wanted to let me know that Adam was feeling better and had been released from the hospital. They'd both be working at the Renaissance White lab today and hoped we could talk further.

"Adam White and Willow Matsumoto are my best leads," I told Dorian. "I'll be back in a few hours."

The Renaissance White lab was in the Central Eastside Industrial District of Portland, only a little over a mile from my house. Rain was still pummeling the city, so I drove to a block of old warehouses that had been converted into mixed use spaces, not far from the Willamette River waterfront.

Past a line of heavy timber structures of dark wood and metal, a red brick warehouse loomed higher than the warehouses next to it. I slowed as I spotted a copper sign with the words "Renaissance White" burned into the metal plate hanging above a steel door. The street was deserted of people in the rain, and there was plenty of space to park on the street.

I slid into my silver raincoat before stepping into the rain. I turned up my collar. Though the rain was falling steadily, I took a moment to press my hand to the brick facade before ringing the bell next to the door. The bricks were old and made of fire clay. Under my palm, I could feel the iron oxide inside the hard clay. The dark red iron was a stable element that didn't decay over time, but I could feel it transforming in the rain.

A few hearty dandelions poked their way through cracks in the concrete next to the building, and two even heartier bees circled near the ground.

A droplet of rain dripped from my nose. I was going to be soaked through in a minute. I lifted my hand and rang the buzzer.

"You're drenched," Adam said as he swung open the door a minute later. A clean bandage was wrapped around his head, another around his left hand. "Sorry about the delay. I'm the only one here right now. Willow barely slept last night. She went home for a nap. I haven't seen Oberon yet today. He's still grieving and never sleeps."

"Grieving?" I asked, but the question was drowned out by the door closing behind us.

Adam showed me a set of wrought iron pegs on the inside wall. The interior foyer was lined in brick like the exterior, and half a dozen oil paintings lined the front wall. None of them were Perenelle's, and I recognized several as reproductions of paintings you'd find in European museums. Two of the copies were of Florentine artist Botticelli, known for his vibrant colors.

"I'm surprised you're at work at all today," I said as I hung my dripping coat.

He crossed his arms and appraised me. "I wanted to ask you more about our paintings when I saw you again. But that hardly seems relevant now. You didn't tell me there'd been a murder."

"To be fair, your wife didn't tell you either."

"She said I needed rest that morning. She's a bit overprotective. Not just of me. Of all of us, actually. She's the one who insisted on so much security in this building. Not that it did any good." He pointed at the thick glass doors in the center of the lobby. "That's our laboratory. I was sure the intruder was going to force me to open the door to the lab."

"There's no room for a factory in here, is there?"

"This is only our lab space, for our recipe testing experiments.

There's enough space that we could make our initial run of paint samples here. We have a factory that's producing the paint in larger quantities. That's why we're getting buzz by giving out free samples to art workshops and schools, then we're launching with a limited run in the Pacific Northwest, and we'll launch nationally as soon as we're able to scale up. We're still perfecting our other colors, which is why I'm here. Our new colors should be ready—"

"This painting." I hadn't meant to interrupt him, but a work of art directly behind him demanded my attention. I stepped closer to the painting of a young girl in the woods. Behind her in the distance, a lake and a small cabin were visible. This painting was different from the others. Not only because I didn't recognize it.

"You painted this." I didn't lift my voice at the end to phrase it as a question. Because I already knew the answer. His intent was evident.

It's not magic to sense something a person has created. It's the energy of intent, one of the core tenants of alchemy. Adam had put so much of himself into this painting that if you knew how to look for the signs, it was impossible not to notice.

Adam looked more closely at me, as if revising his opinion of me.

"Most people don't guess that," he said. "But yes. That's my little sister, when we were kids."

"It's clear how much you love her."

He smiled. "I do. Though I don't know how you can tell, with how flat the white paint is in that dull sunlight falling on her face. Surprised that a scientist can also wield a paintbrush?"

"I'm trying to work out why I can't figure out why exactly this painting feels… unfinished."

"Yes! That's exactly it. Nobody else sees that."

"Because the painting is done, from a technical perspective. But it feels…" I struggled for the word I sought. "Undone," was the best I could come up with.

"The Unravelling," he said. "That's what I call it."

"She's dead," I whispered.

I don't know why I said it, but I was suddenly certain. The girl in the painting was very much alive, but there was something in the way the angelic light danced on her face.

Adam gave a start and looked sharply at me. "Did Willow tell you? She wouldn't have—"

"She didn't." I shook my head. "I'm sorry. I shouldn't have said that. You don't have to say more."

"How did you know?"

"My own little brother. Thomas. He died a long time ago. He's…" I had to stop myself from saying he was the subject of my painting that was stolen. "*This* is why you wanted to figure out how to recreate the lead white that Old Masters used. You want artists to have that magical color without being poisoned. *You* want it."

"You understand." Adam was speaking to me but looking at the painting. "Lily drowned."

"I'm so sorry." I shivered. Rationally, it was most likely my wet hair, but I felt in my bones that it was because I was thinking of the young girl who drowned.

Adam looked back to me. "Your hair. It's soaking wet. How could I not have noticed? Have a seat and I'll be back in a sec." He pointed to an antique chair that had been reupholstered in a beautiful fabric of gold and green, then disappeared down a hallway on our left.

Instead of sitting, I looked around my surroundings more carefully. Windows that were dark from the outside let in plenty of light. Glass doors leading to a laboratory were in the center of the foyer, and another hallway stretched to the right. A red door was crisscrossed with crime scene tape. The office where he was attacked and where the painting was stolen. But it was the painting of Lily that called to me. Adam was a talented artist.

"What was Thomas like?" Adam asked as he handed me a towel.

He hadn't asked what happened. Or offered me either platitudes or bitterness. I can't recall a single person asking me that question. But most people don't lose siblings at a young age.

"He was a cyclone of energy when he was little, and grew into the bravest young man I've ever known." It was Thomas who'd made sure that I got out of Salem before I was jailed—or worse. "He got along with animals better than people. But he was also a heartbreaker who at least a dozen women fell in love with before he—" My voice broke.

"Lily was only fourteen, but she already knew she wanted to be a marine biologist. She loved the water so much… but because of a terrible ear infection when she was little, she'd never learned to swim.... With Renaissance White, I've finally got the right white to do justice to her angelic face. I'm working on another portrait of her now. At least I'm trying to find time to do it. Launching our business has been a lot more difficult than I thought it would be. The only way I'm staying sane—or at least I was before this burglary—was the fact that we succeeded in creating a bright white just as luminous as lead white. One that I can use to do justice to Lily without going back in time to the Renaissance."

"To the good old days when paints could kill you," I said.

"Don't forget dyes," he added. "Dyes were even more toxic, because of how they leached into skin from clothing."

"And wallpaper that would become toxic when the air grew damp."

He gave me a strange look. "You must have the most interesting historical artifacts at your shop."

That shook me out of my reverie from the past. I was saved from answering by the door swinging open.

"We're ruined, Adam." The newcomer said. "We're ruined."

"Zoe Faust," said Adam, "meet the always-dramatic Oberon Salazar. One of our cofounders."

An impossibly thin man with round, oversize glasses gave a start as he noticed my presence. Rain dripped from a raincoat too broad for his sleight frame, but he made no move to remove it.

"Pleasure," he mumbled as he gave me a perfunctory handshake, but he only held my gaze for a fraction of a second before glowering at Adam. "Don't you check your messages?"

"I've been at work in the lab." Adam pulled his phone from his pocket. "What's happened?"

"Someone rifled through my files at my apartment," said Oberon.

"*What?*" Adam nearly dropped his phone.

"I told you from the start," Oberon said. "The painting was only a distraction. They're after our recipe."

"For your non-toxic version of lead white?" I asked.

Oberon turned back to me. This time, he held my gaze for more than a fraction of a second. "Who're you, again? You with the police?"

"I had an old painting stolen two nights ago as well. Mine was an oil painting in a similar style to *The Apothecary's Cabinet,* so Adam and I were comparing notes to try to figure out why our paintings were targeted."

"Just a distraction." Oberon waved his hand through the air. "They want our *recipes*."

"Corporate espionage?" I asked. "A competitor that makes artist paints?"

"But the thief didn't take the encrypted thumb drive from the safe I was forced to open," Adam sputtered. "You know that testing the paintings won't do them any good. Just because science can identify the elements in a paint recipe, it doesn't give us the techniques to bring it back to life. Are you sure a thief was at your place? Your place has been a mess lately. How do you—"

"We shouldn't be talking about this here." Oberon glanced at me as he shrugged out of his raincoat.

"It's fine," Adam assured him. "Will and I have already talked with Zoe about everything we know. She's as much of a victim as we are."

"She knows that the thief will probably destroy her painting?"

I choked. "Why do you say that?" I couldn't lose my painting of Thomas.

"Look," said Oberon, "I'm sure I'm right that a competitor has been trying to steal our paint formulations. We're launching with a big splash, so it's common sense. No scientist is stupid enough to think that when you test an old painting for its ingredients that it means they can recreate it. What's far more likely is that they just took more than one painting to *cover up* the fact that they stole something else. You just happened to get caught up in this since you had an old painting."

I couldn't tell him I knew he was wrong because I was sure they were by the same artist. But I feared he might have been right about one thing. Perenelle's notebook was hidden in the *Brother and Sister* painting. Could someone else know it existed?

"Either way," Oberon finished, "they'll be destroying the paintings."

I attempted to tamp down my rising sense of panic over his words. "Did you tell the police about your theory of corporate espionage?"

"Of course," Oberon said. "Especially just now when they were at my house, sorting through my files."

"Are you *certain* there was a break-in?" Adam asked him once more. "I've seen your house."

"It was them," Oberon insisted. "I told you someone is trying to ruin us."

Pigments and dyes were big business, and always had been. Shortly after my birth, England and Spain signed a peace treaty. The year was 1667, and piracy was big business. Suddenly, hundreds of English pirates—technically "buccaneers"—were out of work. The most lucrative business many of them went into was the dye business. They were well equipped to travel to Central America, where they could obtain the heartwood of logwood trees, a necessary ingredient for an in-demand dark black dye that was used by Puritans.

It was thanks to one such well-traveled trader that my parents encountered the name Zoe, which means "life" in Greek. Nobody else in our village had such a foreign-sounding name, and I sometimes wondered if that was one of the reasons the villagers were so quick to assume I was a witch when they observed how well I could coax dying plants back to life.

There was so much I didn't know back then, before I left Salem Village. I didn't learn of the connection to pirates until much later, when the irony was pointed out by historians that Puritans were desperate for the dye to add a somber color to our fabrics, but that dye came from men thought of as wicked.

Dyes and pigments were traded and fought over across the world, and spies had sometimes been employed to gain access to secret recipes. It wasn't far-fetched to imagine that similar intrigue was happening in the present day. The people who've painstakingly made pigments have always known that it's never been enough to simply have a paint sampling. You needed the recipe.

But did Betty Kubiak's killer who stole the paintings know that? Surely if it was a competitor, they'd know that the paintings wouldn't reveal their secret recipes. They must have been after something else. Was Oberon right that they'd destroy the paintings they'd used to cover up their crimes? I didn't want to think about that possibility.

"Are you sure nothing else was taken from your safe?" I asked Adam.

"I—I think so. I mean, it all happened so fast, and everything I could think of was accounted for."

Oberon stepped closer to me. He was a few inches shorter than I was. He thrust his chin into the air as he spoke. "You're not in the business of replicating lost colors, are you?"

"She's an antiques dealer," Adam snapped. "Not competition."

"Sorry," Oberon murmured. "Been under a lot of stress. And now this. We're doomed." Oberon reached for my hand. Or at least that's what I thought he was doing, until he took hold of the fabric of my sweater cuff.

"This is April's Green," he said wistfully.

Adam pulled him away from me. "Are you drunk?"

Oberon adjusted his glasses and stared up at Adam. "I don't need alcohol to feel this awful. It's our curse."

"Come on, Obe. You need to hold it together. We need you."

"Do you? April was the one who figured it out." He turned back to me. "If you can live without your stolen painting, I'd get yourself as far away from all of us as you can."

"What do you—" I began.

"We're cursed," Oberon said. "There's no other way to explain everything that's happened to us. We're *cursed*."

CHAPTER 28

Adam thought he'd best be able to calm down his friend if they were alone, so I left to meet Perenelle and Gwendolyn. I was already late.

I was disappointed not to be able to ask Oberon more about the curse, but I'd learned something far more important: Arthur Finder might be working for one of Renaissance White's competitors.

When I pulled up in front of the Flamels' house, I saw that any discussion of Arthur Finder would have to wait. Through the rain, I recognized the car in the driveway. The sensible beige sedan belonged to Alessandro Mendoza, the father of Brixton's school friend Veronica Chen-Mendoza.

Veronica had been taking art lessons from Perenelle for the past month, and I didn't realize that today was one of her lessons. She hadn't yet turned sixteen and didn't have her license yet. Even if she did, I wouldn't have been surprised to see Alessandro. His prudent parenting style involved getting to know everyone his daughter spent time with.

I tucked up the collar of my silver raincoat before dashing from my truck to the door. I wasn't sure if the rain would drown out my knocking, so I rang the doorbell, which Nicolas had paid an electrician to reprogram with the opening notes of *Greensleeves*.

Nicolas swung open the front door with one hand, holding a small glass of frothy beer in the other.

"Do join us," he said. "Unless Alessandro has been busy in the few seconds it took me to reach the door, there'll be a smidgen of beer left."

He led me through to the kitchen, where Alessandro was sitting on a bar stool. Sideways rain splattered against the high kitchen windows, and the yeasty aroma with a metallic scent I couldn't place tipped me off that it was Nicolas's home brew.

"Good to see you, Zoe," Alessandro said, raising his glass. "Before I forget, Veronica said she wanted to ask you something. She's having her art lesson with Perenelle."

I knocked on the door of Perenelle's art and alchemy studio. The door flew open a moment later. Veronica stood in the doorway, a wide smile on her face. "Ms. Faust! Want to watch copper grow with me?"

"Is that a real question?"

She laughed and pulled me inside. "It's *so* slow, but Perenelle wants me to get grounded in how to make my own pigments."

Over black leggings and a violet sweater, Veronica wore an oversized men's dress shirt with a ripped pocket. It didn't yet have paint stains on it, but it was the type of shirt you'd wear to get messy.

"It's essential to be connected to the raw materials of art," Perenelle said from behind her. "But we weren't *only* watching the copper in the jar—even though it's had quite a lot of chemical reaction since last week. I was telling her about how to make a green that's both lightfast and nontoxic."

"She said I'd get frustrated by how long it takes to make a pigment, and be tempted to use my paints," Veronica said, "so she made me leave them at home."

"Perenelle is a wise woman," I said. "Speaking of wise women, where's Gwendolyn?"

"She realized she needed to get a lot more of her notes from home in Seattle," Perenelle said, "plus she's packing a larger suitcase since she'll be in town for more than a couple of days. And before you ask, we found her a great hotel."

Even though Perenelle and I were more inclined than Dorian to trust the professor, I was glad Perenelle wasn't willing to open her home to a stranger.

"Dr. Graves is *amazing*," Veronica said. "I got to spend a few minutes with her before she left. Did you know she's spent over fifty years finding evidence to restore the reputations and artwork of women whose work was forgotten or purposefully covered up?"

"I haven't gotten to spend much time with her yet," I said, "but I've read about her work."

"She's visited archives and collections across Europe," Veronica added. "I was thinking maybe I should become an art historian. But I'm interested in so many things."

"You've got plenty of time to decide," I assured her. "You realize how lucky you are to have Perenelle tutoring you?"

"Oh, I *know*. I also know how lucky I am that my little sister isn't here. She threw a fit when I got Perenelle's invitation, so Dad said I had to invite her to come along. Even though I'm the one taking an art class this semester!"

"You didn't refuse her, did you?" I asked Perenelle.

"It wasn't me."

Veronica rolled her eyes. "As soon as Jessica got her way, she read Perenelle's lesson plan and changed her mind. Mom has been taking her to soccer practice while Dad comes here with me."

"I'm surprised he didn't just drop you off after that first day. Especially since it's mid-afternoon."

"He loves Nicolas," Veronica said. "Usually, he's really strict about his work hours, but since he sets his own hours, talking with Nicolas is more important."

I was glad Nicolas was making friends.

"It's weird," Veronica said. "Is he still going to insist on coming over once I have my license?"

"What are you two working on today?" I asked.

Veronica walked me to the window. "I've been making my own verdigris for the past month."

"Copper acetate?"

She nodded. "It's growing on copper strips in a mason jar with vinegar at the bottom."

"Your dad said you had something to ask me."

"Oh. Oh! Um. Perenelle, I'm a bit thirsty from the strong vinegar scent…"

"Say no more." Perenelle said as she closed the door behind her to give us some privacy.

A sense of unease came over me. We thought it was safe at the house, but something had worried Veronica.

"Is Brixton mad at me?" she blurted out.

Ah. "I haven't seen him lately, aside from when he comes over once a week to help me in the back garden."

I knew better than to ask if something had happened, so I walked to the windows and looked out at the falling rain. The earlier torrential thuds had transformed into a gentle patter.

"He didn't want to take an art class with me for an elective," Veronica continued after a moment's hesitation. "So I don't know why he's being so weird about it."

"Have you made any new friends in the class?"

"Sure, but Brix doesn't have anything in common with my new friend Cas, so I haven't invited them to hang out... Oh." She reddened. "It's not like that, though."

"Does Brixton know that?"

"Thanks, Ms. Faust." She walked to the studio door and opened it. Perenelle was sitting in the kitchen with Nicolas and Alessandro, a pained expression on her face as she held a small glass of beer.

She abandoned the glass of dark beer when she spotted Veronica, and scooped up a glass of water to bring back with her.

The doorbell rang. Since everyone else was occupied, I volunteered to get it.

I peeked through the front windows. I've never understood characters on television shows who know there's a murderer somewhere out there, but they still open their door without checking who's on the other side.

I recognized the visitor, though it wasn't someone I was expecting.

CHAPTER 29

From the Typewriter of Dorian Robert-Houdin

```
The Culinary Alchemist's Toolbox

   Beware of unwanted visitors. Cooking and baking
are not team sports. Meals are when you can come
together with those you care about.
```

Dorian reviewed what he had written. This was perhaps too harsh for a cookbook he wished people to buy. His wisdom was correct, of course. If guests nibbled at your carefully measured ingredients, the meal they were waiting for would not be as delectable.

It was mid-afternoon. Zoe would now be with Perenelle Flamel, and presumably Dr. Graves. This was not an ideal situation, for Zoe would not entertain the notion that Gwendolyn Graves could not be trusted. Zoe and Perenelle were biased! Yes, they had lived through times when women were the property of men and had so few rights it was as if they had none.

Dorian understood they were predisposed to trust a woman who sought to right the wrongs done to talented women after their deaths. Yet this did not mean they should overlook her tainted past! What was Dr. Graves hiding?

He wished he could speak with Nicolas. The old alchemist was a trustworthy companion, yet he was entertaining Veronica's father while the girl practiced her painting.

Dorian was deep in thought when he heard the sound of creaking below him. There should not have been anyone else in the house. Another burglar?

On high alert, he wrapped his cape around his shoulders, brandished a carved walking stick as a weapon, and crept down the stairs.

He winced as he neglected to step over the attic step that creaked underfoot. Yet the intruder did not appear to hear. He swept silently through the second floor, yet did not find a soul.

He scampered down the main stairway to the first floor. He walked quickly, as those steps were much more solid and would not give away his presence. Again, there was no one in the house.

The creaking sounded again. It was coming from the back porch.

Of course! Dorian chuckled to himself. Veronica was receiving an art lesson, therefore school had let out for the day. Brixton often came by to tend to Zoe's backyard garden. It had begun as punishment for breaking into Zoe's house. That was before any of them had been properly introduced. How far they had come.

Dorian knew better than to go into the backyard during the daylight hours. He hurried back upstairs, where he used Zoe's computer to text Brixton. Less than one minute later, the boy used his spare key to let himself into the house through the back door.

"Why are you sulking?" Dorian asked when the boy's sullen visage appeared in the attic doorway. "It is raining, so are you disappointed you cannot water the garden?"

"I'm not sulking."

"I will fix you a snack."

"Not hungry."

The boy was definitely sulking. He was always hungry.

"In that case," said Dorian, "you can assist me with a serious problem."

Brixton perked up. "Oh?" Yet his face fell immediately. "If you're talking about looking up who might've seen that burglar two nights ago, Ethan and Harry are on it. They're way better at that stuff than I am. I'm no good at anything."

Ah. This explained the sulking.

The boy was a loyal friend, yet he did not think these words would help at the moment. Nor did an assurance that his skills at the guitar and banjo were more than adequate. If he stuck with it, he would be quite good one day.

"It is not the search for the thief's movements by way of social media sightings," Dorian said. "There is something else I wish you to do. I wish you to be my eyes and ears on the ground."

"What does that mean?"

"You must befriend Dr. Gwendolyn Graves." Dorian explained to the boy that Zoe and Perenelle were already working with Dr. Graves on setting the historical record straight.

"Wicked," said Brixton. "It's about time stuff like that's getting done. But I don't see how I can help."

"Dr. Graves has had a long career. She has published many books and papers, which I am reviewing. I wish you to talk with her colleagues and former students. Say you are doing a class project, and you wish to tell the untold story of Dr. Graves, as a parallel to how she tells the untold story of the artists previously written out of history."

"But I don't know anything about art stuff. Like I said, I'm not good at anything. It's Veronica who's good at art. All she wants to do is practice painting, learn about art history, and hang out with her new art friends."

Ah. A deeper reason why the boy's sulking could not easily be counteracted.

"Yet you possess a characteristic none of them do," said Dorian.

"I do?"

"You are, by nature, *skeptical.* You will assess what you learn with an impartial eye that Zoe, Perenelle, and Veronica do not possess when it comes to Dr. Graves. They *wish* to believe in her, making their judgment biased."

"You know something." Brixton leaned forward.

"I *suspect*," said Dorian. "The truth and what one suspects are two different things. I need you to help me discover if my fears are warranted."

"I'm in."

CHAPTER 30

"I'm glad you're the one who came to the door," Dante said as I swung open the front door of the Flamels' house.

Dante was a neighbor of the Flamels. He'd been a murder suspect when I met him, but I'd always liked him and was glad he hadn't turned out to be guilty. The retired music producer no longer dressed as if he was in a punk rock band himself, but he still walked with a swagger and the zippers of his black pants were subtly adorned with silver skulls. Only one other house was on the hillside, and the mansions weren't in sight of each other. The privacy suited the occupants of both residences.

"That sounds ominous." I stood aside to let him inside.

Dante shook his head. "You up for a walk in the garden? I know it's raining, but—"

"I love walking in the rain." I shut the door behind us and followed him to the path between the stone and flower sections of Perenelle's pigment garden.

"What's going on?" I asked once we were far enough from the house there was no danger of being overheard. A light drizzle of rain made it feel as if we were talking inside a cloud. Here in the hills, we probably were.

Dante didn't speak immediately. When he did, instead of answering, he asked his own question. "Is everything all right with Nicolas and Perenelle?"

I glanced back at the house. "I know they're eccentric, but—"

"Nah, that's not what I mean. They're the best neighbors. They've got strangely colored puffs of smoke coming from their two chimneys sometimes, but the sulfurous smell never lingers—and it inspired me to write a great verse about brimstone the other day, while I was having a pot of tea next to Carla's Venus fly trap—wait, where was I?"

"The Flamels being good neighbors," I reminded him as we continued walking.

"Right. They never complain about our last-minute concerts at the Inferno."

Dante's Inferno was the name of the stone ruins that were all that remained of an older section of his mansion. They'd never been cleared away because they made for a great outdoor concert venue. The previous owner of the Flamels' house had complained about the noise, but Nicolas and Perenelle loved their neighbors' rejection of cultural norms. I was pretty sure they also appreciated having stone ruins nearby.

"They're even into the monster topiary." Dante grinned. "You saw the new dragons they put in?"

"A dragon and an ouroboros." I stopped at the edge of the Flamels' drive, where I could see the ouroboros serpent eating its own tail, and faced Dante. His tall figure loomed above me, and a worried crease dominated his forehead.

"Why are you worried about them?" I asked. "You don't need to worry about the strange smells from their furnaces. They're not harming themselves or going to burn down the house."

He chuckled, but the worried crease was still there. "I love them in the present. It's their past I'm worried about. I got a phone call from someone claiming they were doing a background check on Perenelle related to her artwork."

"A background check for an artist?"

"My thoughts exactly. The woman said she was an art collector thinking of investing in her artwork, so she needed to make sure nothing in her past would get her into trouble, and have the patron lose their money."

"Did this woman identify herself?"

"Said she'd 'rather not say.' So I said back to her that I'd rather not say anything about my great neighbors. Had me wishing she'd called my land line instead of my cell phone, so I could have slammed down the phone on her. You're too young to remember land lines, but it's a really satisfying feeling."

"I've got an old-fashioned phone on each floor of my house. I get it." I had a million questions for Dante, but I didn't know where to start.

"I shouldn't have hung up on her without getting more information. I'm sorry I didn't, but I at least wanted to find out if they were in trouble with anything. I mean, could they be in trouble with the law? I don't even know how long ago they came over from France. I know growing woad on purpose is banned in Oregon, since it grows like a weed in the Pacific Northwest, but that can't be it, can it? She has a legitimate purpose to harvest it to make colors for her art."

"You think the woman who called was law enforcement?"

"Doubt it. Because why wouldn't they just say that."

"So you'd be more willing to cooperate."

He shook his head. "They'd just have sent someone in person to surprise us. Nah, this woman… she was something else."

"Her number," I said. "She called your cell—"

"Tried that. The number is blocked. You okay, Zoe? You know something about this art collector?"

"Maybe. I was burglarized the night before last. I wasn't home," I assured him. "But a painting I love was stolen."

"Valuable to an art collector?"

"Only valuable to me, for sentimental reasons."

"I'll keep an eye on them, and let me know if there's anything I can do."

Dante gave my shoulder a quick squeeze, then swaggered past the serpent, heading back to his house.

The killer already had the paintings. Why would they still be looking into the Flamels? Was this new American art collector a new player in this game I didn't understand? Were we wrong that Betty Kubiak's killer was the one who had the paintings?

"Dante," I called after him as I hurried to catch him. "Would you know the voice of the woman if you heard it again?"

CHAPTER 31

The rain had stopped falling by the time I reached home.

Before coming home, I'd found an online lecture given by Dr. Graves and a press conference featuring Detective Vega, to see if either of those voices had been that of the woman who'd called Dante. They weren't.

I'd also completed the task that brought me to the Flamels' house in the first place: pulling Perenelle aside to tell her about how Renaissance White was worried about a competitor wanting their painting to test for paint formulations. She agreed it was best not to continue with Veronica's art lessons until we were certain the killer wouldn't be back.

There were two more women I was interested in. Willow Matsumoto and April Salazar from Renaissance White. But first, I needed to get Dorian caught up. I needed his help, but I didn't want him unintentionally doing anything dangerous. In the past, he'd managed to do quite a lot while armchair detecting in the attic.

"Was that Brixton I saw riding his bike down the street?" I asked Dorian as I locked up behind me.

"He came by to check on the garden. This is what he told me, at least. I believe he was bored."

"Because Veronica has some new art friends."

"I would not worry too much about the boy. We have a painting to retrieve and a murder to solve."

"About that," I said. "I think I know what's going on. Renaissance White has competitors, and they're worried these competitors might have stolen their painting for their paint formulations."

"Aha!"

"Aha?"

"It was as I suspected! *Recipes* are key."

"But a paint chemist can't simply wave a modern spectroscope—or whatever the technology is called—at a painting and know how to recreate it."

"Of course," said Dorian. "Recipes require training, not simply mimicking a finished product. You appear worried, *mon amie*."

"I *am* worried. Worried that the thief took the paintings because he doesn't know any better. If he's an amateur rather than a big corporate competitor. He might destroy the paintings in trying to get at a paint recipe that's impossible to figure out in isolation, or we could still be in danger when he finds out he can't get what he's after —which might already be the case."

"You have seen someone who might be Arthur Finder lurking about?"

"I don't know if it's him," I said, "but there's a woman who's been asking around about the Flamels."

"A *woman*?"

"'Arthur Finder' might have been a clever alias after all. We were so distracted by the tongue-in-cheek name that we forgot to think about the fact that *he* might not be a man at all."

"*Mon dieu*. You are most correct! A trap far too obvious for the great Dorian Robert-Houdin to have fallen for. I am quite ashamed." He tucked the tips of his wings, giving much the same effect of him hanging his head.

Dorian did, indeed, think of himself as "the great" Dorian Robert-Houdin. Since he'd lived such an isolated life, I was glad for his healthy ego. As long as it didn't go *too* far. So far, his ideas had served us well during our investigations. He focused his energy on cooking at the house, baking for Blue Sky Teas, and researching crimes we'd become embroiled in. I was glad he hadn't raised the idea of publishing any of the Gothic novels he'd started writing. It's not like he could give author interviews as a gargoyle.

"We all made that assumption," I assured him. "A woman called the Flamels' neighbors and said she was an art collector interested in investing in Perenelle's artwork, but she wanted to make sure there wasn't anything she should know about Perenelle that would lower the value of the work."

"*Intéressant.*"

"I found a recording of one of Gwendolyn Graves's lectures, and a press conference where Detective Vega spoke, and played them both for Dante, and he said it wasn't either of them. But there are two other women involved—"

"The women of Renaissance White," said Dorian. "I believe it is time for you to visit them once more."

CHAPTER 32

I turned on my phone's voice recorder before ringing the bell at the Renaissance White office and lab. I hoped I'd be able to get voice recordings of both Willow and April, as well as get more information about the stolen paintings. I didn't update Max about what I was up to, knowing he'd tell me to leave this to Detective Vega, but I did take precautions. I told Dorian I'd call as soon as I left the converted warehouse.

"You again," Oberon said as he opened the door. "Is there a new development?"

"I'm worried that there *haven't been* any developments. My stolen painting has tremendous sentimental value to me… I keep thinking I can do more to help figure out why our two paintings were stolen."

"Understood. Come on in. I could use a break anyway."

"Where exactly did your painting come from? Willow told me you found *The Apothecary's Cabinet* in the Saint-Ouen flea market in Paris. Any details you can remember might be helpful."

"Yeah, it was me," Oberon said, offering me a seat in the lobby and a coat hook for my silver raincoat, neither of which I accepted. I was too wired to sit, and I had no idea how quickly I'd be leaving.

"We used to take vacations together, the four of us," he said. "It was one of those trips. London last year was the last trip we took together, a destination Willow picked so she could fit in research at the British Library. That's the one freshest in my mind, since it was..." He shook off the memory of whatever he was going to say next. "The Paris trip was three years ago, so I don't remember vivid details from the flea market. But I can tell you what I think you're asking about: there was no provenance. No records of any kind about it."

"Oh." I tried not to be too disappointed. How could there be good provenance for a work of art that was originally taken from the Flamels' hastily abandoned home? It was yet another dead end.

"It's an old painting by an unknown artist," Oberon said. "I remember the dealer said she'd picked it up at an estate sale, and there was no paperwork with it. What I remember most was the beautiful day. Adam and Willow were visiting a science museum that afternoon, but April and I wanted to enjoy the glorious weather outside, so we went to the flea market. When April drew me to the crowded stall where I spotted *The Apothecary's Cabinet*, my gut told me the colors were special. It reminded me of Philippe Hayden's work, so for a magical fraction of a second, I thought I might have found a hidden masterpiece in a junk shop."

"But it wasn't."

"Course not. Stuff like that doesn't happen. Especially not to me. But we did have it dated and appraised, just to be sure."

I was going to ask him more about April, who I still hadn't met, but another voice spoke.

"You were right about the colors," said Willow as she stepped through the door to the laboratory behind us. "It inspired Adam to get back to painting and it got us closer to finding our first color formulation."

"We paid the dealer fairly," Oberon added for my benefit. "Adam insists that he's not going to be one of those rich people who screws people over just because he can."

"Our start-up money came from the settlement Adam got for his sister's wrongful death," Willow explained, no doubt seeing the confusion on my face. "That's how we were able to take a chance on setting up Renaissance White. The money was in a trust he got when he turned thirty, three years ago. That's when we all quit our jobs to give the company a go."

"We're not beholden to investors," Oberon added. "Just the four of us. I mean… the three—"

"You were asking Oberon about how he found *The Apothecary's Cabinet?*" Willow cut in, turning her back to Oberon and giving me her undivided attention.

Oberon's face had darkened as he corrected himself from four to *three*. Had he and his wife split up over the stress of the company? Willow clearly didn't want me asking more about it. And there was information I still wanted to get from them. And capturing Willow's voice for Dante to hear. It sounded like I wouldn't be able to get April's voice on tape, since it sounded like she no longer worked there.

"I'm still trying to work out why the thief was after both of our paintings," I said. "Mine means so much to me. I don't want to sit around feeling helpless, and the police are most concerned about the murder. Which I understand."

"But still." Willow nodded. "I get it. I want to know what's going on as much as you do. I nearly lost Adam. This whole year has been a train wreck."

"And now a competitor is going to swoop in and beat us," Oberon said. "It was a beautiful old painting, but not worth anything to an art collector. That's how I know it's one of our competitors who took it. Why else would they want it, if not for the chemical makeup of the colors?"

"That can't be it," Willow snapped. "It's our research they're after. My notes from the British Library trip and yours from your interviews, especially that wild one with the art historian studying the bright colors used on the statues of Ancient Greece."

Oberon's face reddened and he scratched the back of his neck. "I'm uh, pretty sure I was wrong that someone ransacked my house."

Willow's eyes widened, but the look on her face was more angry than surprised.

"I didn't make up what I thought I saw," he insisted before she could speak. "I drank too much and was looking through my notes, like I always do when I can't sleep. I made a mess. When I woke up, I didn't remember anything, but this morning when I found the notebook with my impressions from my interview with that lacquer artist, with some additional notes I'd written in red pen, it came back to me."

"You told this to the police?" Willow asked.

He gave a chagrined nod. "I told that detective I messed up and that mercenary Arthur Finder she told us about—or whoever it is that's after our secrets—didn't search my house after all. She wasn't as mad as I thought she'd be. Said a mistake like that could happen to anyone."

Willow glared at him. "She was just being nice."

"You're angrier than she was. I knew I was right to leave you and Adam on your own in the lab just now. Even if you're working so hard you're going to—"

"I'm not angry," Willow insisted, but it was less than convincing since she was near shouting. When she spoke again, she'd gotten a handle on her emotions. "I'm sorry. I miss her, too."

Oberon looked at the floor. "I need an aspirin." He shuffled down the hall without another word.

"Sorry you're seeing all our dirty laundry," Willow said to me.

"We're all under a lot of stress," I said. "I think we'll all feel better if we figure out what's going on. It *is* related to our paintings somehow. It has to be."

"But *why*? It doesn't make any sense."

"You don't think Oberon could be right about the corporate espionage?"

"He might be right, but he's wrong about the paintings. Any of our competitors would know that paintings don't give up their secrets."

"You mentioned you were doing research at the British Library. Not the British Museum. You weren't looking for artwork?"

"We each have our specialties related to chemistry." Willow walked over to the portrait of Adam's dead sister. She ran her fingertips across the gilded frame. "We're all chemists who work in the lab. But in addition to that, Adam is an oil painter, Oberon and April studied art history, and I'm interested in the history of science. That's why we all found each other as grad students. None of us wanted to spend our free time winning pub quizzes. We wanted to explore our humanities interests. The four of us went to museums and art galleries when most of the people in our cohort were either still in the lab or winning free pitchers of beer."

"The history of science," I said. "A huge field itself."

The hint of a smile appeared on Willow's face. "I'm a chemist by training and a hopeless romantic by disposition. Did Adam and I already tell you we think of ourselves as modern alchemists?"

"You did."

"Art and science are so much more intertwined than people today realize. The history of chemistry is bound together with the history of creating color for art. And right before modern chemistry, the people making true scientific breakthroughs were alchemists."

"When you were at the British Library," I said, catching on, "you were looking for their forgotten paint recipes. Written ones."

"Recipes for pigments and dyes, to be precise." She broadened her hesitant smile. The excitement of her passion tentatively peeking out through the mess we were in. "There are countless pigment and dye recipes lost to history. *Colors* lost to history. So far, we've only perfected one color that replicates a brilliant color from the past. Our testing of old works of art tells us a lot, but it doesn't give us the recipes. So I've been looking in places others might not have thought of. Trying historical texts that weren't specifically related to art."

"So not Cennini's *The Craftsman's Handbook*," I said, referencing the famous fifteenth-century Italian manuscript that recorded painting methods from the medieval ages. It, like so many books and works of art, had been lost to time, but it was rediscovered in the 1800s and an English translation from the 1930s has been popular ever since.

"Exactly," said Willow. "Cennini wrote that for artists. Historians also look to monks, who worked on illuminated manuscripts at monasteries. But most people overlook *early scientists* as a source for recipes for lost colors. People only seem to care about the Latin written by monks, but they forget the scientists."

Her enthusiasm was contagious. "Did you find any of the recipes you were after?" I asked.

"Not exactly," Willow said. "Apprentices mostly learned verbally and through live instruction. Everything written down in manuscripts and journals is so vague that it's nearly useless. There's still some Latin I need to translate. Nothing is going to give me *all* the answers, but everything I track down is another piece of the puzzle to creating our paints."

"A modern way of recreating the vibrant colors people have been finding and then losing for millennia." I looked at Adam's portrait of his sister. Even though he'd used modern, mass-produced paints in the oil painting, it was still a powerful piece. I hadn't noticed before that the trees, cabin, and lake all had a subtle soft focus compared to his sister's face.

"A modern method to get at our favorite colors from the past that *doesn't* involve poisoning either the people who use it or the people who make it," said Willow. "With how much those scientists and artists of the past used toxic elements to create pigments, it's no wonder so many of them died so young."

"You said Oberon had an interesting interview with someone who studies the paints of Ancient Greece?" I'd hoped to follow up with Oberon, but he hadn't returned.

"Oberon should write a book about that guy. Or at least an article. His work is fascinating, but not helpful for us. He works with people recreating the old arts, but not in colorfast, mass producible ways. Like a blue verditer that's created by leaving a jar of copper, ash, and lime outside during the coldest months of winter, agitating it by hand, and watching for when you need to stir it so it doesn't turn from blue to green. It's fun to learn about. But not a recipe we can create for artists in large volume in a factory." Willow twisted her dark hair around her finger and lowered her voice. "I wish I knew if someone had really broken into Oberon's house. That would help narrow things down."

"You think he rationalized away the ransacking, since the thief didn't take a notebook he initially thought was missing?"

Willow shrugged. "I don't know what to think. Oberon hasn't been the same since April died."

"His wife *died*?"

Willow's focus drifted away from me as she turned toward the lab. She lifted her arm slowly, as if in a trance. Her index finger slowly straightened as she pointed towards the laboratory door. "April died right here. Oberon found her on the floor of our lab. Ever since then, nothing has been the same."

CHAPTER 33

Back in my truck parked outside Renaissance White, I turned off the audio recording on my phone and rested my forehead on the steering wheel. The more I learned, the more questions I had.

Before returning my phone to my bag, I looked up April Salazar's death. Nothing popped up. Surely Willow wouldn't have lied about that, would she? Did she lie to get rid of me?

Willow had given me a few more details before I left. She told me it wasn't a lab accident that killed April, but a heart defect. April had been drinking coffee and energy drinks nonstop, while barely eating. They were close to perfecting their recipe for a brilliant white pigment, so April had pushed too hard, and her heart had given out. Willow was clearly shaken by talking about her friend's death, and I didn't think I was going to learn more, so I'd thanked her and left.

In case Willow, Adam, or Oberon was looking through one of the front-facing windows, I drove around the corner before parking out of sight and calling Dante. I was hoping to play a snippet of the voice recording of Willow's voice for him and hear what he thought, but he didn't answer. I tried once more before giving up. I found a clip where Willow was speaking about the history of color and sent Dante the audio file. I didn't want to miss it when he called back, so I changed the settings on my phone so the ringer would sound for all callers.

Next, I called Dorian to ask him to use his armchair research skills to find out what had become of April.

"Dead?" he repeated when he picked up the phone. "Oberon's wife is *dead?*"

"Her name is still on the website," I said. "I didn't think of questioning that she was alive. She had to be in her early thirties like the rest of them, so it never occurred to me that she'd be dead."

"What a fool I have been to not dig deeper into the lives of the two couples who make up Renaissance White! *Je suis désolé, mon amie.*"

"There's no need to be sorry," I said. "I did a brief search and didn't find her. Willow said she died of cardiac arrest after basically working herself to death."

"I have fallen victim to yet another logical fallacy. Since Adam White was a victim, we made a grave error in failing to consider the entire Renaissance White collective as serious suspects."

"But with one of them dead," I said, "there's more we need to learn."

~

I was back home ten minutes later. Dorian looked up from my laptop as I stepped into the attic.

"I have not had time to conduct a full search," he said, "but I have already learned why you did not find news of her death. Before her marriage, April Salazar was April Rowe. Her Rowe surname appears to have been used on official documents, but Salazar was how she wished to be known. Her name on the Renaissance White website and minor publications is Salazar."

"I don't care what she calls herself. Is she really dead?"

"*Oui.* I regret that she did indeed die. There was not much news about the young woman's death, as it was reported as congenital heart disease leading to heart failure."

"Which is a tragedy," I said. "Not suspicious."

"That," Dorian said, "remains to be seen." He turned to his murder board and removed three handwritten notecards. "Renaissance White. Founded three years ago by married couple Adam White and Willow Matsumoto, with their married friends Oberon and April

162

Salazar. They met as PhD students in chemistry. There is not much about them online. This is the first suspicious fact."

"There are a lot of reasons people don't have a big social media presence," I pointed out.

"They have a shared Renaissance White account in which they post about art, as well as their line of oil and acrylic white paints that are launching this fall on the West Coast of the United States, and across the country very soon. Yet there is much more to their story. Though they do not discuss personal matters online, many of their friends *do*."

He tacked the first notecard back onto the cork board and read from the second. "The four friends were married in a joint ceremony, which they called a Chemical Wedding. As in alchemy! This is suspicious, is it not?"

"Willow made it clear they think of themselves as modern-day alchemists. They draw from the knowledge of the past, but disregard what they believe the alchemists got wrong. They must have meant it symbolically, since a Chemical Wedding means the union of opposites, the sun and the moon, with different energies coming together. Not suspicious."

Dorian sighed. "You are most likely correct. The Chemical Wedding was simply play on words. They are chemists interested in the history of alchemy, *alors*, they called their wedding a 'Chemical Wedding.' I have only had ten minutes to conduct my research. Give me time, and I will discover more."

"I'm about to give you more time. I'm due to meet Max when he closes his shop."

"There is too much food in the refrigerator. Bring some to Max, or there will be no room for me to cook more food."

"Why do you need to cook more food if the fridge is full?"

Dorian flapped his wings. "We are *investigating*, Zoe. A mystery is afoot, and I do my best thinking while cooking. And we now have so many suspects to investigate."

"I know," I said. "Five people. Adam, Willow, and Oberon from Renaissance White, the mysterious Arthur Finder who sent a thief to break into our houses, and the woman claiming to be an art collector."

"You are forgetting the art historian," said Dorian. "Surely you are not forgetting Gwendolyn Graves, whose expertise and secrecy places her in the middle of this conundrum."

"She's not—"

"Nobody," said Dorian, "is above suspicion. Not even a respected professor. That leaves us with six suspects. Three scientists, two art collectors, and one historian."

"Which one of them," I said, "is a thief and killer?"

"And," said Dorian, "do not overlook the most intriguing fact of all. April Salazar died late at night while in a *locked* laboratory." He paused for dramatic effect. "A locked-room murder! I have not solved such a crime since Paris."

I was the one who solved that Paris case, but I didn't need to quibble.

"Please ask Max to have Detective Vega look more closely at her death," Dorian said. "Is it not suspicious that someone with a weak heart drank so many energy drinks?"

This mystery might have begun long before we imagined.

CHAPTER 34

I reached The Alchemy of Tea a few minutes before closing time. Max rang up two customers before flipping the sign on the door to CLOSED.

He greeted me with a kiss. "Staying out of trouble?"

"I even brought snacks." I held up a small paper bag holding two crèmes brûlées I'd found in the fridge.

"Why does that sound like a deflection?"

"A lot's happened today."

Max swore. "What's happened? You should have called. Your short texts barely told me anything. You—"

"I'm fine. There's so much to say that I don't know where to start."

"I *knew* I should have shut the shop." He ran a hand through his hair and surveyed the shop.

"How many customers did you have today?" I followed his gaze to the nearly empty glass containers and empty spots on the shelves that he'd need to restock.

"It was another good day," he admitted. "A great one. Every day the shop's popularity seems to grow. But it's hardly the most important thing in life. If anything were to happen to you—"

"Max. Nothing is going to happen to me. You've put so much of yourself into setting up the shop of your dreams. I'm not going to let you ruin that for me. Especially when I'm safe, and when your expertise is best served here, not digging through historical research."

"Historical research?"

"It turns out that my stolen painting has historical value beyond the sentimental value it has for me."

I told him about Perenelle's notebook, Professor Graves's research, and how we were going to prove the truth about Philippe Hayden—the truth about *Perenelle*.

Though it was only that morning that I'd outwardly resolved to set the historical record straight, the idea had been bubbling up inside me for the past year, ever since I'd learned the full truth about Perenelle's path. And the *desire* had been in me for centuries. I hadn't known it was linked to exposing the truth about Philippe Hayden. But there was a pattern of women artists and scientists like Perenelle not being recognized. A history I'd seen unfold over the centuries. Now that I'd voiced the desire aloud, there was no going back.

"I always knew you were an amazing woman, Zoe Faust." Max's broad smile held such pride and excitement that I wished I didn't have to break the spell and tell him about the rest of my day.

"I wish Perenelle would have told me everything earlier," I said. "The timing is awful, but meeting Professor Graves is the silver lining. If we can get the *Brother and Sister* painting back, it will go a long way in both solving a murder and revealing an important hidden truth from history."

"You would have told me right away if any progress had been made in locating the stolen paintings."

"I don't know if it's progress, exactly, but I did learn more. Adam White of Renaissance White is out of the hospital, so I was able to talk with him and his coworkers, Willow Matsumoto and Oberon Salazar, about our stolen paintings. Oberon is worried that competitor chemists might have wanted both paintings for the chemical compounds in the paint."

"Why steal a painting rather than simply take one of the tubes of paint they've given out before their launch? Or break into their lab itself?"

I shook my head. "Paint formulations don't work like that. Which is why Adam and Willow disagree with Oberon. You can't recreate a paint from the finished product. It can give you clues by showing you the secrets of the ingredients, but without a recipe, you don't have the method. You need a *recipe*."

"Did they steal a recipe along with the paintings?"

"That's the weird thing. Betty Kubiak wasn't interested in the thumb drive in the safe next to *The Apothecary's Cabinet* painting when she robbed Adam, just like she didn't take anything else from my shelves of Elixir."

"So we can presume that she was only tasked with stealing the two paintings," Max said.

"Which are more connected to Perenelle than Renaissance White." I rubbed my temples. My energy was fading.

I grabbed one of the small spoons Max kept for stirring tea samples and broke through the caramelized sugar on top of the crème brûlée. I winced at its bitterness as the dessert hit my tongue. The flavors were so burnt that I could barely taste the coconut cream custard under the charred top. It was unlike Dorian to have ruined a recipe so badly. It was as if he'd used a flame thrower to crisp the top. But I'd been so busy that afternoon I needed the sugar to keep going, so I took another bite.

"Let's make dinner at my house," Max said. "Give me ten minutes to clean up the shop, then we can head over."

"Can I help?"

"You can help by telling me more about what you learned today. Have a seat and enjoy your pudding. But keep talking."

"April Salazar, one of the four cofounders of Renaissance White, died last year in the lab."

Max swore.

"Natural causes," I added quickly. "A congenital heart defect combined with overwork and way too much caffeine. Dorian wondered if someone might have forced her to drink a dangerous amount."

"I can ask Vega about it," Max said. "April was working on the paint formulation that the surviving scientists think a competitor is trying to steal?"

"Looks that way," I pointed at his unmoving broom. "Keep sweeping."

Max muttered something under his breath that I didn't catch in its entirety, but I was pretty sure was something about not letting me out of his sight.

"There's one more thing that happened today," I said. "A woman with an American accent, who identified herself as an art collector, has been asking questions about the Flamels' past."

"Not Arthur Finder, then."

"Probably not. But who knows, since it's an alias. Maybe it's been a woman the whole time. This woman called their neighbor, Dante, but we don't know her identity."

"I don't like the fact that there's more going on here than makes sense. Maybe it's time to leave everything to Detective Vega. I was in favor of investigating a theft, but now that there's at least one murder, maybe two? I don't like this at all."

"I don't either, but we can't tell Detective Vega the whole truth," I pointed out. "We have way too many unanswered questions. I can't give up. There's too much at stake."

CHAPTER 35

The sun hung low in the sky by the time Max and I stepped outside of The Alchemy of Tea. The sidewalk was covered in a rainbow of damp leaves after the heavy rains earlier that day, but the air was now cool and dry.

"Look at that green." I pointed at a ginkgo tree that was filled with yellow leaves, with only a few green leaves remaining. "That's the exact shade of green in the dress I'm wearing in the portrait with Thomas."

"I know that painting means a lot to you. I've been thinking about something. You've never told me much about Thomas. Even though I've seen the painting, I can't really picture him. I know what he looks like and how much you loved him, but not much more than that."

"It's hard for me," I admitted. "And before I got the painting of him from Perenelle, it was hard for me to conjure him in my mind. I only had that locket-size portrait of him. I know that sounds terrible—"

"It doesn't. I still grieve for Chadna, and I'll always love her. It doesn't hurt less that she's gone, but so many times when I think of her it's the good times, not the tragedy. I'm still sad, but I can move forward. But if I lost Mina, I wonder if losing a sister would be like losing an arm."

Max's wife Chadna had died many years ago in an accident. He knew the pain of losing someone far too soon.

"Or an eye," I said. I hadn't thought of it like that before, but Max was right. "That's how I feel about Thomas. He saw the world differently than I did. When I was with him, I got two sets of eyes. Thomas was so mischievous that I wanted to strangle him as much as I wanted to hug him. He was the night to my day. It was nearly impossible to get him to come inside at night, so twilight was our favorite time of day. Our shared time, before I got tired and as he was truly coming alive."

"He was the moon to your sun."

"The moon usually rises during daylight," I said. "That's how I can make both solar infusions and moon infusions with herbs. People who aren't paying attention don't notice that."

"Hey." Max put his hands on his hips in mock outrage. "Are you saying I'm not observant?"

We reached Max's front door just as I hiccupped.

"How many rings am I wearing today?" I asked as I hid my hands behind me. The bag of creme brûlée ramekins knocked into my side as I hiccupped once more.

"Trick question. You don't wear rings. Only your locket necklace."

I stuck out my tongue at him.

"Zoe Faust. Are you *drunk*?"

Oh no, the creme brûlée… I lifted the remnants of the nearly empty ramekin from the bag and sniffed. It wasn't just burnt sugar.

"Chocolate and alcohol." I groaned. "There's chocolate liquor in here."

I don't tolerate caffeine well at all. And a mix of sugar, caffeine, and alcohol? It was amazing I was still standing. I hiccupped again. Dorian would have warned me if he saw what I'd taken from the fridge, but he'd stayed in the attic doing research.

"Let's get you inside and sober you up." Max unlocked the door and pulled me inside.

"We might as well make the best of it," I said. "I'm going to crash in a bit, but before then, let's go skinny dipping in your backyard."

"I don't have a pool."

"I bet that clover groundcover is super soft."

"That clover is deceptive."

"Evil clover? Are you hiding a villainous leprechaun in your backyard?"

Max's whole body shook with laughter. "You've been spending too much time with Dorian. You're starting to sound like one of his Gothic novels."

I frowned. "He lets you read his novels?" Dorian hadn't shown me anything he'd written.

"I may have taken a peek while we were playing chess in the attic and he went downstairs to get more tea."

"I had no idea you could be so mischievous, Max Liu."

The man in question sighed. "If it wouldn't literally keep you up for days, I'd make you drink some coffee."

"Did you know that even though Thomas lived until he was twenty-six, he never fully outgrew his mischievous streak? He was a charming heartbreaker. Not unlike a certain former-detective-turned-tea-alchemist who's standing in this peaceful living room. Did anyone ever tell you it looks like you can step right into the forest in these paintings?"

"Maybe a cold shower would work."

"Anything but that!" I ran to the kitchen and flung open the doors of the kitchen cabinets. Carbs. Something with carbs would sober me up. Wouldn't it? I pulled flour and yeast from one shelf before realizing how shocked I should have been. I stared at the five-pound bag of flour in my hand, gobsmacked by its presence in Max's kitchen. "When did you stock your cabinets?"

The last time I'd rummaged through Max's kitchen had been a year ago when he came down with a bad cold. To make him a healing soup, I had to think creatively. I'd harvested wild nettles from his backyard, and cooked them with the garlic, shallots, and spices in his sparse cabinets, blending the result for a smooth soup filled with healing ingredients.

My own philosophy of cooking is much simpler than Dorian's. I don't follow recipes. Instead, I think about which plants would give me energy and how different elements would combine. I grow my own vegetables and herbs, make my own infused oils and vinegars, and buy high quality legumes, grains, and spices. To be fair, he's a far better cook and baker than I am. My simple, healing meals have sustained me for centuries, but Dorian has given me the gift of joyous food these last two years.

Max gave me a shy smile. "The stocked cabinets are a new development. When I was setting up The Alchemy of Tea and transforming the tea plants I'd grown into special dried teas, my senses became elevated beyond tea. My taste buds are more attuned to the food I eat. I still grab lunch from one of the restaurants near the shop, but when I'm not eating breakfast or dinner at your house with Dorian cooking, I've started cooking for myself."

I set down the bag of flour in my hands and kissed him. "We're going to figure out the recipe for pumpkin croissants that Dorian hasn't gotten right! Won't that be a great gift for the gargoyle who gave us both the gift of good food?"

"Um, Zoe, neither of us knows how to bake. Especially not croissants." He put the kettle on and lifted a tin of chamomile tea from a cabinet.

"I've watched Dorian do it plenty of times," I said. "And there's this newfangled thing called the internet. I hear it has recipes."

Max laughed. "I don't have any fresh pumpkins."

I frowned. "I have some on the vine at my house… I'm not sure if they're ready to pick… Hmm… Oh, good. Pumpkin puree. That'll do."

"A shortcut? I'm shocked."

I waved aside his concern. But as I did so, a niggling thought flickered at the back of my mind.

Max took the canned pumpkin from my hand. "You okay?"

"A shortcut," I murmured.

"I was joking. I'm pretty sure recipes for baking with pumpkin all recommend canned pumpkin."

"Unless you're in France," I said automatically. The product that was ubiquitous in the US was surprisingly difficult to find elsewhere. "But that's not what I meant. Something about shortcuts." My temple began to throb.

"Let's go sit down in the living room. Tea will be done in a few minutes."

Max led me to his serene living room. A large white couch and pewter-topped coffee table were the main pieces of furniture on the hardwood floor. The room overlooked the backyard through a sliding glass door, and the walls held oversize paintings of forests, making it feel as if you were relaxing in a forest.

"The thought is gone," I said, leaping up from the couch as soon as we sat down. "I have too much energy to sit still. It's either skinny dipping on clover, or baking. I know what we'll bake. A nut bread with the nettles in the back corner of your backyard."

"Uh…"

"Zucchini bread works, so why wouldn't nettle bread? Oh! I have a better idea. Parsnip bread. Thomas loved parsnips. He loved their sweetness."

"Sweetness?"

"You, Max Liu, have a very twenty-first century notion of sweetness." I bopped him on the nose with my finger.

"I'm sorry to say I don't have any parsnips. You look overly disappointed. I promise if you still want to bake a parsnip loaf tomorrow, I'll buy you parsnips—"

"It's not that." I couldn't shake my worry about shortcuts. There was something I'd learned… Something out of place. "What am I missing?"

"A lot of ingredients. Even though my pantry is no longer empty, it isn't stocked for baking."

"That's not what I meant." The idea was gone.

Max handed me a cup of chamomile tea. I closed my eyes and breathed in the steam. The dried blossoms infused in hot water smelled like an orchard filled with bees. Subtle notes of sweet apple and honey were what gave me that impression. I opened my eyes and took a sip.

Before I could take another, my phone trilled. I lunged for my bag, spilling half of my tea in the process. Max's eyes flashed with concern until I showed him the screen. I knew he wasn't worried about the spill, but who was calling.

"Dante," I told Max as he took the mug from my hand.

"Was your phone shoved into the bottom of your purse when you made that recording?" Dante asked as soon as I picked up.

I winced. "Probably. Too muffled?"

"Too muted to tell for sure," he said. "But that might have been the woman who called me earlier."

"Thanks for trying."

"Hey, are Nicolas and Perenelle all right?"

"Why?" I gripped the edge of the couch. Why was Max's living room spinning? "Has something happened?"

"Carla and I invited them over for a sunset cup of tea. They bailed at the last minute. I heard tires screeching as they drove off."

CHAPTER 36

I tried calling the Flamels yet again. I'd been trying them both for the last fifteen minutes, and each time their phones went straight to voicemail.

Night had fallen, and Max was driving to the Flamels' house. They'd left in a hurry, so we wanted to make sure there were no signs of them being taken forcefully.

As we crested the top of the hillside near the Flamels' house, our headlights bounced off of the monster topiary. The dragon, kraken, and sea serpent on the hillside looked more life-like tonight, but I knew it was a combination of a trick of the light and my frazzled mental state.

"Their car isn't here," I said as we reached their drive. I was nearly sober. Fear is a surprisingly good antidote to drunkenness.

"Looks like they left on their own," said Max as he parked. "Which is as we suspected, since they canceled their plans with Dante and Carla."

I leapt out of the car, hurrying past the pigment garden to the front door. "Locked. And I don't see any windows broken."

We searched the perimeter of the house and didn't see anything amiss.

"Car coming," Max said unnecessarily as I heard it as well. We made our way back to the front of the house, and the Flamels' silver 1968 Volkswagen Beetle appeared a few moments later.

"Something tells me we missed a great deal while we were out," said Nicolas as he stepped out of the small car.

"I was worried since Dante said you canceled on him and Carla," I said.

"Change of plans." Perenelle squinted in the light of Max's cell phone flashlight. "We thought it more important to have drinks with someone who claimed to be an art collector who was very interested in my work."

Max lowered the light. "Arthur Finder?"

"Joni Mitchell," Nicolas clarified. "Not Arthur Finder. But we believe her to be a *faux* art collector as well."

"The famous folk singer?" Max gaped at Nicolas.

"She could be a real art collector," I added.

I'd seen Joni Mitchell perform many times, and in addition to enjoying her music, I'd always admired her resilience. A childhood bout of polio permanently weakened her left hand, so she had to invent unique ways to play the guitar. It contributed to her signature style playing her acoustic guitar, and gave her a life perspective that made her wise beyond her years. How else could someone so young have written songs like *Both Sides Now* that perfectly captured the duality of life?

"She gets that reaction to her name sometimes," Nicolas said. "But they simply share a name."

I was strangely disappointed, though also relieved the musician wasn't involved in this mess.

"She showed up at Elements Art House," said Perenelle. "She told Sameera she was interested in my artwork, so Sameera passed along the message to me. We thought it was best to humor her that we believed her to be an art collector."

Before moving into this larger house, Perenelle had rented studio space at Elements Art House, run by Sameera Reddy.

"Why do you think your Joni Mitchell isn't a real collector?" I asked. "Couldn't she just be someone who's new to collecting?" I didn't believe it myself, but it was possible. Perenelle's work was masterful enough to attract interest during any era.

"It wasn't a lack of knowledge about art," said Perenelle. "It was the fact that we were being interrogated."

"Subtly, of course," Nicolas added. "But it was clear it wasn't Perenelle's artwork she was most interested in. She was keen on gathering *information*."

"Let's get inside," I said, suddenly feeling very exposed under the moonlight. I looped my hand through the crook of Nicolas's elbow to get our little group moving into the house.

"What type of information?" Max asked once we were gathered inside. The living room was filled with hazardous towers of books that looked like they might topple at the slightest provocation, so we were in the kitchen.

"That is the curious thing," said Nicolas.

"And why we were curious enough to stay for a second drink," Perenelle added. "She had no focus. At least none that I could determine. She was trying to make it sound as if she were simply a friendly woman."

"If we had not lived through so much inquiry ourselves in the past," said Nicolas, "we no doubt would have believed her act. She was very good."

"I don't suppose you got a photo," Max said.

Nicolas grinned and held up his phone. "I pretended to be looking for a photograph of one of Perenelle's recent paintings, but really I took her photo."

I looked over Max's shoulder at the photo. A woman of medium build who was maybe in her late sixties, with short brown hair that had a slight wave, and only the subtlest touch of makeup. The most distinctive thing about her was a bright magenta blazer with a beautiful pewter broach. Which was to say, she was completely nondescript outside of two items of memorable clothing.

"Someone who doesn't want to be remembered," I said.

"Or someone who simply isn't distinctive," said Max. "But in this case, with the Flamels' instincts, I'm inclined to agree with you. American accent?"

"Midwestern America, I believe," said Nicolas.

"He has been studying dialects," Perenelle added when she saw the skepticism on Max's face.

"Her *name*," I said. "It makes perfect sense why she'd use that name, even though at first glance it seems like it would only bring more attention to herself."

"Because we can't easily look her up," Max said.

I nodded. "If we suspect she's disingenuous—which we do—we won't find her online, since the more famous Joni Mitchell, who's also an older American woman, will crowd out all the search results."

"You should send her photo over to Detective Vega," Max said.

"I'm glad you agree," said Perenelle, "because I've already done so."

"My dear," Nicolas said, "I believe Zoe is unwell."

"Accidentally drunk," Max said.

"I'm not drunk," I insisted. "Okay, fine. I *was* drunk. I mistakenly ate a dessert with chocolate liquor. I'm better now, but still not feeling my best."

"Let's get you home," said Max. "There's nothing else we can do tonight."

"Isn't there?" asked Nicolas. "We have many more books to go through."

"You," Perenelle said to her husband, "are getting some sleep as soon as we have a light supper." She turned to us. "He thinks he can stay up all night like he did when he was only 100 years old."

"I'm still getting used to this," Max whispered in my ear.

I was still getting used to a lot of things. Like being surrounded by people I loved and could trust. I'd felt wretched when I thought something might have happened to Nicolas or Perenelle, like my whole life was being ripped away from me again. I wasn't going to lose them again. I wasn't going to lose *anyone* I loved. That included my biggest remaining connection to Thomas. I needed everyone I loved to be safe—and I needed that painting back.

CHAPTER 37

From the Typewriter of Dorian Robert-Houdin

The Culinary Alchemist's Toolbox

One must experiment to succeed. Experimentation comes with failure. This is not a flaw, but a necessary step.

Zoe had called to tell Dorian she would be staying over at Max's house that night, so the tea alchemist could care for her during her hangover. She had foolishly taken one of Dorian's failed culinary experiments in which he was testing the line between peak flavor extraction and distasteful ash. Fire brought out the best in food, but it also obscured the truth when it went too far and turned a culinary delight into only bitter, charred remnants of a once-great creation.

Before ringing off, Zoe also told Dorian about the Flamels' adventures with their "Art Collector #2" suspect, for whom they now had a name. Joni Mitchell. An unhelpful name, but still, it was a start.

Dorian remained convinced that everyone besides himself was overlooking Gwendolyn Graves as the primary suspect. Why was her trip to Seattle to retrieve her notes taking her so long? Zoe maintained it was because an elderly person might wish to spread a long drive across two days. *Pfft.* In spite of arthritis, the professor was quite capable. She might very well be up to something else.

Though the sun had set, it was not yet late in the evening. He called Brixton to find out if the boy had learned anything of interest.

"You were right," Brixton said. "I talked to three professors who were happy to share their ideas with a high school student interested in art history. I told them I'd heard about some scandal from fifty years ago. Only one of them had heard about it, and he said everyone makes mistakes when they're young."

"Good work," Dorian said. "This is a promising start. Keep at it."

He bid the boy goodnight, then paced back and forth upon the attic floorboards. In this ruminative state, he tapped his fingers together as he paced, then clasped his hands behind his back. After much contemplative thought, Dorian hatched a plan. His little gray cells had done their work. Now he needed Nicolas Flamel's assistance.

"We must gather evidence of Gwendolyn Graves's wrongdoings," he told the old alchemist. "The professor alluded to the fact that the evidence is at her office. As soon as I am done baking for Blue Sky Teas, we must drive there to seek it out."

And so it was that Nicolas Flamel and Dorian Robert-Houdin secretly borrowed Zoe's truck for the three-hour drive to Seattle.

It was four o'clock in the morning when the gargoyle and the old alchemist arrived at the university.

With Dorian's claws, they made quick work of the inconsequential lock on the office door of Emeritus Professor Graves, and on the locks on her file cabinets.

Dorian was pleased he was correct in his assumption that Dr. Graves kept paper records of her research. He was not a gargoyle who wished to stereotype based on age. The woman herself had said she needed to return so she could bring boxes back with her. This wording indicated her preference for paper.

"I'm still unsure what you hope to find," Nicolas said as they began searching through the beige file cabinets. "Gwendolyn is willingly bringing her research on Hayden back to Portland tomorrow. Er, I suppose I mean *today* at this point."

"Willingly bringing only the documents she *wishes* to share with Perenelle and Zoe."

"Looks like her Hayden research is already gone." Nicolas drew Dorian's attention to an empty drawer that squeaked as the older alchemist pulled it all the way open.

"Not quite." Dorian reached inside the nearly empty drawer. There was one well-worn file folder at the bottom of the drawer. A few dust bunnies fluttered to the floor as he lifted it in his clawed hands.

"This drawer was kept under lock and key."

"For good reason," Dorian exclaimed, the little gray cells in his mind spinning so quickly he could barely contain himself. "I believe I have found our secret society!"

Nicolas peered over his shoulder. "The Brushstrokes and Brimstone Society." There was a note of reverence in his voice as he read from the top of a yellowed, typewritten page.

Dorian spun around, nearly knocking Nicolas over with an outstretched wing. "You have heard of this society?"

Nicolas scratched his scruffy chin. "Not exactly. But it's similar."

"Similar to *what?*" Dorian prompted.

"I'm mistaken. Never heard of it." He tapped his temple. "Many centuries of facts up here. They get jumbled sometimes."

Dorian sighed. His exciting breakthrough was somewhat marred by the fact that Nicolas's health had not recovered.

"Night will be turning into day soon," Nicolas said. "We should be on our way. Gwendolyn has already been here to take what she needs, so we can safely take this with us."

"There is not much to read. Only one page remains."

It was five o'clock as they locked the door behind them. The hallway was dim, but bright enough that they need not use the torch from Nicolas's mobile phone.

"Can I help?" a deep voice called.

Nicolas raised his wild eyebrows as they exchanged a brief look, before hurrying around a corner, pretending not to have heard.

"Stone," Nicolas whispered.

Dorian agreed, and quickly turned to stone.

"Professor?" the voice called.

"It must be a security guard," Dorian whispered back, and a moment later, he was fully stone.

"Never fear," Nicolas whispered. "I will talk our way out of this."

Dorian was not certain the old alchemist would be able to do this, but what choice did he have but to have faith?

Nicolas straightened his lapels and turned to face the guard who was quickly approaching.

"Hello, good man!" Nicolas beamed at the uniformed man. "I'm so sorry to have startled you from your rounds. I couldn't get back to sleep, so I thought I'd do some work."

"With a statue of a Gothic Revival-style gargoyle as your muse?" The guard pointed at Dorian.

"Ah, you recognize the style!"

Dorian's stone faced the guard, not Nicolas, so he could not see his friend's expression, though he detected delight in the old alchemist's voice.

"Notre Dame Cathedral, right?" said the guard. "Eugène Viollet-le-Duc's 1860s renovation."

"Quite right, good sir."

The guard chuckled. "Let me guess. You specialize in art history going back a ways. Not modern art."

"There is *much* to be learned from history."

It was all Dorian could do not to come back to life to nudge Nicolas. Why was the man making mundane small talk with the lowly guard? The man had clearly assumed Nicolas was a professor, so there was no need to speak further.

"Agreed," said the guard. "But I don't agree that modern scientific advancements should bow down to 'expert' connoisseurs. Your sculpture, for example. It looks like limestone, like those cathedral gargoyles, but if you were to claim it was really that old, that doesn't mean nobody should test it."

"Quite," said Nicolas. "Yet I do not believe modern science can tell us everything we need to know about art history. Those we think of as experts need to be checked. Tell me, what era of art do you study?"

The guard hesitated.

"I did not mean to pry," said Nicolas. "If you don't wish to share your research—"

"It's not that." The man's bravado turned almost bashful. "Most people… They assume I'm just a security guard."

"How could they think that after speaking with you?"

The man chortled. "You assume students and professors talk to me."

"That's distressing to hear."

The guard shrugged. "I'm glad visiting professors at least are open minded. Can I help you with your statue? What are you doing with it anyway? You're sharing that big old office with Professor Graves?"

"You know her?" Nicolas asked.

"She's mostly retired, so not much."

"The gargoyle is related to some research that Dr. Graves worked on in the past. She's doing research in Portland at present, so I'm retrieving him."

"*Him?*"

"Does he not have enough personality to merit more than an *it?*"

The man chuckled as he lifted Dorian in his strong arms. "Sure does. And I see what you mean about scientific analysis being checked. This gargoyle, even if the stone dates back to the time the cathedral was being renovated and the rock is placed to come from those limestone quarries, this little guy is far too small to be one of those gargoyles on the cathedral."

Dorian, in spite of suffering the indignity of being carried by this muscular man back to the car, could not help but be impressed by this line of reasoning.

During the walk to Zoe's truck, Nicolas learned that the man had been in the military and was now returning to school to earn his bachelor's degree.

"You giving any lectures I can attend?" he asked as they reached the parking lot.

"Afraid I'm only visiting for research. But please do feel free to call me if you wish to discuss your research. I'm technically retired, but always happy to mentor a bright young pupil." Nicolas handed the man a card. "My name is Nicolas. Nicolas Flamel."

"Like that fictional alchemist?"

"Ah! Have you done adequate research to be sure he was indeed fictional?"

The guard chuckled and wished Nicolas a safe journey home.

"You do not mind giving out your name?" Dorian asked once the man had gone.

"Why would I? It's the name on my identification. I believe the expression is that I am 'hiding in plain sight.' After all, who would believe I'm six hundred years old?"

Who, indeed. Nicolas would surely make a good front for Dorian's chart-topping work of culinary genius. But first, they must confront Gwendolyn Graves.

"Have you seen the news this morning that the media has now connected Betty Kubiak's murder with two art thefts?" Dorian called from the kitchen as I let myself into the house after having breakfast at Max's house.

I was nursing a sugar-caffeine-liquor hangover, but Max's ministrations had helped me at least feel human this morning. Plus, it helped that it was a sunny day.

"Max read the news while I was sleeping." I pushed open the swinging door to the kitchen and found Dorian standing on his stepping stool, kneading dough on a floured wooden cutting board. "But don't worry. Theo worked quickly and already set up a better online history for the Flamels. I don't know how he does it, but their close-to-true backstories are now more believable, if reporters connect us to the crimes and started digging."

Dorian hopped off his stepping stool and faced me. "I am glad to hear the criminal came through for you. But this is not what I wish to discuss this morning."

"You found out more about April Salazar's death?"

"No additional information is available to the public," he said. "But I do not believe Renaissance White's possession of a Perenelle Flamel painting was pure happenstance. There is a tangled web afoot with more tentacles than we can yet imagine."

He'd combined a dizzying number of mismatched metaphors, but I had no desire to quibble with the sentiment.

Dorian cleared his throat. "But you are not mistaken about my having made progress during the night. I have indeed made a step forward in our investigations. It does not relate to Renaissance White. It is Gwendolyn Graves. She is not what she—"

"I get it," I cut in, cross with the untrusting gargoyle. "Gwendolyn isn't what she seems. She's a complex human just like the rest of us."

"*Alors,* she has told you about the Brushstrokes and Brimstone Society?"

"The *what?*"

"The name of a clandestine, secret society of women artists. Gwendolyn Graves attempted to share their secrets with the world— and it nearly ruined her career."

I stared at the gargoyle. "The hooded figures you mentioned?"

"That has yet to be confirmed." He lifted a file folder from the kitchen table and handed it to me.

I sank into a chair at the table as I flipped open the folder. The letter-size sheet of paper had yellowed with age, but the black ink hadn't faded. My guess was that it hadn't seen sunlight in decades. The mark from a rusted staple had left a dark red stain in the upper left corner. Though a reference to 4,000 words was noted on this cover page, it was the only sheet of paper that remained. It was a research paper titled *The Brushstrokes and Brimstone Society.* The author? Gwendolyn Graves.

I looked up at Dorian. "Where did you get this?"

"It is by Dr. Graves."

"I can see that. You've read it?"

"It is quite fascinating. I wonder why she did not tell you about it." He rocked back and forth on his heels.

"She'll be back from Seattle today. I'm meeting with her and Perenelle this afternoon." I looked back at the faded page. "This is from fifty years ago. This is the paper she presented before she finished her PhD. The one that made her a laughingstock."

Dorian blinked at me and frowned. "She has told you of it?"

"I'm sure she's embarrassed by it. You never answered my question. Where did you get this?"

He dismissed my question with a wave of his hand.

I was about to press further when my phone screamed from the bag on the floor next to my feet, causing my headache to return. Sometimes I really despised the twenty-first century.

"I'm sure it's nothing to worry about," said Nicolas, his voice chipper. "But we've been asked to return to the police station."

"Is it optional?" I asked.

Even though Theo had come through with online breadcrumbs that would confirm their identities if the police dug deeper, it was still an unwelcome development.

"I'll meet you there," I said.

The Flamels were already meeting with Detective Vega when I arrived, and I had to wait half an hour to see them.

"She had a few follow-up questions for us," Nicolas said when they emerged from their meeting. "But the main purpose of the visit was for the detective to assure us that the art dealer we met with was nothing to worry about."

"But also that Joni Mitchell won't trouble us again," said Perenelle.

Something was going on. What was Detective Vega keeping from us? She couldn't already have the results of the toxicology on the paint sample, could she? Did she already know if it was poison? Even if it did, would that tell her who stole the paintings and killed Betty Kubiak?

"Are you still feeling unwell?" Perenelle asked me as we walked to the police station parking lot. Her red curls were pulled back in two hair clips, one silver and one gold.

"I'll feel better once I understand what's going on," I told her.

"And I," said Nicolas, "wish the detective would tell us more about what she's learned."

"You think she's learned more."

"I'm certain of it."

I'd parked next to them. We reached our cars, and keys jingled like wind chimes as Nicolas unlocked the passenger side door for Perenelle.

Perenelle lifted her ankle-length indigo blue skirt of silk taffeta to step into the small car, revealing white silk stockings and silver Mary Jane shoes with golden buckles. Most people wouldn't be able to pull off the combination of colors, but for her, it worked.

The powerful Perenelle Flamel had once kept many things from me. She believed it was for my own good at the time, but had since realized the error of her ways. Was there more she was keeping from me?

"What's the Brushstrokes and Brimstone Society?" I asked before she could step into the car.

A flash of recognition passed over her face, but it was gone as quickly as it had appeared.

"You know something," I said.

"I'm an old woman, Zoe. One who has lived for many centuries. I know many things."

"What do you know about the secret society?" My head throbbed, but I didn't look away from her or shield my eyes from the sun.

"Secret society?" She blinked at me, confused. That wasn't what she'd expected me to say.

I glanced at Nicolas. His face held the same expression of open curiosity that he wore most of the time.

"Brushstrokes, brimstone..." Nicolas repeated. "Can't say I've seen it."

They got into their little car. The engine revved for a few seconds before they drove off.

Nicolas said he hadn't *seen* it. Why would he have said it like that? What were Nicolas and Perenelle keeping from me?

CHAPTER 39

I went home to eat lunch and get more information from Dorian before I headed back to the Flamels' house, where I'd be meeting Perenelle and Gwendolyn this afternoon.

I found Perenelle in her art and alchemy studio, an empty canvas in front of her, but no paint on a pallet or paintbrush in her hand.

I stepped closer and saw she'd primed the canvas and added a stormy blue-gray sky that looked like Payne's Gray, but I knew it would be a formulation of Perenelle's. The rest of the canvas was blank.

"You think I lied to you earlier," she said without turning.

"Did you?"

She turned, and her face looked older. With the brightest light coming from the high windows behind her, I knew it was a trick of the light. But it was also the heavy expression she wore.

A gentle knock on the studio door sounded.

"I believe you have another visitor," Nicolas said, popping his head into the studio. "She's out front and hasn't yet knocked on the door."

"We'll go." Perenelle's deep indigo skirt rustled as she hurried outside.

Gwendolyn was standing in the pigment garden, both hands on her cane, her eyes closed as if she was absorbing the energy of the plants.

She opened her eyes and smiled as we approached.

"What's the Brushstrokes and Brimstone Society?" I asked.

Her face paled and she gripped her cane more forcefully. "Where did you hear that name?"

"It's the idea that nearly cost you a tenure-track job," I said, "isn't it?"

She gave a sharp intake of breath. "You know about that?"

"When you got in touch—" I broke off and cringed. "When the *fake* you got in touch, I looked into you. I wanted to make sure I wasn't walking into a trap—even though I was. In addition to looking you up online, I visited a local art history professor."

"That must have been Jonas."

I nodded.

"He's the only one left who's old enough to remember," she said. "The only one local, at least. What did he tell you?"

"He didn't remember the details. Just that when he was a graduate student attending a conference, around the bar in the evening talk turned to gossip from recent years."

"And *I* was that gossip."

"He doesn't even know the substance of the paper you presented, because it wasn't something he saw himself. He only remembered that grad students further along in the program told him that everyone said you'd been reading too many Gothic novels. That you'd presented a paper that was more fantasy than fact."

"The Brushstrokes and Brimstone Society," she laughed bitterly. "A secret society of women artists. This is the danger of falling in love with your own theories. I truly don't know how my students these days are ever going to overcome their mistakes. The internet didn't exist when I wrote that damn paper, yet it still haunts me."

"Where did you hear about it?" Perenelle whispered.

"I never found a primary source," Gwendolyn hissed. "It's a phantom I was chasing. You're the one with real proof about Hayden, Perenelle. You've confirmed the truth about Hayden, not my fanciful ideas from badly cited research. I didn't want to tell you about my mistake. I've spent more than half a century trying to undo it." She pointed to her car. "Three boxes of real research, plus more I have online. Can I show you?"

Nicolas, Perenelle, and I each took a box from the trunk of her car and carried it into the house.

Nicolas offered us tea bought at Max's shop or beer from his home brew. We all asked for tea.

"We should start with this box." Gwendolyn lifted the lid off one of the three banker's boxes we'd set on the dining room table.

"First," said Perenelle, "I need you to tell me what you know about the Brushstrokes and Brimstone Society. Gwendolyn. Please. It's important."

Perenelle knew more than she was telling either of us.

Gwendolyn's gaze darted between us as she accepted a cup of green tea from Nicolas. "Long before I realized it was just one artist passing along the tradition to another," she continued, "I had another idea about how it was done… a foolish idea."

"It's not foolish." Perenelle smiled at her. "Sulfur was always a key ingredient in my—er, *her*—pigments. Alchemical ingredients made their way into both her artwork and the paints used. Art and science are linked. People used to know this but have forgotten."

Gwendolyn looked away from Perenelle, as if she couldn't face her. Only when she was turned away from both of us did she speak. "I saw scribbled writing in a painting, and I *wanted* it to be real. Can you understand? I wanted too badly for it to be real."

"A scribble in a painting?" I repeated as a car driving over gravel sounded in the distance. Perenelle's *The Red Queen?*

"It's not real," Gwendolyn said. "Please, can we look at my other research?"

"You've been lying to yourself for so long that you've made yourself believe it," Perenelle said. "A brushstroke over the symbol for brimstone was one of the many puzzles my predecessor hid in a painting called *The Red Queen*, along with the words *société des femmes* —society of women—that could only be seen from certain angles. She used the technique of anamorphosis to create a hidden puzzle."

Gwendolyn stared at Perenelle, wide-eyed. "The symbols were really there?"

"They were. As were the words. Hidden with a trick of perspective."

"My photographs didn't capture it." Gwendolyn's voice was

shaking now. "And the painting was one kept in archives, not on display. I was a starving graduate student and couldn't easily get back to Prague."

"You didn't imagine it." Perenelle gripped her hand. "As soon as we find the stolen painting with the notebook passed down to me, we can prove—"

Gwendolyn failed at holding in a stifled sob.

"Are you all right?" I wondered if I had an herbal preparation that could help.

"Aside from once being young and foolish," Gwendolyn said, "I'm fine. In your research, you didn't come across a copy of my paper itself, did you?"

I shook my head.

"That's why you think everything is fine, and that I simply spotted some clever puzzle. You don't understand what I did next."

"It wasn't foolish to share the words and symbols you saw in the paper," Perenelle assured her. "The world wasn't ready—"

"You don't understand." Gwendolyn slammed her teacup onto the table. "I *made up* the Brushstrokes and Brimstone Society. Because I didn't have photographic evidence of what I'd seen in the painting, I pretended a *real society* existed—not just the ideas in the painting. I said I'd found evidence of the Society of Brushstrokes and Brimstone, a society of women artists."

"You made up what you thought *should have* existed," Perenelle said, and I could see the pride in her eyes. That's why she had painted those symbols and words into one of her paintings from Rudolfine Prague and hadn't made it clear that it was a Hayden. She wanted it to be true as much as Gwendolyn did.

"But you lied," I said gently. "You falsified your research."

Gwendolyn met my gaze, a desperate, haunted look in her eyes. "I've spent my whole career being overly meticulous to make up for that one stupid mistake. For making up the Brushstrokes and Brimstone Society."

"But it's not made up."

We all gave a start at the sound of a new voice. Someone who wasn't supposed to be there. Veronica stepped into the room.

"I know about the Brushstrokes and Brimstone Society," Veronica said as she dumped her backpack at her feet. "I know it's real. Because I was invited to one of their meetings."

CHAPTER 40

"You shouldn't be here," Perenelle said to Veronica. "It's too—"

"Too dangerous?" Veronica crossed her arms. "I don't know why everyone insists on treating me like a child. I know you told me you'd let me know when it would be safe for me to have another art lesson, Mrs. Flamel, but I had Ethan drive me so I could check on my verdigris. It's a good thing I came over."

Veronica wasn't someone who made things up. She wouldn't have pretended to know anything about the secret society if she didn't. She was pushing against her strict father's rules, and I was certain Alessandro didn't know she was here now, but that was different from outright lying.

"You can't be serious about the Society." Gwendolyn's hand shook on her cane as she stepped towards Veronica. "The Brushstrokes and Brimstone Society doesn't exist."

"It does," Veronica insisted. "It's a secret society of women artists and scientists." She reached into her backpack, searching for something.

"A secret organization of artists and scientists?" Gwendolyn asked in a reverent whisper.

"I don't know its history or how long it's been around," Veronica said as she rummaged through her bag. "But today, I told my art class about the verdigris I'm making. After class, I found a note in my backpack. A real old-school note, not a text." She stood up holding a thick piece of paper in her hand, which she gave to me. "An invitation."

Veronica, you might like to join the Brushstrokes and Brimstone Society of women artists and scientists.

Next meeting: When moonrise overlaps with night on the next full moon, OMSI.

"I don't think it's a joke," Veronica said. "There's no printer in Ms. Fairchild's classroom, but the important part of the invitation is printed."

The personalized first line of the invitation was handwritten and hastily scrawled, but the second line was a printout in a standard font. I read the invitation aloud.

"It's real?" Gwendolyn whispered. "It can't be real."

"Someone must have created it," I said. "You're not the only one who saw the symbols and words hidden in *The Red Queen* painting."

Gwendolyn let out a sound in between a gasp and a squeal. "I was invited to join," she said. "A decade ago. I thought… I thought it was a cruel joke. Someone who remembered my paper and wanted to mock me because I was making so much progress in exposing the truth about misattributed works of art. I ignored the invitation."

"OMSI?" Perenelle asked.

"The Oregon Museum of Science and Industry," I said. Which was only about a mile from Hawthorne Bridge, where hooded figures were seen earlier this week.

"It's for scientists as well as artists?" Perenelle asked.

Veronica shrugged. "The intersection of art and science, I guess. Like what you're teaching me with making my own pigments. And how STEM became STEAM while I've been at school. Science, Technology, Engineering, and Math, but the 'A' for Arts was added since creative thinking is so important for those other fields. Ethan is in a class where they're using creative ideas as much as engineering to build robots—Ethan! I totally forgot he and the guys are waiting in the car for me. Brix was hungry so we're going to get some food. I should check my verdigris and go—"

"Yo, V." Brixton stood in the doorway. "You said you'd just be a minute. Oh, hey, Zoe. Perenelle. Nicolas let me in. I, uh, I think I interrupted?"

"Go get your friends," Perenelle said. "Nicolas baked a fresh loaf of bread with the spent grains leftover after brewing his beer. There's plenty of bread and preserves for everyone."

"Even a car filled with three teenage guys?" he asked.

Perenelle smiled. "Nicolas and I were capable of feeding Zoe's brother. That young man ate more than any other person I've known. We'll be fine."

Brixton grinned before disappearing from view. His mischievous grin reminded me of Thomas, as did Perenelle's accurate description of his appetite. Thomas had walked at least twenty miles a day, both running errands and exploring while I learned alchemy, coming home with a ravenous appetite. My brother had never been interested in being indoors, even at night. I was the one who followed the sunrise and sunset closely, and Thomas stayed up late at night watching the moon, following its cycles and telling me all about what he'd observed. Even though he didn't enjoy formal studies, he was curious about the world around him and would have done great things if he hadn't died far too young.

I had to remind myself I was in twenty-first century Portland, Oregon, in a situation that was quickly slipping out of my control.

I was inclined to trust Gwendolyn in spite of her faults, but I was biased. Dorian was right that we couldn't be sure she wasn't involved in the theft and murder in some way we didn't yet comprehend. The kids were teenagers with drivers' licenses, but they were still kids. They shouldn't have been here. But I didn't see how I could make them leave without piquing their curiosity and making them investigate behind my back. I had a feeling they were already doing so. Dorian's information about late-night sightings of robed figures didn't come from the newspapers and was most likely something one of the teenagers had found via social media. At least here, I could help them understand what was going on and make sure they didn't act rashly.

"I didn't mean for us to invite ourselves over like that, Mrs. Flamel," Veronica said, her face turning crimson.

"Not to worry," Perenelle said. "We need you to help us figure out this latest development."

"You don't have any idea who put the invitation in your bag?" Gwendolyn asked her.

Veronica shook her head. "We were painting today, looking at the ways different white paints are different from each other when you look closely, so everyone was up at the sink washing their brushes."

"*When moonrise overlaps with night on the next full moon,*" I said. "That's what the invitation said."

"I don't follow lunar cycles," Veronica said, "and I didn't look it up, since there's no way my dad would let me follow a mysterious, anonymous invitation to a late-night meeting."

"Today's moon has already risen," I said. "The overlap of night would be—"

"Sunset," Gwendolyn finished.

"The society that doesn't exist," I said, "will be meeting in two hours."

CHAPTER 41

Fifteen minutes later, all that was left of the hearty loaf of brown bread was a few crumbs on the wooden serving platter. Before Veronica would try it, she looked up its alcohol content online. Satisfied that there was no alcohol in the bread in spite of its grain being initially used to make beer, she ate nearly as heartily as Brixton, Ethan, and Harry.

"When did you learn how to bake bread, Nicolas?" Brixton asked as he licked strawberry preserves from his thumb.

"That's gross, Brix." Veronica kicked him under the table as she looked at his sticky hand.

Ethan handed Brixton a linen napkin. Brixton rolled his eyes at both of them, but wiped away the strawberry preserves with the bright white napkin.

"Perenelle and I used to live in the countryside," Nicolas answered. "The middle of nowhere, you'd call it. It was the kind of place where you would never waste ingredients."

"What can we do to help with this historical mystery you're working on?" Harry asked as he carried empty plates to the sink.

The lanky young man wasn't just being polite. Harry had grown up at the Oregon Gold History Museum that his parents ran, and he'd been interested in history since he was a young child. The interest was solidified when, at twelve years old, he was playing with a metal detector and discovered a prospector's tools that were 150 years old.

I didn't know Harry Cabot nearly as well as Brixton, Veronica, and Ethan. The three friends had met him last year when Harry's family was embroiled in a mystery that began during the Gold Rush and ended with a present-day crime. At seventeen, Harry was one year older than the others. He also went to a different high school, but he and Ethan had been dating, so he could often be found with the group of friends.

Harry didn't know Dorian was a gargoyle, but I wasn't worried about anyone at the dining table revealing his secret. Both because Gwendolyn was there and because in case anyone slipped up and referenced Dorian being a gargoyle, Harry would rationally think they were being insensitive jerks by describing a physical deformity so crassly.

"Yeah," said Veronica, speaking to Gwendolyn. "Tell us more about Hayden. We promise we won't reveal anything about her being a woman until you publish your findings."

The others added their agreement as Gwendolyn beamed at them. They'd moved her three banker's boxes filled with research to the side of the table while they ate their afternoon snack.

"I still don't understand how getting Zoe's painting and an old notebook back can prove something from hundreds of years ago," Brixton said. "I mean, won't people just refuse to believe it?"

"It's a good question," said Gwendolyn. "Let me share an example with you. Judith Lester was a famous artist who lived in the Netherlands in the 1600s. She was an accomplished painter who was part of what's known as the Dutch Golden Age, known for artists who painted realistic oil paintings of average people and settings, using dark, rich colors. Judith Leyster's work was equal to that of the men around her."

"But they didn't like her work?" Brixton asked.

"Worse," said Gwendolyn. "She painted many works of art that people loved, but after her death, her work was often attributed to either prominent artist Frans Hals or to her artist husband, Jan Miense Molenaer. But there was purposeful misattribution of her work for more than *two centuries* after she died."

"How'd they find out the truth after two hundred years?" Ethan asked.

"We only know the truth," said Gwendolyn, "because of a scandal from 1892. For historical context, Grover Cleveland was the US president that year. You probably haven't thought of that name since you had to learn it in the fifth grade. Over in England, where this scandal takes place, it was the year Arthur Conan Doyle published *The Adventures of Sherlock Holmes*, collecting his famous stories that had appeared in *The Strand Magazine* into a single collected volume."

The professor knew how to capture the attention of young minds. None of them had reached for their phones to get a faster answer to what fate had befallen Judith Leyster.

"That year, a painting known as *The Happy Couple* was sold to a British art dealer. But this was no ordinary painting. It had the signature of renowned artist Frans Hals. His work was similar in style to that of Judith Leyster, but not indistinguishable. The subject matter was the first clue that something was amiss. On closer inspection, Hals' signature in the newly sold painting looked suspicious. Yes, there was definitely something suspicious about this painting."

Gwendolyn shifted in her seat, and everyone at the table followed the small movement with rapt attention. "When the painting was tested, it was revealed that a forged Hals signature had been added *on top of* Judith Leyster's own signature. A distinctive monogram that could not be disputed. As you can imagine, a court case ensued. But here's what I'm sure you'll agree is the most interesting part. The art dealer who'd been tricked went to court *not* because of the forged signature itself, but rather, his argument was that the painting was now *worthless*."

"Because it was painted by Judith instead of Frans?" Veronica asked.

Gwendolyn gave a single nod. "That 'worthless' painting now hangs in the Louvre."

Veronica's face took on the wistful expression it did whenever Paris was mentioned. "Brix, did you see it when you were in Paris?" she asked him.

"I, uh, wasn't really sightseeing." He fidgeted in the dining chair.

I knew Brixton wanted to forget about his ordeal in the catacombs underneath Paris, so I prompted Gwendolyn, "Don't forget to tell them what else happened after that court case."

The professor smiled. "The scandal forced the art world to look more critically at paintings that were most likely hers. A year later, several more paintings of hers were correctly attributed, and she's now taken her rightful place in art history. Which is what we're hoping to do for Philippe Hayden, who we believe chose to pretend to be a man for the opportunity to be a painter in the Court of Rudolf II in Prague."

"That's amazing," said Veronica. "I mean, it's so messed up what happened to these women, but amazing you're going to prove the truth."

"If following clues gives us enough of the truth," Gwendolyn said. "We know that women in the late 1500s didn't have the same access, the subjects and puzzles in many of Hayden's paintings have been documented, and we have subtle clues from historical accounts of Hayden in Rudolfine Prague. But we need definitive proof first. None of it is definitive on its own, which is why we're putting the puzzle pieces together and also looking for key pieces of evidence that prove she taught apprentices who continued to create color with her recipes and learned to paint in her style under her tutelage."

Gwendolyn was in her element explaining what she knew. I could tell she'd been a great teacher. Whatever she'd done wrong as a young woman, she'd done so much good for the world since then.

While the kids were asking more questions, I slipped outside to let Max and Dorian know what was happening.

I sent Max a text message, because I knew if I spoke with him he'd try to talk me out of it.

I called Dorian, both because he didn't have a cell phone and because he would never try to talk me out of investigating. On the contrary, he might convince me to do something more ridiculous than going in search of a secret society at sunset on the night of the full moon.

"But you cannot trust her!" Dorian insisted after I told him what we were doing.

"You don't seriously think Professor Graves murdered Betty Kubiak," I replied as calmly as I could.

"She has a hefty cane that could be used as a weapon," he replied. "But no, I agree it is unlikely. There is also April's death, supposedly of cardiac arrest. We must find out the true cause."

"Max asked Detective Vega to look into if there were any suspicions about April's death. He—" I broke off abruptly as the red and yellow leaves of a nearby Bigleaf maple tree shifted in the breeze and sunlight hit my face. The sun was lower in the sky than I thought.

"Zoe! Zoe? *Mon dieu.* Are you being attacked? I will call for assistance!"

"No, I—"

"I beg you," Dorian pleaded. "Tell me what is happening."

"I'm trying. If you'd let me talk, I'm fine. I'm worried that it's later in the afternoon than I thought. I need to get to the museum."

CHAPTER 42

Veronica had to get home in time for dinner, so as much as she wanted to join us, she agreed it would be best for Ethan to drop her off at home. Perenelle, Gwendolyn, and I would be the ones to check out the Brushstrokes and Brimstone Society.

We took Gwendolyn's car. Hers was the least conspicuous. Not many people had the original 1960s Beetle, which I'm fairly certain the Flamels had fallen in love with for its silver paint as much as its counterculture history they'd learned about, and even fewer people had a 1940s pickup truck like mine.

As we parked on a nearby side street near the river's waterfront, a cold rain began to fall. It already looked like it was going to be difficult to find a good spot to hide with a view of the front entrance of the museum. Now that it was raining, that would be even harder. I didn't know if that's where members of the Brushstrokes and Brimstone Society would enter, but the museum had closed at 5:30, so it was possible they had an after-hours meeting space here. About half a dozen cars were parked in the lot, but we hadn't gone early enough to know if they were staff people or members of the secret society.

Perenelle grasped my arm. "There's someone walking across the parking lot."

The figure wore a hooded cape, only partially sheltering them from the rain that was now pelting down. I shivered under my wool sweater and silver raincoat. The crimson cape only reached their waist, and was more of a fashion statement than the type of cape I'd imagine for a secret society disguising the person underneath.

The figure crossed the deserted lot. As the wind lifted the cape and its hood, I recognized her.

Before I could think, I ran forward, calling out as I did so. "Willow?"

It was Willow Matsumoto from Renaissance White.

She turned our way. After a moment, she broke into a wide smile.

"Dr. Graves? Are you *finally* taking me up on my invitation to join the Brushstrokes and Brimstone Society?"

CHAPTER 43

Twenty minutes later, the four of us were seated in a cozy corner booth, warming up with bowls of ramen. The walls of the small restaurant had absorbed decades of flame-charred toppings and now emanated a scent not unlike brimstone.

Our coats and Willow's crimson cape hung on a nearby coat rack, dripping water onto the linoleum floor. The ferocity of the storm had caught us off guard, though after nearly two years in Portland, I shouldn't have been surprised. Max had given me a handmade hat that he'd bought at one of the small shops on Hawthorne, not far from The Alchemy of Tea, but I never remembered to take it with me. A subconscious forgetfulness, no doubt. I loved the fact that Max had bought me the knit cap woven with a dozen shades of green, and I could feel the loving intent that had gone into the knitter's needle-work. But I also loved feeling the sun and rain on my face and the freedom of my hair blowing wild in the wind. I loved the hat from Max, but I'd never be a hat person.

Willow's hands were cupped around her ceramic bowl filled with warm broth and squiggly noodles, and despite her chill, she couldn't stop smiling. She'd already texted the Brushstrokes and Brimstone Society members who were expecting her that she wouldn't be joining them tonight. Perenelle was sitting next to Willow, and Gwendolyn and I were across from her.

"Clearly we have much to talk about," said Perenelle, "but now that our food is beginning to warm us, why don't you start at the beginning?"

"The beginning can mean a lot of things." Willow adjusted her glasses, unbothered by the spots left behind from the rain. "But since I know you're all in search of our stolen paintings, I know where I should start. I've spent my life devouring everything about the history of science. There's a big part of that history that most professors gloss over. Alchemy."

I drew a sharp breath and exchanged a look with Perenelle, but Willow didn't seem to notice.

"Alchemy is central to the history of science," she continued. "And also to the history of art. They were so connected in the past, but people forgot. Those artists and alchemists were so advanced for their day. But then society lost their way. At Renaissance White, one of our central ideas is using alchemical principles to recreate lost colors. We approach color formulations giving equal weight to chemistry and art. We consult historical sources for clues about color, interview people practicing traditional techniques, and source ingredients in more traditional ways, like people had to do when apothecaries were pigment suppliers."

"When you tested *The Apothecary's Cabinet*," I said, "you wanted to know what ingredients were used to create the colors, even though you knew it wouldn't give you the recipes."

"Exactly. There are alchemical symbols in that old painting, and Adam and Oberon realized right away that the colors were so much like pigments from the past that we can't buy today."

"You learned from it," said Perenelle. "It taught you through both its subject matter and its materials."

Willow nodded. "I know alchemy as we think of it today isn't real —there's no such thing as immortality, and there's no stone that makes gold."

She was right about that. Alchemists who've found the Elixir of Life aren't immortal just because we've stopped aging. And the philosopher's stone isn't a one-time experiment that creates a stone that magically creates gold. Ongoing hard work and intent is necessary to keep our bodies healthy and to create gold. The thought reminded me that I needed to nourish myself, regardless of what was going on around me. Especially since the sun had already gone down. I took a sip of my twig tea and ate my soup as Willow continued.

"So much real science came out of alchemy," she said. "Isaac Newton was a practicing alchemist, which is how he made his optics discoveries. And the foundations of lab work, like distillation and calcination, came from alchemical experimentation. Inspired by those who came before me, one summer during grad school I went to Prague to dig deeper into the history of alchemy. Rudolf II was known as the Mad Alchemist, and he really did support the work of a bunch of alchemists in his court. When I dug into archives in Prague, I saw a painting called *The Red Queen*."

"That's the painting," Gwendolyn whispered. "The painting with Brushstrokes and Brimstone."

Willow nodded. "I found symbols for Brushstrokes and Brimstone, and the Latin words *societas feminarum*. Together, the words and symbols give us the Brushstrokes and Brimstone Society of Women."

"That's what was intended," Perenelle said. "Not the alliteration, since English wasn't the artist's mother tongue. But the idea of powerful women artists."

Willow's lips parted in surprise. "How do you know that?"

"The knowledge was passed down to me from my mentor," Perenelle explained.

"Your—?"

"Finish your story first."

Willow hesitated, her curiosity for what Perenelle hinted at clashing with her enthusiasm for telling us about the Society.

"I loved the name," Willow said. "*Brushstrokes* to recognize art, and *brimstone* for power. Fire. Sulfur. Traditionally a male element in alchemy. But here, this represented women at a time when we were so far from being equal. The idea stayed with me. On that trip, I didn't find any chemical recipes that worked, but when I was seeking out kindred spirits in grad school after I got back from Prague, I invited a few people to join the Brushstrokes and Brimstone Society."

"It was really you who invited me a decade ago?" Gwendolyn asked.

Willow gave her a warm smile. "Your work is renowned. I heard about your presentation from an archivist I met during my research, a woman around your age, so I thought the Society had once been real but was now defunct. The archivist thought it was terrible the way you were treated, by the way."

"I thought your invitation was a joke," Gwendolyn said.

"I'm sorry about that." Willow cringed. "I wasn't organized enough to follow up with people, so nothing came of my idea of resurrecting it. Not then. I was too busy with my lab work and dissertation, followed by working way too hard for a company that drained all my energy."

"But you resurrected it," I said.

Willow nodded. "It was only once Adam got money for us to start the Renaissance White lab that I thought about bringing back the Society. It's a word-of-mouth kind of thing. I make it clear it's for creative and artistic thinkers, *not* a book club with wine and gossip for burned-out scientists."

Rain began falling harder, drumming rhythmically on the window next to our booth.

"The rule," Willow continued, "is that the Brushstrokes and Brimstone Society stays analog. Too much of the world is online, so it's for people who want to meet in person. Sometimes we only meet every few months, and sometimes it's more frequent. I've called the group together a few times lately, because Adam, Oberon, and I have been struggling in the lab. I wanted an infusion of new ideas."

"Only when it's a full moon?" I asked.

"Tonight was a last-minute idea, after I was shaken up by the theft and attack on Adam earlier this week. We had a meeting that night, but I went home early because I've been so tired from spending so much time in the lab. I know it's a bit woo-woo to meet on the full moon and to have referenced it in my invitation, but honestly there was some powerful energy the last time we met on a full moon. Planetary pulls are real, and alchemists were right about some of their ideas, so why not try it? It's usually only three to five of us at a time who can make it. Busy lives, you know. One of our members works at OMSI, so we can use a meeting room after hours."

"And a local high school teacher is a member," I said, remembering something Veronica had told us this afternoon. "Ms. Fairchild?"

I'd realized that it must have been Veronica's teacher who put the note in Veronica's backpack. Not only because the most likely person to have done so was the adult in the classroom, but because of something I should have seen far sooner.

Willow narrowed her eyes. "How did you know? Cynthia hadn't arrived yet when you saw me."

"Renaissance White couldn't possibly have given out paint samples to each high school in the Pacific Northwest," I said, "or even all the schools in Portland. There had to be a reason Veronica's art class received paint samples for all the students."

Willow sighed and looked out the window into the dark storm. "I guess you know our secret, then?"

I looked to Perenelle and Gwendolyn. They didn't look any more enlightened than I felt. A secret having to do with Renaissance White's paint samples?

"You'll know soon enough anyway," Willow said. "The reason I've been asking to meet with the Society so much is because of April. She was my coconspirator in resurrecting the Brushstrokes and Brimstone Society. And my best friend." Her lip trembled.

"When April died in the lab, she was perfecting the formulation of Renaissance White," Willow said. "Her last act on earth was recreating the beauty of lead white but without its toxicity. And it killed her."

"I'm so sorry," Perenelle said.

"She left a beautiful legacy," Gwendolyn added.

"Don't you see?" Willow's voice was now venomous. "We don't have her recipe. We can't recreate what she did. We thought the last ingredient was rotten eggs, because that was the last note she wrote, but it was such a strange ingredient, and it didn't work. We only have enough paint to meet our soft launch West Coast shipments. But the Nationwide scale we promised to fulfill before Christmas?" She shook her head. "Adam, Oberon, and I have been working so hard in the lab, and I've also been trying to get help from the Society, because just like those damn secretive alchemists of centuries past, *April didn't write down her recipe.*"

CHAPTER 44

Rain beat furiously on the window next to our table as Perenelle, Gwendolyn, and I stared at Willow. A gentle din of voices surrounded us at the restaurant, but the world outside of our table fell away.

"You mean that April made enough of your paint formulation for samples that got people interested," I said, "but not enough for mass production?"

Willow nodded. "We *thought* we had her recipe, because she did write down a lot of detailed notes. The white pigment she created was the most luminous shade of white, and it mixed so well with binders to make both acrylic and oil paints. We were walking through life in a haze after April's death, so we weren't thinking about how foolish it was to begin working with a factory to create the pigment and package both oil and acrylic paints at scale. At first, we thought we had the recipe, because it looked almost the same at first. Then, we kept thinking we were *so close* to recreating it. But each time it failed to hold together and lost the vibrance of what April created."

"Were there pigment recipe secrets hidden in *The Apothecary's Cabinet*?" I asked.

"Not that got us anywhere," Willow said. "Oh! You were asking Perenelle, not me?"

"I was."

Perenelle shook her head. "Only for the inward journey of alchemy."

"My mind is being blown on so many levels tonight," said Willow. "A few minutes ago, you talked about your mentor… You and your mentor trained in the methods used to create color like the ones in our stolen paintings?"

"They did!" Gwendolyn could barely contain her excitement. She'd been vindicated twice this week.

"I know I only just met you all," said Willow, "and I haven't consulted Adam and Oberon about this, but I'm sure if you could help us with our recipe, we could cut you in on the profits."

Perenelle shook her head. "I'm afraid it doesn't work like that. The method I use to create my pigments isn't something that can be mass produced."

"She has a pigment garden," Gwendolyn added with enthusiasm. "With dozens of varieties of flowers and rocks. It's heavenly. Like something out of a painting. Sorry to interrupt. I won't do it again." With her hand, she made the motion of zipping her lips shut.

"I make my own paints," said Perenelle, "as part of creating a painting. I use fire and my intent to bring the natural world into a canvas."

Her words described how she painted vivid representations of life, but her word choice also hid a secondary meaning. How she had the power to move elements of the natural world into a canvas.

"I get it," Willow said. "The more I found out about how alchemists worked, the more I came to believe that their recipes, even if successful, would only produce a small amount. But there has to be a way. April succeeded."

"You'll figure it out," Gwendolyn said. "Modern science has come so far. And with a group of great minds, how can you fail?"

I didn't share her optimism, but I knew why she felt so hopeful after everything she'd learned this week.

"We shouldn't have moved forward before we were ready," said Willow, "but you're right. I know we'll get there. Please don't let it go further than this table that we're behind our production goals."

"Does Detective Vega know?" I asked.

"Adam opened up the company's finances to her, and we showed her our personal finances as well. She wanted to rule out insurance fraud. Not that our stolen painting was insured. We didn't pay much for it, and beautiful but anonymous paintings aren't worth much." Willow turned to Perenelle. "You said you know more about the artist who painted *The Red Queen*. Is it related to this week's stolen paintings?"

"I don't know if it's related," Perenelle said truthfully. "The professor has a theory we're still researching."

Willow blinked at her. "That's all you're going to say? I told you everything—"

"I'll tell you," Gwendolyn said, "because you already know the answer. If you know about my paper that nearly got me blacklisted, you know the truth."

Willow's hands flew to her mouth. "Philippe Hayden was truly a woman? She was the instigator of the Brushstrokes and Brimstone Society? But our painting was made a century later."

"By her apprentice's apprentice," said Gwendolyn.

Willow remained speechless, but a wave of elation spread across her face.

"Please don't say anything until I can *prove it* this time," Gwendolyn added.

"I won't." Willow glanced at her phone. "I could talk with you all night, but I should go. The group is probably still meeting, and I want to run a couple of ideas by them while they're together."

We exchanged contact information and wished her good luck as she left. When we asked for the check a minute later, the server told us Willow had already paid and left a big enough tip that the server insisted on bringing us complementary desserts.

"She's not a killer," said Perenelle.

Gwendolyn gasped. "You thought that young woman could be the killer of my impersonator?"

I didn't look away from Perenelle. "You think Willow is innocent because she's a kindred spirit?"

"No. Because she understands that intent is necessary in alchemy. She had no reason to steal the *Brother and Sister* painting."

"I don't think she's guilty either," said Gwendolyn as she bit into a strawberry mochi dessert. "She's a big tipper. No way is she a cold-blooded killer."

CHAPTER 45

From the Typewriter of Dorian Robert-Houdin

The Culinary Alchemist's Toolbox

If you are ready to listen, your ingredients will tell you their secrets. You must use all your senses to coax these confidences.

Touch a vegetable to feel if it is firm or soft, and the texture it holds.

Listen as your knife slices or your wooden spoon smashes.

Sniff the air to detect additional scents that have been released.

Watch for how the interior reacts once exposed.

Finally, taste at each stage.

Elements change as they react to other ingredients, air, fire, and time. The secrets yielded at the start will be different than the secrets revealed at the end.

Zoe, Perenelle, and the morally questionable Professor Graves were chasing down the secrets of the Brushstrokes and Brimstone Society. Veronica had wished to accompany them, but her parents insisted she arrive home for dinner. Not that they would have allowed her to traipse across Portland's underworld in search of secret societies, had they known the substance of her desired trip.

Dorian was left to his own devices, which was most welcome at present. He was pleased that Zoe was making real progress. It would allow him time to work on *Culinary Alchemy*.

Alas, it was not to be. Before he could settle in to focus, the door-bell rang. Dorian glanced to the ceiling and his skylight escape hatch. Rain pummeled the glass. It was not a desirable evening to crawl through the window.

"It's me!" Brixton's voice called out from below. "I've got Nicolas with me."

Dorian would need to discuss spare key etiquette with the boy at some point. But at this moment, he did not mind. The kitchen fridge and counters were bursting with food. He hoped Nicolas and Brixton had not yet eaten dinner.

"Did Zoe tell you what's going on?" Brixton asked as he burst through the attic door. "It's wild."

"Manners, young man," Nicolas said as he paused in the doorway. "May we join you?"

"Dorian wants to know what's going on," said Brixton. "Right, D?"

"I appreciate your thoughtfulness in keeping me informed," said Dorian. "Zoe called to update me about their excursion to unmask the secret society."

"That explains why you didn't answer when I called. I thought you were out investigating, but you were on the phone."

"Alas, I am confined to the attic until the hour grows late. Nicolas, stop hovering in the doorway. You know you are welcome. But may I suggest we adjourn to the kitchen? Have you two eaten?"

They had not, and they eagerly accepted bowls of autumnal stew with crispy onion flakes on top. After a dessert of carrot cake with carrots from Zoe's garden, they retreated to the attic once more.

"Let us discuss the case over a game of chess," Dorian suggested. "I take it you both would have shared if you had received any text message updates from Zoe or Perenelle?"

"Only from Perenelle before we arrived," said Nicolas, "to assure me they were well and would be eating dinner out."

"They've totally forgotten about us." Brixton scowled at his phone.

"I expect they are busy bringing about the demise of a treacherous secret society," said Dorian. "This endeavor might take them a few hours."

Nicolas chuckled. "I wouldn't put it past Perenelle."

"Or Zoe," Dorian added. "She is more devious than she first appears. You realize she entered the criminal underworld to help you this very week, Nicolas."

"I'm glad Zoe thought of it. Our histories now hold up to much more scrutiny." Nicolas leaned over the chess board and picked the white queen. "I've always thought it a shame there's no red queen. Perenelle might have enjoyed the game more."

"The queen is still the most powerful piece in chess," Dorian said.

"Except," said Brixton, tapping on the figure of the hapless king, "she only uses that power to protect the king. That's totally messed up."

Nicolas chuckled. "He has a point. A powerful queen should not be relegated to protecting her husband above all else, nor should she be confined to the chess board."

"We are here," said Dorian, "to discuss the case, not philosophy."

Brixton crossed his arms in a hostile stance. "You were the one who wanted to play chess."

"Because it enables the mind to enter a state of deep thought. We are at an impasse. We must open our minds. With your contributions, my little gray cells will surely see the way forward."

"Veronica is better at this stuff than me. She's forgotten about me, too. Her new friend Cas, from her art class, is going over to her house after dinner so they can paint together. I bet V will be the one to solve the mystery, helping Perenelle, Zoe, and that professor." Brixton turned to Nicolas. "Don't you feel sidelined?"

"Of course not." Nicolas blinked at the boy. "They haven't abandoned us."

"Veronica has this new passion she loves, and new artist friends at school."

"When you love someone," Nicolas said, "they are still their own person."

"I didn't say that I—"

"You wear your heart on your sleeve," Nicolas said. "I believe that is the English expression, is it not?"

"Yeah, whatever." The boy rubbed his nose in an attempt to cover the redness spreading across his cheeks.

The phone rang. Dorian waited to make sure it was Zoe calling with her coded rings, then picked up.

"You have news?" he asked. "Have you brought about the downfall of a wicked secret society that seeks to destroy us all?"

"Not exactly," Zoe said. "But I need you to help with your murder board. Willow is the mastermind of the Brushstrokes and Brimstone Society."

"*Mon dieu.* You are lucky you escaped with your life when you were alone with her earlier in her evil laboratory!"

"Actually, it sounds like it's a perfectly harmless women's club. But unrelated to the secret society, Renaissance White lost the recipe for their paint that's about to go on the market. I imagine they're desperate. I called Detective Vega to make sure she knew, but their finances are fine, so I don't think she realizes how important it could be. I need your help."

"You wish me to break into their laboratory in the darkest hours of night?" Dorian asked in all seriousness.

"I have something else in mind."

CHAPTER 46

It was late and I was exhausted. But I wanted to see Max.

Everything happening around us had to do with lost and forgotten art, so the task I gave Dorian before leaving for Max's house was to look up more of this lost history. What previously cherished pigments had been lost and never found again?

Max's door swung open before I knocked. I was bracing myself for his frustration, but instead he drew me into his arms and kissed me.

"Remind me to seek out secret societies more often if that's your reaction," I said once I broke away, breathless.

"You can thank Perenelle. She already called me, expecting I'd be worried. She reminded me that she was with you."

"That's all you need to make your worries disappear? For me to be with the all-powerful Perenelle Flamel?"

"You know what? I *do* think she might be the most powerful person I've ever met." His smile faltered. "I do worry about her, though. Does she seem… restless to you? Like she's being held back and needed something like this to happen?"

I stared at Max. "Don't tell me you think *Perenelle* set this in motion on purpose."

"Of course not," he assured me. "But I know about the danger of old alchemists losing their humanity. I'm not saying that's happened to her already, but those powerful skills of hers…"

"Alchemical paint." I didn't want to give power to my fears by voicing them aloud, but I agreed it was a dangerous talent to be able to use her intent to move objects and people into a canvas. Perenelle hadn't abused the powerful ability, but she *could*. One of the reasons I wanted her to feel vindicated by having her artwork properly attributed was to quell the restlessness I'd seen in her as well.

"The danger of losing my humanity is one of the many reasons I'm sticking to the alchemy of tea," said Max. "Nothing more. But I do wish our tea plant cuttings would grow a bit more quickly."

"You know better than that." I wagged my finger at him, glad for the playful banter that washed away my fears. "It's only been a couple of months." The rescued tea cuttings in Max's backyard were the last of a once-vast garden of special *camellia sinensis* tea plants from Max's childhood home in Astoria, Oregon.

"See? I'd make a terrible alchemist." He gave me a mischievous smile as he slipped my silver coat off my shoulders. "I'm confiscating your coat and bag so you'll stay a while and I can remind you why you don't want to lose your humanity. You're soaking wet. You got caught in that downpour earlier?"

"I warmed up on soup. Since you're not peppering me with questions, I take it Perenelle already told you about Willow?"

"And April's discovery. I was thinking, maybe April was practicing alchemy. They talk about it so much. But that doesn't quite fit. Someone who knew intent mattered wouldn't have kept themselves awake with energy drinks. That's a backward way to think of alchemy. She'd have known better."

"It also doesn't fit that April would be into real alchemy," I said. "Willow was the one obsessed with the history of alchemy. April and Oberon were art historians. They're the ones who thought Perenelle's painting they found looked like a Hayden that Adam would like. I got the feeling that Willow is the only one who really believes that intent matters. Unless…"

"Unless?"

An idea that had been swirling around my mind suddenly stilled. Artwork. History. Alchemy. Pigments. Paints. It all fit. It fit *horribly*.

"You said it was a *backward* way to think of alchemy," I said as I reached for my bag with a buzz of equal parts excitement and dread.

"Who are you calling?" Max asked as I clutched my phone.

"Willow. She gave me her number tonight. If I'm right, she has a big piece of information that can help us figure out what's going on."

"About *April's* death?"

"I think April's death last year is connected to Betty Kubiak's murder and the stolen paintings."

"Zoe?" Willow said when she picked up. Her voice sounded far away. "Hang on. I'm driving home. Give me one sec to pull over."

While she did so, I put the phone on speaker phone so Max could hear, but pressed my finger to my lips so he wouldn't try to join the conversation. If my theory was right, this might be a delicate conversation.

"Okay," she said. "What's up?"

"What was the name of the strange book you found at the British Library?" I asked.

"I read a lot of books in their reading rooms."

"Did you read a Latin alchemy book that presented the idea of working *backwards*."

"That was a strange one. I remember it because I wanted to photograph the bizarre woodcut illustrations, but had a yellow slip, meaning I wasn't allowed to photograph it. It was a new acquisition without proper provenance, so the library didn't have copyright sorted out yet. But I have some notes saved to the cloud. Give me a sec."

My heart beat more furiously by the second as I waited.

"Got it," she said. "*Non Degenera Alchemia.*"

I closed my eyes and wished, more than anything, that she'd spoken any other words than the title of that monstrous book. The backward alchemy book that had brought Dorian to life before nearly killing him. The book we were so sure no longer had power after its tie to Notre Dame Cathedral was severed.

Non Degenera Alchemia could no longer transfer energy unknowingly, but that didn't mean the words were invisible. People could still learn dangerous ideas from it. Like the idea of shortcuts, told through woodcut illustrations of birds with broken necks and bees circling in a counterclockwise rotation to symbolize the death rotation. The Latin that accompanied the disturbing illustrations hinted at the twisted idea that you could take energy from a person to give it to someone else. Or *something* else. Like *paint.*

That's why April hadn't left behind a full recipe for others to follow. She'd died by draining her life force and transferring the energy into the most luminous white paint in the world.

That was the secret ingredient of Renaissance White's paint. April's *life.*

CHAPTER 47

April had unknowingly given her life by listening to the whispers of backward alchemy. But I couldn't believe she'd have given up her life on purpose. Even if she wanted to sacrifice herself, what would have been the point, for an unreproducible result?

Non Degenera Alchemia didn't explicitly state that a person had to die for backward alchemy to be realized. Like all alchemy, its lessons were shrouded in obscure clues. When I'd studied the book, all I'd been able to glean were hints that gave me enough information to keep Dorian alive while we searched for a real solution.

That was the problem of backward alchemy. *It didn't last.* Like anything in life that's too good to be true, backward alchemy's "quick fix" was only a temporary solution.

The book of backward alchemy had been stolen from Dorian over a year ago, and now I knew that it had somehow ended up at the British Library. How that had happened was a question for another day. For now, I had to figure out if my theory was right. And if it was, how it had set in motion the events of this week.

"Did April know about your research?" I asked Willow. "And about that book?" I wished I could see her face, but this phone call would have to do.

"I guess so. We share each other's research in a secure online filing system. April was much more interested in the history of art than the

"

history of science, but she was still a scientist, so she was interested in anything that could help her lab experiments. What does that strange book have to do with anything? It barely looked like alchemy, so I wondered if it was a spoof. Something a bored monk with a macabre sense of humor had created. Like how nuns sometimes painted humorous self-portraits into the margins of illuminated manuscripts. But a monk would have had access to more resources to create a whole book of satire. Zoe? Did I lose you?"

I hesitated before answering. I didn't yet know who was involved in this week's thefts and murder. Willow was an unlikely suspect, but she wasn't someone to underestimate. Conversely, if I assumed she was innocent, I didn't want to give her information for how to read the dangerous clues from *Non Degenera Alchemia* if she hadn't yet figured them out.

"I don't know exactly how the book fits in," I said. "But it's an alchemy book I've encountered before."

"How?" Willow's voice had taken on a sharp edge that hadn't been there a moment ago, when she was caught up in her ideas about medieval satire. "That alchemy book was one-of-a-kind. A new acquisition that wasn't available in their online archives."

I grimaced. I was trying to say something innocuous that wouldn't raise her suspicions, but it had backfired.

Max scribbled a note to me. *Say you read about it somewhere?*

I shook my head. It was a decent idea, but one that would lead me down a path of lies. It was always best to stay as close to the truth as possible.

"I think the reason the library doesn't have provenance," I said, "is because the book was stolen from a friend of mine a year ago."

Willow's intake of breath was loud enough for me to hear over the phone. "The book is valuable, then? How does it involve us?"

"I honestly don't know," I said, "but thefts of historical items related to alchemy got me thinking about the book. I'm going to ask my friend more about it." It wasn't completely a lie.

"You'll keep me posted?"

"I will." *That* was a lie.

I tossed my phone aside after hanging up and looked to Max.

"Backward alchemy?" he asked me.

"Maybe. The book doesn't have all the answers, though. It's not a step-by-step guide. April had to have something else to go on if that's how she really died."

"Why would the medical examiner lie?" Max asked, but he was speaking mostly to himself.

"I doubt they lied. People see what they want to see. What they're ready to believe. April probably *did* die of heart failure from her weak heart after drinking way too many energy drinks and not sleeping left her in a weakened state. Whoever examined her body would have overlooked clues about her life force being drained out of her, because signs of backward alchemy, like rapid aging, wouldn't make sense rationally."

"I'll ask Vega if there were any anomalies noted in the autopsy."

"Later. First, we need to go to Veronica's house."

Max raised an eyebrow.

"She has a tube of the Renaissance White paint sample," I explained. "I was going to ask Willow for one, but she was already suspicious of my questions, and I wouldn't have been able to tell her why I wanted one."

"Why *do* you want one?"

"If that paint was made with backward alchemy, it'll start deteriorating sometime soon."

It wasn't yet nine o'clock at night, so later than was socially acceptable to stop by someone's house, but far from the middle of the night.

Alessandro answered the door, scowling at the unexpected visit so late, but he let Max ask Veronica about her paint.

"What's going on?" she asked with her parents and little sister looking on.

"You have a tube of Renaissance White paint?" Max asked her.

"Yeah. Why?"

"Have you used it?" I asked.

"Not much. Since Perenelle is tutoring me, I'm using paints I'm mixing myself from natural dyes Perenelle is helping me turn into color-fast pigments. But I've used it at school, and my friend Cas and I were painting with it earlier."

"You have some left?" Max asked.

"About half the tube?"

Alessandro stepped to his daughter's side. "What's this about?"

"The paint," said Max, "might be relevant to a criminal investigation."

A squeak escaped from Veronica's lips.

"Give it to Max, *tesoro*," Alessandro said before turning to Max. "Is she in any danger?"

"I don't think so," Max said. "And as soon as she gives us the paint, definitely not."

We left with the wrinkled tube of white paint. The rain had moved on, and the dark sky was clear above us. I twisted open the lid under the light of the full moon, looking for any sign of separation of the pigment from the binders.

The sensation that washed over me wasn't one I was expecting.

Brimstone.

"Do you smell that?" I asked Max.

"Smell what?"

I guess that answered my question. He didn't smell the sulfuric scent of rotten eggs. Max eyed the window of the Chen-Mendoza household, where Alessandro was scowling at us through the window.

"Come on," Max said. "Let's get out of here."

We climbed into Max's jeep and drove down the deserted residential street.

"You didn't tell me what you smelled," he said as we came to a stop sign.

"I must have imagined it," I said, half believing it. I no longer smelled anything foul. I dabbed a small amount of the acrylic paint onto the back of my hand.

Immediately, my hand began to burn.

My skin burned as strongly as if it had caught fire, though I could see no visible flame. Terrible memories flashed through my mind. Fires that had caused destruction and killed people I knew. I gasped in pain as I felt my skin blistering in the heat. Desperate, I reached for a tissue from the box in between the seats.

"What's happening?" Max yanked the emergency break and helped me wipe away the paint.

There was nothing wrong with my palm. No blisters. No burn. Only the sensation of fire.

"Burning," I croaked. "My hand. It was burning."

"You're all right," he said gently as he lifted my hand. "We got it off in time. Something caustic in there?"

"As it's breaking down. It'll be far worse than the toxic paints they were trying to replicate safely. If anyone touches this paint, they'll be severely burned."

This was no longer about an inward-looking goal of saving my beloved painting of Thomas, helping Perenelle set the historical record straight, or even catching a killer who'd used a desperate woman. This was bigger than all of that.

A major product about to be released by Renaissance White would harm thousands of people. And the more the paint broke down, the more damage it would do.

CHAPTER 48

"I detect nothing dangerous." Dorian pointed at the glass test tube suspended over a flame. "This white has a distasteful smell. You are mistaking this foul scent for acid."

It was fifteen minutes after I'd felt as if my hand was on fire. Max, Dorian, and I stood around a simple wooden worktable in my basement alchemy lab. I hadn't wanted Max to test the paint on his own skin, so the next quickest solution was my alchemy lab.

"It's not just the scent of brimstone," I said. "That quickly dissipated. But the paint burned my skin."

Dorian took hold of my wrist and held my hand close to his black eyes. "I see no ill effects."

He was right. Though I'd felt my skin sizzling as if on fire, there was no mark.

"No test can detect all substances," said Max. "No offense to either of your skills as an alchemist, but we need a more drastic test." He held up the tube of paint to his own arm.

"No!" I tried to snatch the paint from Max's hand, but he dodged out of my way.

"There." When he lowered his hand, a dab of bright white paint rested on the opposite forearm. "I'm fine."

Dorian sniffed the air. "His skin is not burning, Zoe."

"You don't feel like your arm is on fire?" I leaned closer to the small blob of paint.

"I thought I caught a whiff of something sour," said Max. "Like a sewer line backed up. But it quickly disappeared."

"That it is a sour scent is an apt description," Dorian said. "What came to mind was that I had spilled an entire jar of black salt onto a meal."

"I need to show it to Perenelle. She knows paint best. If anyone can find out what's going on in this paint, it's her."

"Distasteful," Perenelle declared half an hour later.

"Corrupted ingredients?" I asked.

She pursed her lips in disgust. "Mass produced paint."

I frowned. And also tried not to yawn. It was far too late for me to be awake. "You're sure it's not dangerous?" Could I really have been so wrong?

"I'm certain. There's nothing harmful here. Only the philosophical danger of artists being separated from their raw materials."

"You're sure?" Max asked. "Zoe was certain she felt something—"

"She might be allergic to one of the ingredients. That's why it made her skin feel like it was burning, but yours didn't." Perenelle kept her voice soft. Nicolas was asleep and we hadn't woken him. "Your mind was primed to suspect something amiss because you learned that Willow and the others read about backward alchemy. Even if that vile book gave them ideas about dangerous shortcuts in alchemy, sacrificing April's life wouldn't have been enough to create transformation, because the book of backward alchemy no longer has power. Get some sleep. Things will look clearer in the morning."

"It is not your fault," Dorian said from beneath a blanket as Max drove me and Dorian home. "Your mind is not sharp once the sun has descended."

I shook my head. "I know why nobody else can feel it."

"Do I need to turn around?" Max asked as the headlights shone over a rainbow of fallen leaves alongside the narrow road leading away from the Flamels' house.

"There's nothing we can do until morning. The pain hasn't yet deteriorated. Because of my connection to the sun, I think I was feeling what *will* happen when the paint hits sunlight in the morning. The moonlight wasn't strong enough."

Max swore. "You're sympathetic to the natural world, so you feel it first."

"This is why she is a good healer," said Dorian. "But a terrible night owl."

"Why didn't Perenelle sense it?" I asked.

"She was distracted," said Max. "Didn't you both notice? She's worried about Nicolas."

"But you both believe me?"

"I believe that *you* believe it," said Dorian.

"I believe you." Max reached across the seat and took my hand in his.

"If you two are kissing," said Dorian from beneath the blanket, "please do me the courtesy of turning on the radio so I am not subjected to this public display of affection."

"The inside of a car is hardly public," said Max. "But sadly, no time for kissing."

"How does one get a product pulled from the market?" I asked.

"No idea," said Max, "but we can get it figured out as soon as we confirm it's breaking down and going to burn people." He tossed me his phone.

"Who am I calling?"

"Vega. If a dangerous paint is about to hit the market, we're not waiting until morning for us to prove it."

CHAPTER 49

For the first few moments after waking up, I was in the blissful state where I didn't remember the challenges of the previous day. All I was aware of was the sunlight awaking me, and Max's warm body beside me.

I bolted up. *Sunlight.*

Max rolled over and mumbled something I didn't hear. I shook him. "Time to get up and test for the paint to catch fire."

At the word *fire,* Max's eyes popped open.

Max got the fire extinguisher from his kitchen before we stepped into the backyard and felt the rising sun on our faces.

In alchemy, the sun represents many things. Gold, sulfur, the alchemical king, and here, the important symbol was *uncovering hidden truths.* Sunlight revealed all.

Last night, I'd put half of the remaining paint into a small glass jar before handing over the tube to Detective Vega for testing. She put a rush order on testing, but the results wouldn't be immediate. I didn't want to wait. Not while there was something I could do.

I carried the small vial of paint into Max's backyard and stepped away from the house, onto the clover.

"Careful," he said as he stood by with the fire extinguisher in one hand, a box of tissues in the other. He'd left a first aid kit on the tiny table with two chairs.

I unscrewed the lid of the glass jar. This time, I didn't smell anything. Had I truly imagined it?

I spread a small dab on the skin of my forearm. Yet again, it felt as if it was burning. Max stepped forward as soon as he heard me gasp, but I motioned for him to stay put. I needed to see what the paint would do.

"Tissue!" I cried out when I couldn't stand the burning any longer.

"There's no mark here, Zoe." Max's black hair was askew, and a shadow of stubble darkened his face. We hadn't taken time to get ready for the day, since this was more important.

Only it *wasn't*. Because apparently, I either had an allergy or I'd imagined it.

I took the fire extinguisher and tissues from Max as he tested the paint on himself.

"Nothing," he shook his head. "It feels like a cool gel." He raised his arm higher into the sunlight, but nothing changed.

"I was so sure," I whispered.

"Maybe the sun isn't bright enough."

We fixed tea and sat hand in hand on the back porch as the sun grew brighter. Max believed me. There wasn't one shred of proof, and all evidence pointed the other way, but he still believed in me.

At shortly after eight o'clock, a full hour after sunrise, we did one more test.

Nothing.

"I have a little while before opening the shop," Max said. "I'm going to go check with Vega. I'll harass her until she harasses the lab."

Sunlight shone on my skin as I stepped out of my truck in the Flamels' driveway. I still felt the spots on my hand and arm where the paint had touched my skin. How could I have been so wrong? If I was suffering from an allergy, wouldn't I have seen a mark?

Water droplets from yesterday's rainstorm made the pigment garden sparkle as brightly as a rainbow as I walked to the house.

"I can't find my blasted glasses," Nicolas said as he opened the door for me. Two pairs were sitting atop his head, though to be fair, both were nearly obscured by his hair.

I plucked out one pair of glasses and handed them to him.

"Brilliant girl." He kissed my cheek.

Perenelle gave him a loving yet exasperated smile before turning to me. "Join me and Nicolas for breakfast?"

"There's nothing wrong with the paint," I said. "It looks like everyone was right that I'm allergic to something in it."

"You could have told us that over the phone."

"I wanted to see if you two were all right."

"Don't worry about my forgetfulness." Nicolas tapped his temple. "This is how I've always been."

It was true.

"Our Nicolas has too many ideas running through his mind, as always," Perenelle added. "But I believe Zoe is referring to the theft and murder."

"Dreadful business," said Nicolas. "Oh! I should let you know that we arranged for an anonymous donation for Betty Kubiak's nephew. The young man will never have to worry about monetary support, and will receive the finest care for as long as he lives."

He frowned. "You seem troubled by this."

I shook my head. "I'm happy about your donation, which was generous."

"Has something else transpired?"

"Only that I feel like the more I learn, the less I understand about what's going on. With everything that's happened... please promise me you'll be careful."

"We get ourselves trapped by a villain *once* during hundreds of years of being careful," said Nicolas with a sly smile, "and Zoe thinks we need looking after. I'll have you know we've made great progress going through the research Gwendolyn has compiled over the years. Though most of her work isn't relevant. Not to Perenelle specifically."

"She hadn't narrowed it down."

Nicolas chuckled. "I heartily endorse hoarder tendencies. Did I use that word correctly?"

"You did," I assured him as he made a note of the modern vernacular in his commonplace notebook.

"Gwendolyn isn't a hoarder." Perenelle shook her head with a smile. "She's a meticulous researcher. If we'd had time to prepare our records before we were unexpectedly attacked by Edward Kelley, Gwendolyn and researchers like her would have been able to piece together a lot more. She's pieced together so much history over the years, with so little to show for it. There are still so many misattributed artists who should be recognized."

"We'll get there," I said. "It's a backward way of getting there, but the truth about Philippe Hayden is sure to get more attention for the cause."

"You're still thinking of Renaissance White's paint," Perenelle said.

"If it was created with backward alchemy, it would be breaking down in unstable ways," I said. "But you're right that even if April had used her intent as she died, that wouldn't have sacrificed enough energy to create the beautiful paint. There's *something* going on with that paint."

"I'm as powerful an alchemist as you are," Perenelle said. "I don't sense anything in it."

"You're *more* powerful, Perenelle." I stared at her cascading red waves of hair hanging loose around her resolute face, and I knew what was wrong. "You're *too* powerful. Your paints use sulfur and mercury."

"Of course. They're part of alchemy's *tria prima*. How could I not?"

"Those are dangerous substances modern manufacturers can't use in their products. You can't sense the beginning of any toxins leaching out *because they won't harm you*."

That's why nobody else sensed it. As an herbalist and healer, I've always been able to sense toxins that will cause people harm. Dorian had detected a faint sulfurous odor, but he'd only found true alchemy a little over a year ago. And Max had said it smelled faintly like a sewer line, but he only used alchemical principles to cultivate tea. Perenelle, however, was on the other end of the alchemical spectrum. She was over six hundred years old. She was too powerful an alchemical artist to sense anything amiss, *because it wouldn't harm her*. Her own alchemical transformations rendered toxins inert in her finished paints.

With a sickening sense of dread, I knew what had happened.

"Renaissance White was in possession of *The Apothecary's Cabinet*," I said. "They tested its paint. Paint that you created. *They knew what was in it*. But they didn't know how to safely recreate it. Their paint won't only burn when it breaks down. It's *poison*."

234

CHAPTER 50

I'd left the remains of the glass jar of paint with Max. I needed to see him and get my remaining paint sample, but he wasn't answering his phone. He was probably too busy at the shop. It was shortly after ten, so it would be open by now.

But when I arrived at The Alchemy of Tea, the sign on the front door of the shop was set to CLOSED. He hadn't opened the shop that day. He must have been running late because of me. He wasn't kidding about harassing Detective Vega until she got answers about the paint.

Since Max wasn't answering his phone, I called the detective.

"Like I already told Max," she said with an exasperated sigh, "the lab doesn't work that quickly."

"Is he still with you?"

"He left a while ago. I appreciate the tip about the paint, but you two really need to leave things to us now. If I find out you're—"

"All I'm doing is looking for Max," I said truthfully.

"He was talking about a cabinet before he left," she said. "So if he's not at his shop, maybe he was stopping by a hardware store to fix one of his cabinets."

"Maybe," I murmured as I peered through the glass. The shop was dark inside, but in the dim light I could see the cabinets and shelving. Nothing was broken.

"Leave things to us, Zoe," the detective said before hanging up.

"Max?" I rattled the handle. "Are you restocking? This is important!"

I shook the handle once more. Even if he was in back, the front lights should have been on.

"Max, the paint isn't just prone to catch fire," I cried. "It's poison!"

There was no reply. It was a small shop. He would have heard my shouting even from the back. Something must have happened.

"What did you just say?"

It wasn't Max's voice.

I whipped around, cursing myself for my foolishness shouting about poison when I was next door to a popular café. But the woman who'd spoken hadn't walked out of Blue Sky Teas. She was hurrying over from across the street.

"You," I whispered when she reached my side. I recognized her. It was the mysterious art collector, Joni Mitchell. The suspect Detective Vega had said wasn't under suspicion. Where had she come from?

"FBI Special Agent Mitchell," she said, showing me her ID. The woman's surname was truly Mitchell, though she had a different first name.

She was a law enforcement agent. That's why Detective Vega had told the Flamels she could be trusted. And also why she'd made sure her clothing was the most distinctive thing about her when she'd met with the Flamels.

"You're investigating the Betty Kubiak homicide?" I asked.

"Something like that."

Unlike the woman in the photo Nicolas had showed me, this version of Special Agent Mitchell was dressed like a backpacker. With scruffy sneakers, a jean jacket covered with hand-sewn patches of national parks, a small backpack that clipped onto her hips for stability, and two walking sticks she held in one hand, she looked like she could have stepped off a hiking trail on Mount Hood, not out of an office where she was looking into a murder that had taken place in the city.

"I haven't come across poison in my investigation," she said. "What were you yelling about?"

I wasn't worried about Special Agent Mitchell being an imposter.

Detective Vega had vouched for her. But how much could I tell her? It was clear I needed help, but asking for help was difficult when the reasoning was based in alchemy.

Detective Vega had told me more than she'd realized. I hadn't noticed it at first either. She said he'd been talking about a *cabinet* when he left her. None of the shelving in his shop was damaged. But there was another cabinet central to this investigation. *The Apothecary's Cabinet.*

"I'll tell you about the poison," I said, "but I also need your help. My boyfriend has a theory about what's happening. And now he's missing."

CHAPTER 51

"The sidewalk isn't the best place for us to talk." Special Agent Mitchell stepped aside as a woman attempted to open the door to The Alchemy of Tea. "My car is across the street."

I hurried after the agent to an old car with a few layers of mud on the bumper and tires. She tossed her gear into the back before sliding into the driver's seat.

"Door's open," she said as I stood on the sidewalk.

"Let me see your ID one more time."

She stood and held it over the top of the little car, close enough for me to see but not grab.

"Dora," I read. "Special Agent Dora Mitchell."

"Friends call me Mitch. You can call me *Special Agent Mitchell*. Ms. Faust, we're wasting time." She gave an exasperated sigh. "You said your boyfriend is missing and there's poison—"

"You already knew my name when you came over to me."

"A perk of being in law enforcement. Can you get in the car?"

I stared at her over the top of the dirty car. Max's shop and Blue's café were in my line of sight, but they barely registered as I looked at the special agent in a new light. *I knew who she was.*

Special Agent Mitchell wasn't trying to kidnap me. She was indeed who she said she was. But she was also so much more.

"The given name Dora," I said. "Isn't that often a diminutive for a more formal name?"

She scowled at me. "I'm not in the mood for riddles. Were you being serious about poison and Mr. Liu being in trouble?"

"I'm going to tell you what's going on," I said, now certain I was right. She knew Max's name in addition to mine. "I'm going to be truthful with you. Because I need your help. I think you understand a big part of what's going on, from information you've already collected, so I can get you up to speed quickly. But you need to get us into Max's shop, so we can make sure he's not hurt."

Without a word, she pulled open the car door. But she wasn't getting inside. She reached into the glovebox and put something in her pocket.

"Let's go," she said as she held up her arm to stop the car that was driving down the popular street. She did it with such authority that the driver didn't even honk as they stopped for us.

I jogged across the street after her. "There's a back door in the alley. Less conspicuous."

She didn't break stride as she went around to the back. By the time I reached her side, the door was already open and the overhead light on.

"Max?" I called out. The shop's back room was small enough that I could immediately tell he wasn't there. Dorian would have pointed out that one of the cardboard boxes was large enough for a body, so I reluctantly peeked inside. A dozen boxes of tea pots rested neatly inside.

"Talk while we look around." Agent Mitchell quickly scanned the small room, then poked her head into the tiny bathroom.

"The idea for poison starts with Perenelle Flamel," I said. "But she's not the one who created it. You can think of her as my godmother, to understand my relationship to her. She's an artist who knows a special process to create beautiful pigments for oil paintings. She's originally French, from a line of artists who passed down these secrets. Her secret recipe involves principles from alchemy, so it's very complex. It can't simply be written down as a recipe and copied. And it involves dangerous ingredients that are rendered inert when handled properly."

"Which is where poison comes in," said Special Agent Mitchell.

"Exactly. Well-meaning people who handle the pigment recipes incorrectly can accidentally create poisoned substances. A new line of artist paints from Renaissance White already has hundreds of samples out in the world, and thousands more are about to go on sale, with even more planned if they succeed."

"Sounds like a bad business model."

I shook my head. "I don't think they realize it's poison. The poison will only take effect once the paint breaks down. I don't know exactly how long that will take, but it was created with a corrupted process and is already starting to break down. The same night I had a work of art stolen, the Renaissance White lab was burglarized and a painting stolen. Both paintings were from that line of artists Perenelle is descended from."

"Made with pigments from this secret technique that'll result in poison if it's done incorrectly."

"Exactly. The paintings are known as *Brother and Sister* and *The Apothecary's Cabinet*. Max was checking in with Detective Vega of Portland PD, who's having a paint sample tested for poison, and before he left her, he said he had to go deal with a *cabinet*. His shop doesn't need a cabinet."

"But it's shorthand for one of the stolen paintings."

"And he's not answering his phone." I checked my phone for messages. Still no Max. "He might have left his shop closed for something important, but he would have told me. And he wouldn't have gone offline like this."

Special Agent Mitchell shook her head. "He doesn't have any specialized knowledge here. It sounds like Mrs. Flamel is the one who's in danger."

I froze. She was right. I dialed Perenelle's number. It went straight to voicemail. I frowned at the phone as I called Nicolas.

"Zoe, my dear!" The sound of his voice put me at ease.

"Perenelle isn't answering her phone," I said.

"But isn't she with you and Max?"

"She's not home with you?"

"She left when Max called," Nicolas said. "Is something wrong?"

Something was *very* wrong.

"Keep me posted if she calls you," I told him before hanging up.

"She's missing too?" A look of real concern showed on the agent's face.

"Let's stop playing games. You know more about Perenelle Flamel than I do right now. You've been investigating both her and Nicolas."

I wasn't worried that the FBI was investigating the Flamels for a crime. The agent had called the Flamels' neighbors and contacted them using the fake identity of art collector Joni Mitchell *right before* the Flamels' backstories came through online. Special Agent Dora Mitchell was looking into whether they were worthy of her help disguising their identities.

"Thank you for helping the Flamels," I said. "Thank you, Theodora Mitchell. Or should I call you *Theo?*"

<h1 style="text-align:center">CHAPTER 52</h1>

Special Agent Mitchell only hesitated for a moment before smiling. "Do you know in all my years of helping people, nobody's ever guessed the truth?"

"Nobody receiving your help would want to prod too much," I said.

The people who went to Theo were desperate. They were escaping something from the past. Tobias had told me that Theo was a former FBI agent who'd quickly become disillusioned. *Always stay as close to the truth as possible.* I had a feeling that nearly everything Tobias had told me about Theo was true. Everything except that she was a woman and she still worked for the FBI. She also didn't need to be the expert hacker we'd assumed of Theo. She had access to resources from within the agency.

"I'll deny it, of course," she said as she knelt to examine a spot on the floor. "You don't have proof."

"I don't want anyone to find out. You've helped so many people. I don't have any family left, but Tobias, Nicolas, and Perenelle are just about the closest I have. You've helped them as well as so many innocent people who needed to start over. Thank you."

She acknowledged my thanks with a slight nod as she stood up. "Thought that might have been blood on the floor. It's just ink."

"Where *is* he?" I glanced at my phone. Still no word from Max. I looked back at the agent. "I can't stop thinking of you as Joni Mitchell."

"My middle name really is Joan. It's a great way to automatically respond to the name but also have it impossible for anyone to find out information about me online. Everything is crowded out by the famous Joni Mitchell. You see anything out of place?"

"Nothing…" I trailed off as I was hit with an idea that should have already occurred to me. "Why are you still here?"

"I don't want to see innocent people poisoned any more than you do."

"I mean why were you still here *at all*? You should have been done looking into the Flamels. You already manipulated online data to give them more thorough backstories. Why stay?"

"Having access to resources to help people was only one reason I stayed on the job. When I looked into the lives of people who desperately needed help, by default I often found out about very bad people. The people my clients were hiding from. That pointed me in the direction of big cases to pursue. I'm known for having a sixth sense for sniffing out baddies. It gives me a bit of free rein to look into cases that interest me."

"And you found something of interest here?"

"Nothing definitive. But a young woman died last year."

"April Salazar."

"Why doesn't it surprise me that you've been investigating? You're right, there were some curious details in her autopsy. The medical examiner dismissed them, because there was a clear, explainable cause of death."

"But you aren't satisfied."

"The skin was wrinkled and shrunken."

Exactly how it would have been if she was aging quickly and prematurely, as backward alchemy would do to someone when it unraveled. But I couldn't tell the agent that.

"It was dismissed as extreme dehydration," she continued, "but there's something funny about it. There's evidence that leads me to believe hydrogen sulfide contributed to her death. It can be highly toxic."

"*Brimstone,*" I whispered. That's what I'd smelled when I sniffed the paint sample, but the scent had been so fleeting that I wasn't sure if I'd imagined it.

She gave me a strange look.

"Sulfur," I clarified. "Brimstone means the same thing. I think of sulfur by the archaic term."

"In confined spaces in high concentration, it's highly poisonous and can cause cardiac arrest. But it dissipates quickly. There were other reasons for the Medical Examiner to believe her cardiac arrest was caused by something more common."

"Her underlying medical condition plus all the empty energy drinks they found."

She nodded. "Whereas hydrogen sulfide is a natural gas created by a volcano, or sewage, or some types of industrial work."

"Rotten eggs," I said. "She wrote down *rotten eggs* before she died. From the hydrogen sulfide."

If hydrogen sulfide was there during the paint transformation, it might surface again when the paint finished breaking down. Then it would become a deadly poison for anyone using it indoors. I knew about the toxic gas because it was identified by the same chemist who'd created a highly toxic green pigment, Scheele's Green, a vivid green color that poisoned people through arsenic. Scheele's Green was popular throughout the Victorian Era despite its toxicity. Perenelle didn't use arsenic in creating her pigments, but she did use mercury and *sulfur*. Sulfur was a key element of hydrogen sulfide— and it smelled strongly of rotten eggs.

"It kills quickly and barely leaves a trace," Special Agent Mitchell said, "so that's my bet for what killed Mrs. Salazar last year. But I don't see it being a danger to anyone using it. Only people making it. I can check with our experts, but I'm pretty sure that gas is only deadly in high concentration, like what she did in her lab."

"You don't understand," I pleaded. "There's a special technique. A dangerous one that I think was used to create this paint. It means that the paint will break down quickly and return to its natural state— releasing all the toxins used to create it."

She reached for her phone. "This is bad."

"Who are you calling?"

"Detective Vega. I've stayed in contact with her. She and her team are making strides into the murder of Ms. Kubiak, and their lab is testing the paint sample you gave them, but now we can tell them what to test for."

"Except it might not reveal the poison. Not until it breaks down."

She swore. "Is there anything you can tell me? Anything we can use as proof?"

"Not yet. Maybe that's what Max was after, with *The Apothecary's Cabinet* painting."

"Voicemail." She cursed and shoved her phone back into her pocket. "Wait. That was one of the paintings that was stolen. You think he knows where it is?"

"I don't know." I tugged my hair in frustration. I breathed deeply, inhaling the calming scents of tea surrounding me. Honey, caramel, and citrus. *Where was Max?* Why wouldn't he have told me if he'd figured out where it was? Where could the two stolen paintings be?

"Could he be going after proof of this poison?" she asked. "It's difficult to implement a recall. And without clear evidence? We'd need to get Renaissance White to come clean that it's poison."

"I don't think they realize it's poison."

"Maybe they do," Agent Mitchell said as she read a message on her phone. "Vega wasn't answering because she's made an arrest. Willow Matsumoto has been arrested on suspicion of murder."

CHAPTER 53

From the Typewriter of Dorian Robert-Houdin

```
The Culinary Alchemist's Toolbox

   Cooking is a form of nurturing, and it shows
others that you care for them. Yet cooking is not
all of life. Do not neglect the people who
need you.
```

As soon as Zoe called, Dorian set aside his soon-to-be mega-bestselling cookbook. It had taken up so much of his energy lately that he was not 100 percent devoted to the crimes afoot. Crimes that were now being solved without him! *Culinary Alchemy: The Art of Transforming Simple Ingredients into a Feast of the Senses,* was a foul temptress indeed.

Willow Matsumoto had been arrested for murder, yet Zoe did not believe her to be guilty. Detective Vega found evidence that Willow had lied about her whereabouts the night of the murder. The detective believed Willow to have been out the night of Betty Kubiak's murder, contradicting Willow's earlier statement in which she said she was at home sleeping. But now she was caught in a lie. A lie Dorian had learned about earlier, but he had not realized its significance. Members of the red-caped secret society had been observed the night of the murder. Willow had explained to Zoe that she had gone home after that meeting and had not joined her friends on their midnight waterfront stroll. The question was whether Willow was lying. Was she indeed at home asleep when her husband was being robbed by Betty Kubiak, or could she have been an accomplice to the dead thief?

The truth would be determined soon enough, but did they have time? Max and Perenelle were missing.

The familiar rumble of Zoe's old truck's engine sounded. *Bon.* She was home.

"Dorian?" Zoe's voice called out less than a minute later. "It's just me."

He scampered down the stairs and met her in the living room.

"The detectives did not let you sit in on Willow's interrogation?" he asked.

"I didn't want to," Zoe said. Her expression was bleak. "They think the best way to find Max and Perenelle is to get Willow to confess."

"Yet you do not believe she is guilty."

"I don't know... I can almost see the truth, but not quite." Zoe collapsed onto her beloved green sofa, leaning her head against the cushions.

"You must separate your worry from the truths that we know. Max mentioned the *cabinet.* This suggests the painting. Could it mean anything else?"

Zoe shook her head. "There were no damaged cabinets in his shop. He wasn't going to the hardware store or a furniture store. Neither would make him disappear."

Dorian clasped his hands behind his back and paced back and forth. "Why would *The Apothecary's Cabinet* be of interest to Max, but not *Brother and Sister*? Would he not care more about getting your painting back?"

Zoe's body jolted upright, as if she were a marionette being jerked awake by the strings of a puppet master.

"How are the paintings different." She spoke the words not as a question, but as if she knew the answer.

"What have you realized?"

"Oberon Salazar. He was the one who found his wife's body. He's the one who would have seen that something was wrong with the body—and what was unexpectedly there in the lab."

"What was there?" Dorian asked in rapt attention.

"*The Apothecary's Cabinet* painting. That was the last ingredient in her recipe. That's where the poisoned gas came from—pure alchemy being corrupted by backward alchemy."

"*Mon dieu.*" Zoe had solved the murder! Dorian was pleased if she was indeed correct. Yet he could not but feel slightly rebuked. It was on his watch that Zoe's beloved painting had been stolen. He had hoped to solve the crime, or at least play a pivotal role in helping Zoe. Perhaps his murder board had helped her put the pieces together, but he still felt he had let her down.

"Oberon loved April so much that his suspicions wouldn't have been waved away by the convenient answer," Zoe said. "And he's the one who would have seen that April used part of the painting to complete the recipe. He might not know the term 'backward alchemy,' but he wasn't wrong when he called it a *curse*. He wanted revenge."

Dorian did not understand how stealing Zoe's painting would bring about revenge. But Zoe now held her mobile phone to her ear as she made a telephone call, so he could not ask her to elaborate.

With deliberate, anxious steps, she walked the length of the living room while she telephoned two different detectives. From what he could hear, both attempts were in vain. She left a voicemail message for Detective Vega, and then for Agent Mitchell. This was wise of her —or so he thought, until he heard the words she spoke as she reached the end of her message to Agent Mitchell.

"But you cannot go in search of the degenerate killer yourself!" Dorian cried after she hung up.

"They know where I'm going," the foolish alchemist said. "I can't wait around for Oberon to kill Max and Perenelle like he did Betty."

Dorian watched helplessly as she left.

This would not do. He must save Zoe from herself. As the foolish alchemist backed out of the driveway, he called for backup. Which, in Dorian's case, meant three 16-year-old students and a 600-year-old absentminded alchemist.

CHAPTER 54

As I drove to Renaissance White, I thought through what I knew.

Oberon was the one who found Willow. He would have been the one to find the painting with April when she died. That's why it went into the safe. Not that they were worried about theft, but because it had been damaged.

Pigment from Perenelle's painting *The Apothecary's Cabinet* was the shortcut necessary to make the temporarily beautiful Renaissance White paint. An ingredient from the painting *itself* had been the last element in April's recipe that killed her. The sulfur in the painting was stable, but mixed with their other and backward intent ingredients, had released a toxic gas in the enclosed space. By the time April was found, it had dissipated.

Oberon knew there was something wrong with April's death. He wanted revenge. But… revenge against who? Adam and Willow? He hadn't framed them, and he'd continued to work for Renaissance White. Why steal my painting? Why kidnap Max and Perenelle? Was that what had happened, or could I have been wrong about why Max hadn't opened his shop and the two of them were offline?

I didn't have all the answers. But that's why I was headed to Renaissance White.

My tires screeched as I pulled to a stop. I checked my phone. The detective and agent hadn't called me back. They must have still been questioning Willow. I hurried from my truck so quickly that I didn't shut the door behind me. I was prepared to bang on the front door, but it was ajar. Maybe because the police had arrested Willow here, and nobody had locked up afterward?

"Hello?" I called out.

Silence.

Taking a step further inside the lobby, I was again struck by the beauty of the painting that Adam had made of his beloved sister. Her angelic face in the foreground, the forest setting of the trees, cabin, and lake in the distance. It was an act of love and a beautiful memory, like my painting of Thomas. I understood his desire to have the colors he believed could give a true representation of his sister he'd loved so much. But it didn't matter that the oil paint used here was slightly different than a paint Perenelle would make. Adam's love for his sister came through in his execution.

"Hey, Zoe."

I spun around and faced the person who'd spoken. I'd been so absorbed in Adam's painting I hadn't heard Oberon approaching.

Oberon wasn't pointing a gun or any other weapon at me. He stood with slumped shoulders, his thumbs looped around the belt loops of jeans that hung loosely on his thin frame.

"Now's not a really good time," he said. "There's some screw-up with the police and they think Willow was involved in killing that thief."

"Did Adam go with her?" I asked as I backed away slowly, towards the door.

"Nah. Haven't seen him this morning. He's been working so hard in the lab that I thought he crashed here, because he wasn't at home when the detective took Willow. That's what I came to check. But he's not here."

I stared at Oberon. He was grieving, but this didn't look like a man seeking revenge. I had so many unanswered questions about Oberon as the killer because it was entirely possible I was mistaken about him.

"I won't take up much of your time," I said, "but I have a couple of important questions. Difficult questions." *Life or death* questions.

"Um, sure? But then I really need to find Adam."

"When your wife died, did you find anything surprising next to her?"

"Stop victim-blaming!" he erupted. "I know she drank too many energy drinks. That doesn't mean it was her fault."

Even as he lashed out verbally, he didn't lash out physically.

"That wasn't what I meant," I assured him. I didn't want to lead his answer, so I tried to think of how I could ask him about the painting without referencing it. I needed to know if I was right that April was using pigment from *The Apothecary's Cabinet* as her last ingredient.

"Oh," he said. "Do you mean the ashes?"

Ashes? "Like ashes from a heating source, or from something that was burned for a chemical reaction?"

"Ashes with fragments of paint."

"Next to a painting?"

He shook his head. "We don't bring any of our artwork into the lab. There was no painting with her."

I was wrong about April using a *sample* of the painting. She needed the whole thing. That's why they needed another painting. The *Brother and Sister* painting was my last connection to Thomas. At another time, I would have been devastated knowing that my painting was about to be destroyed, if it hadn't been already, but right now all I cared about was getting Max and Perenelle back safely.

"The whole painting was destroyed," I repeated aloud. I knew that fact told me something else important, but I was so distracted by my worry that I was having trouble grasping it.

"What?" Oberon said, shaking me from my worry.

"When was *The Apothecary's Cabinet* moved into your safe?"

"Why does—"

"Please. It's important."

"Sometime right around when I lost April. That period of my life is a haze, so I don't know exactly. Adam was taking care of everything then, since Willow and I were so messed up with grief."

"Did you or Willow ever see the painting again?"

He blinked at me. "I don't think we ever took it out. If you don't have any more weird questions for me, I need to find Adam."

"So do I." Because Oberon had given me the last pieces of the puzzle. So many pieces of my theory hadn't fit Oberon being the killer, because he wasn't.

Adam was attacked by Betty Kubiak when she supposedly stole *The Apothecary's Cabinet*. But with her dead, we only had Adam's word for it that the painting still existed.

There was more that pointed to Adam. It could have been any of them who pretended to be Arthur Finder. Except for one thing. Adam was the only one of the Renaissance White team who was an artist. *The only one who would have known Betty Kubiak.*

I doubted "Arthur" was looking everywhere for a painting he believed had similar colors to their destroyed painting, *The Apothecary's Cabinet.* He'd invested his money into his company and wouldn't have the time or resources to fly around the world seeking out similar artwork, but as a member of the local art community, he would have seen Perenelle's work and known the artistic style that inspired her. Local artists knew her name, and it was public record that one "Nicolas Flamel" had purchased *Brother and Sister* in France. Adam pieced together that the Flamels were the ones who bought *Brother and Sister.*

Adam wouldn't understand that backward alchemy had created the paint. But as a scientist and artist, he could have easily believed that adding a unique pigment from the old painting had been the missing ingredient they'd needed. He needed another painting with the same pigments.

I didn't yet know why he'd killed Betty, or what he'd done with Max and Perenelle. I needed to find him.

"Where are you looking next?" I asked him.

He shrugged. "There's a café he likes not far from here."

Adam wasn't at a café. My eyes fell again to his painting of his sister. The painting born of love that had twisted his ideas about how important it was to recreate lost color.

"The cabin at the lake in the background," I said. "Is it real?"

"Sure. It's his family's cabin. The four of us went up there for a cheap honeymoon after our dual wedding. April fell into some poison oak."

"I need the address."

CHAPTER 55

Before leaving for the cabin, I tried the police once more. I left a message with a confused dispatcher, then sent Oberon to the police station to convey the urgent message about Adam. Oberon wasn't completely convinced about Adam's guilt, but it made more sense to him than Willow. I reasoned that even if he told the detectives that a crazed woman with dyed-white hair was going to a cabin to attack his friend, that was fine.

I also called Dorian to tell him where I was going. I was surprised he didn't insist on me stopping at home to get him, but he did recommend I bring a weapon. I didn't carry weapons around with me, so I picked up a loose brick in a flowerbed near the warehouse lab.

My phone's GPS told me Adam's cabin was less than an hour away. I reached it in just over 30 minutes.

Pebbles and small branches crunched under my tires as I turned onto the dirt road less than a mile from the cabin. I pulled over behind a dense grouping of trees. I didn't want Adam to hear me approaching, so I put the brick in my bag and continued on foot. I kept clear of the road all together, making my way towards the cabin through the trees. I spotted the poison oak Oberon had mentioned, which was deep red at this time of year and blended in with the crimson leaves shedding from the nearby dogwood and maple trees.

I knew I was in the right spot when a small cabin came into view that looked exactly as it did in Adam's painting. A solitary black car was parked in front.

I listened for a full minute, but I didn't hear any voices. I couldn't stand not knowing if Max and Perenelle were inside, and what had become of them, so I crept to the window.

My breath caught. The wooden shelves in this front room were nearly identical to ones in *The Apothecary's Cabinet*. Thick glass jars lined the smooth shelves. Each jar was filled with a colorful pigment or dried flowers. There was a gap where it looked as if an apothecary had removed half a dozen jars for their work. Looking through the glass windowpane, it was as if I'd been transported to the French Farmhouse where I'd lived with the Flamels.

I pried my gaze from the eerily familiar scene. Besides the uncanny shelves, there was a laminate kitchenette, a few pieces of mismatched furniture that had seen better days, and an open door leading to a small bathroom. There was one more door, but this one was closed. I crept around the side of the house. The second room's window had been boarded up. I gave a tug, but it didn't budge.

I made my way to the front door. It was unlocked. A trap? But Adam had no way of knowing I was coming, did he? I couldn't think about worst case scenarios. If he was in the back room with Max and Perenelle, it was worth the risk.

I hurried inside and to the closed interior door. This one was locked. If Dorian had been with me, he would have made quick work of the lock with his claws. But I was on my own. I knelt at the handle, and that's when I heard it. A creaking noise came from behind me.

Before I could turn around, strong arms grabbed my shoulders and threw me to the ground, hard, knocking the wind out of me. Before I could recover, I felt myself being shoved once more. Through a doorway that was now open. This time, I caught myself with my hands and rolled onto my side. Adam White stood above me, a mixture of confusion and rage on his face. He didn't come at me. He did something worse: he slammed the door.

"No!" I screamed as I scrambled up and yanked in vain on the handle.

"Are you hurt?" a familiar voice asked. I was so flustered that I hadn't realized I wasn't alone.

Perenelle rushed to my side and helped me up.

"Only my hands." I winced as I stood. I had scraped my palms, and my shoulder would surely have a bruise, but otherwise I was unharmed. I scanned the small room as I stretched to make sure.

A solitary wooden stool stood in front of a table filled with equipment. It looked like a section of a chemistry classroom ready for its next experiments. A Bunsen burner, glass vessels, jars of minerals and pigments, a scale, a metal pot, a mortar and pestle, a notebook, and dozens of other items cluttered the table. The *Brother and Sister* painting rested on the table as well, supported by the wall behind the table. There were no other doors in the room. *Where was Max?*

"You're not drugged?" she asked.

"Drugged?"

"That's how he got us. It's my fault for not keeping up with modern science. He sprayed something in our faces, and we woke up here."

"Where's Max?"

"He's safe." Perenelle paused and pressed her ear to the door. "I think Adam has gone in search of him once more."

"Max *escaped*?"

"Not exactly."

"Could you stop speaking in riddles?" I tried not to let frustration creep into my voice. I was upset with myself, not Perenelle.

"I have to make sure Adam is gone first," she said. "I think he is."

"Did Max escape or didn't he?" Maybe I'd knocked my head without realizing it, because nothing made sense.

"Max is safe," she said once more. "Adam knows I understand more about pigment recipes than he does, so he wants me to create the paint formulation for him. He threatened to hurt Max if I didn't help him, so while Adam was gathering jars from the shelves in the other room, I helped Max hide."

"Help should be on the way," I said. My bag with my phone inside it was on the other side of the locked door.

"I'm not sure how long he'll search for Max before giving up."

"Why did you two go see him alone, before telling anyone?"

She frowned. "We didn't. Not exactly. Max wanted to get a look at their lab to check an idea about the poison, *because he believed you.*

With my connection to the stolen paintings, Max thought I'd sense the ingredients if they were there, so he took me along. We didn't think we'd be in danger or that he'd catch us off guard. We didn't realize Adam was a killer." As she spoke, she'd begun to mix colors together on a wooden pallet.

"You're not going through with making his recipe, are you?"

"Adam says he doesn't care about the money the paint formulations will make him," Perenelle said. "And I believe him."

"He thinks the brilliant colors will bring him closer to his sister he cherished," I said. "But you can't mass produce your paint, even if you wanted to."

"No," she said as she dipped a small paintbrush into a daub of paint. "But I don't want Adam to be able to use my love for you against me. When he doesn't find Max, he's going to threaten you to make me do his bidding. I'm making sure he can't do that."

Perenelle touched her left hand to my cheek, then lifted the paintbrush in her right hand to the *Brother and Sister* painting.

CHAPTER 56

I wasn't aware of leaving my earthly body, or even of the passage of time. All I was aware of for the first few moments of arriving inside the painting was an overwhelming sensation of *love*.

Love from Perenelle's sacrifice to resume this dangerous process she didn't undertake lightly, because she thought it was her best chance at saving my life.

Love from my brother, who Perenelle had painted with so much love. Thomas wasn't here in this painting with me, but the alchemy that had transformed raw materials into vibrant pigments was from the farmhouse where Thomas and I were living. Everything was connected.

Is that how I also felt love from Max? Or was I right that I sensed him nearby.

"Zoe." His voice was a whisper. Or was it a shout? It was all the same.

But I was sure of one thing: Max was *here in the painting*.

And I knew how we'd both gotten here. Perenelle always wore her full skirts with plenty of hidden pockets, which Adam wouldn't have known to search. She had her alchemical paints with her when he kidnapped her.

"Max?" I called back. The sound rippled, as if through water, both silent and a scream.

I looked out of Thomas's eye, orienting myself. My sight was simultaneously crisp and blurred. It was difficult to focus. If I hadn't seen Perenelle's paintbrush touch the canvas, I wouldn't have realized I was a reflection in Thomas's eye.

Where was Max?

Feeling the natural elements of the paints surround me, I directed my intent on seeing them. I closed my eyes and reached for the core alchemical elements: sulfur, mercury, and salt. They were all here.

I opened my eyes and found myself looking into a mirror. No. This wasn't a mirror. It was *an earlier version of myself*. The young woman who'd escaped Salem with my little brother, fled to dirty London where I'd made herbal tinctures for the ailing, and been offered an apprenticeship with Nicolas Flamel. It was Zoe in the French countryside I was looking at. The young woman next to Thomas in the painting.

Perenelle had painted this portrait before Thomas died of the plague, and his mortal body had died the following year. The paints brimmed with energy and life. A sulfurous red vermillion in the hearth. A mercurial brightness of the white light shining through the window onto my face. A mix of blue lapis lazuli and yellow ochre that created the green of my dress. Burnt ashes for the black that cast a shadow in my eye, rising like brimstone...

That wasn't a shadow. It was another person reflected in my eye.

Max.

Of course. Perenelle hadn't the time to paint full portraits of either of us with the small amount of alchemical paint she had with her. But she'd captured *our essences* with the quick, masterful brushstrokes that brought us into the world of the portrait.

"I see you," I called to Max.

"Where are you? I feel your presence, but I can't..."

"Look to the reflection in Thomas's eye," I said as I leaned forward to see him more clearly. I couldn't move from where Perenelle had placed me.

"I can see Perenelle when I look out of the painting, but here... I'm in a fog. I taste the earthy sweetness of flowers, feel the coolness of metals, and smell ashes. But I can't see beyond shapes inside here."

"Don't worry. You haven't been practicing your tea alchemy as long, but your senses are doing great."

"How long have we been here?"

"A few…" I began before trailing off. I had no idea. The concept of time was something I once understood… wasn't it? *Time…* "We have something important to do. We need to stop something bad from happening."

"Poison," Max said. "We have to stop poison from being released through the paint."

That was it. How could I have forgotten? The ashes were so thick in here they created a fog. Had the poison already gotten out? Had we been here for years?

"Zoe?" Max called. "Can you hear me?"

"I can."

"I didn't mean for things to end like this for us. I was going to—" He broke off, but quickly regained his composure. "I always thought we had time. But I was a fool to think we could get a happy ending."

"Don't say that."

"There was so much more in life I wanted to do with you." Max's words were filled with both hope and despair.

"We're getting out of here," I said, but before I reached the end of my sentence, I knew I was wrong.

"You don't believe it yourself."

I didn't know how to answer. I was confined to a tiny reflection, but I was surrounded by love. Had Max spoken seconds ago, or years ago? How could I possibly know?

Feeling the heavy weight of moving my head, I looked out of the painting. Perenelle was still there. And the door was opening. Adam was walking inside. He hadn't aged, so not much time could have passed.

I turned back to Max. "Perenelle will get us out once it's safe."

"I don't think that's going to happen. Look."

I pulled my gaze from the small form of Max's reflection back to the outside world. Adam's movements showed me he was screaming, even though his voice sounded like a whisper through the veil of the painting.

He held a glass test tube filled with a granulated substance. I couldn't tell what it was, but I knew in every fiber of my paint-created body that it was poison. Adam tossed it into Perenelle's eyes.

She screamed, and this wail I could hear. The howl pierced the two worlds and nearly shattered my eardrums and broke my heart.

Adam had blinded the woman whose life was color and who was the one person who knew Max and I were inside the painting.

CHAPTER 57

I screamed, but Adam and Perenelle couldn't hear me.

"We have to get out and help her," cried Max. "Why can't I move?"

My heart—whatever it was made of right now—tightened in my chest. Max didn't fully comprehend our predicament. We weren't simply hiding in a painting. We had truly transformed, but it wasn't our own intent that had changed us. It was Perenelle's power with color, pigments, and paint that had brought us into the painting. We were helpless.

"We're not helpless," Max said.

I would have fallen to my knees if I hadn't been trapped in suspended animation. "You heard me?"

"You were talking to me."

"I was only thinking about what I should tell you. I wasn't using my voice."

"Zoe. You have no voice here. I understand enough to see it's our essences that are here—our spirit and soul combined—but our physical bodies are only representations."

"Our vocal cords don't exist." I felt my way through what Max had said. He was right. And it meant far more than he imagined. "It's our *intent* that matters here."

"You have an idea. I can tell."

I looked out of the painting. Perenelle was on her knees, her hands grasping helplessly at her eyes.

"We can't help her until we get out," said Max. "How do we do it?"

"I don't know if it will work," I said. "But you know about the penultimate step of an alchemical transformation."

"When the opposing elements finally come together," he said, "right before transcending into something new—the elixir or the stone or the new pure element the alchemist was working to create."

"Exactly," I said. "The Chemical Wedding, when sulfur and mercury, the sun and the moon, have gone through all of their challenges—all the chemical steps of alchemy—and are able to join forces."

"The opposites have united."

"The rational and the intuitive?" asked Max.

"You're talking about the two of us now."

That was the challenge Max and I had to overcome from the start. He'd consciously chosen a life of rationalism, rejecting anything that couldn't be fully understood. I followed my heart and let my senses lead me. It's how I'd discovered my aptitude for plants long before I had a mentor to teach me.

"You were already talking about us," said Max.

Was I? I'd been thinking about Nicolas and Perenelle. Traditionally in alchemy, sulfur is the male solar energy, the Red King, and mercury is the female lunar energy, the White Queen. But with Nicolas and Perenelle, nothing was average about them, even their alchemy.

Nicolas had the mercurial, curious personality, a "Renaissance man" before the Renaissance existed, always wanting to understand the whole world around him, but never interested in wielding power. Perenelle was filled with a sulfurous fire that burned in her to escape the narrow confines of what was expected of a talented woman of her time, erupting in her passion to be so talented a painter that the hidden alchemical messages in her artwork would be displayed for people who weren't the chosen few to study alchemy if it called to them.

The Flamels didn't flip the rules of society or of alchemy, but they bent them. The White King and the Red Queen were the most powerful alchemists who'd ever lived, and they were the ones who'd raised me in their alchemical training. Nicolas was the nursing mentor, and Perenelle the jaded protector. With them as my guides, I'd achieved the final stage of alchemy far younger than perhaps anyone alive.

"You're their alchemical child," said Max, sensing my thoughts. "The final step of alchemy. If anyone can get us out of this painting, it's *you*."

"No," I said. "You're wrong. The only way I'm getting us out of here is with your help."

Max and I were the opposites who together might just be powerful enough to break free. He and I weren't the same as Nicolas and Perenelle. Max was sulfur and I was mercury, but I was the sun where he was the moon. We weren't balanced enough on our own, and we were so much younger than the Flamels. But together?

I tried to lift my legs, but I didn't even know if I had legs. If I could only get to Max, we could try—

"Hold out your hand to me," he said.

"You're too far away."

"I'm right here."

I felt his hands on mine, and then I felt a band of copper slip onto my ring finger. A malachite stone of swirling green was set into the band.

Malachite. The stone of transformation.

"This wasn't exactly the proposal I was planning on," said Max. "I can't get down on one knee, because I can't feel my knees. But… Zoe Faust, I don't know how much time we'll have together, but I love you more than the sun and the moon and everything in this world that I don't claim to understand. I was hoping for a real wedding, but even if an alchemical Chemical Wedding is all we get… Will you marry me, Zoe?"

My body buzzed, and I could feel every molecule of my paint-formed body down to my toes. Toes? I could feel my toes!

"Yes," I said as I jumped into his arms.

I'd moved from Thomas's eye to young Zoe's eye. It *was* possible to move.

I kissed Max. He tasted of copper and fire and flower petals and quicksilver and a hundred other elements that I was at one with. But the strongest of all was the green malachite.

"How did you keep the stone with you?"

"It's a copper mineral."

"And copper is one of the elements in Perenelle's paintings. She sensed it. I don't know how much time is passing, but while we still have a chance, we need to try and get to her."

I also needed to save something important to her. Her notebook. I couldn't see it clearly, but I felt its energy. It was a new addition to the painting, like me and Max. I reached out and felt my fingertips grip the thick parchment. I sensed the oak galls of the ink in its pages. This was her notebook.

I kissed Max one last time, not knowing if it would be the last time. I didn't know what would happen when we tried to pull ourselves out of the painting. Would we leave part of ourselves behind? Would we break our bodies, spirits, or souls? This was untested territory.

Focus your intent on getting us out, I said to Max in my mind, *us saving Perenelle, and having a life together.*

I know you'll miss Thomas.

He's not really here. It's his memory. You're the one who's really here. You and our life outside of this painting.

I shared my intent with all the elements I could sense around me, grabbed tightly hold of Max, and pulled as hard as I could.

CHAPTER 58

From the Typewriter of Dorian Robert-Houdin

```
The Culinary Alchemist's Toolbox

   Patience is critical, as transformations cannot
be rushed. All elements have their natural rates
of change. However, there is sometimes a need for
speed. When you have less time at your disposal,
choose  a  recipe  accordingly.  Select  one  with
elements  that  may  be  prepared  and  reach  their
state  of  perfection  in  less  time.  Or,  in  an  emer-
gency,  added  heat  might  be  the  right  decision.
```

"Does this old car not drive any faster?" Dorian peeked out from underneath a scratchy tartan blanket to scowl at Nicolas Flamel from the cramped space at the foot of the front seat.

"From what I've read of the Beetle's history," the old alchemist said, "I don't believe it has ever gone as fast as other cars on the road."

It was Friday, so Brixton and his friends were in school, unable to assist in the rescue. That meant they did not have Ethan's fast car.

The boy's car was shiny, new, and expensive, so at least Dorian *assumed* it was fast.

"Can you not press the foot pedal harder?"

"It's pressed," Nicolas said, his voice terse, "as far as it will go."

"This is a poor choice for an automobile," Dorian muttered as he attempted to free his clawed foot from the undercarriage of the seat. He was worried that Zoe had not answered her phone as Nicolas attempted to call her on their drive. *Drive?* Were they going fast enough to be legally permitted on the highway? *Stroll* was more like it!

"This little car has a history of transporting curious souls like ourselves," Nicolas added.

"At this rate, the police will reach the cabin before us!"

"Wouldn't that be a good thing?"

Pfft. Dorian felt responsible for Zoe's painting being stolen, which set in motion this week's tragic events. He wished to redeem himself. Zoe had been the one to solve the crime—with his invaluable assistance, of course. Was it too much to ask that he be the one to rescue his friends and capture a killer?

"Of course I wish the authorities to come to the rescue," Dorian said aloud. Nicolas must have been worried for his beloved wife, so Dorian did not need to add insult to injury.

As the old car sputtered on the highway, Dorian was filled with such trepidation that it barely crossed his mind that during this time on his own with Nicolas he might broach the subject of the public authorship of his cookbook. This was not the appropriate time for such discussions, no matter how noble the project might be.

After what felt like an eternity, the rumbling motorcar down-shifted, and the sounds of other cars fell away.

"We have arrived?" Dorian peeked out from the coarse blanket once more.

"According to my phone, we're nearly there."

A faint humming sounded, followed by tires skidding to a halt.

"The killer!" Dorian cried. "He is escaping?"

"Not quite," said Nicolas, and his voice now held a note of hope. "I believe the expression is that the cavalry has arrived."

"Did we make it in time?" Brixton asked a moment later.

Dorian tossed off the blanket and uncurled his cramped body. Looking out the window, he saw all three friends. "You escaped the confines of your educational prison?"

"Of course," said Ethan.

"We all happened to have family emergencies come up," said Veronica. "What's happened? How can we help?"

They proceeded in Ethan's car with the quieter engine and room for the five of them. Minutes later, they reached the small cabin in the woods. Dorian was hiding, so he could not see it, but he knew they had arrived when they were greeted by the horrifying sound of a scream.

Before the car had come to a full stop, Nicolas flung himself out of the car. Dorian pulled his cape over himself and followed the others out of the car. Nicolas rushed into the cabin like a berserker in a trance. The others followed with only slightly more trepidation.

The site they found inside was most curious indeed.

Max was on the floor, wrestling with Adam White, while Zoe clutched a small notebook and attended to Perenelle, who appeared to have suffered an injury to her eyes. Nicolas ran straight to his wife, ignoring the fact that Adam was holding a vial of a foul substance above Max's face. In another moment, the glass vessel would tip enough to spill onto Max.

Before Dorian could think rationally enough to hide beneath the voluminous hood of his cape, he flapped his wings and took flight. Swooping over the two men, he yanked the glass vial from Adam's hand. As Dorian touched down with the caustic mixture safely intact, the teenagers charged Adam, knocking him over and holding him down.

Max, for his part, moved sluggishly. Dorian presumed he had been drugged. With the brutish Adam no longer above him, Max rallied. He flung open the kitchen cabinets, as if searching for something. Dorian hoped it would be a lid for the jar of whatever it was Adam had wished to harm Max with, but instead, Max retrieved a spool of duct tape from beneath the kitchen sink.

Nudging Brixton and Ethan from where they were sitting on Adam, and Veronica from where she held the man's arms, Max twisted Adam's arms behind his back and wrapped his wrists with tape.

"I can take that," Zoe said to Dorian as she gingerly lifted the glass vial from his hands. "You saved Max. Thank you."

As sirens sounded in the distance, Dorian beamed at his friend. Perhaps he had not failed her after all.

CHAPTER 59

I felt a surge of affection for Dorian. He'd swooped in to grab the caustic granules Adam had been about to toss onto Max's face, saving him from suffering the same fate as Perenelle. The vial held a synthetic mixture I couldn't identify beyond sensing its toxicity, so I found a cork stopper that fit the lid.

Nicolas was caring for Perenelle, so she was in excellent hands. My own hands shook as I made sure Dorian was covered by his cape. I couldn't quite grasp the gravity of what had happened.

"I believe it is time for me to take my leave," Dorian said as the sirens grew louder. "Will you be safe? What is that foul smell? Is something on fire?"

"The *Brother and Sister* painting," I said, feeling a catch in my throat as I spoke the words aloud. "Adam burned it as soon as I got out of it. All that's left is ashes." I pushed back a wave of emotion threatening to seize control. The situation wasn't yet under control.

"You were *inside* the painting?" Dorian blinked at me.

"I'll fill you in later," I said, eyeing Adam.

He was on the other side of the room, squirming under his restraints. He seemed to be focused on Max, but it wasn't a wise idea to explain the full series of events to Dorian right then. Adam thought Max and I had come from a secret back door in the cabin that he hadn't known about. Since people only see what they're ready to believe, it never occurred to him that we'd been inside the painting. He only thought we'd damaged it as we rushed through the hidden door to rescue Perenelle. Knowing he was about to be overpowered, he lit it on fire to capture the ashes that he believed were a necessary ingredient for the pigments he desperately wanted to create.

"We're safe enough," I told Dorian. "Perenelle is badly hurt. I think it's beyond what Nicolas and I can do. I hope that's an ambulance."

As the wailing of multiple sirens became almost deafening, Dorian slipped out the window.

Veronica rushed up to me, saying, "There are some smoldering ashes in the other room. I told Brix not to splash water on them. We didn't know what materials were in there, so was that right?"

I expected to feel my insides twisting with anguish as she talked about Thomas being reduced to smoldering ashes. But I didn't. Because it wasn't really Thomas in the painting.

"Leaving the ashes alone was the right thing to do," I assured Veronica.

"I failed her," Adam moaned. "I failed Lily."

"It wouldn't have brought her back," I said, thinking of Thomas. "Painting your sister's image, no matter how beautifully, will never replace her."

"You don't understand. I should have been with her that day when she went swimming. But it was summer. I wanted to have fun with my own friends. There was supposed to be a lifeguard on duty." Adam choked back a sob.

The sirens stopped, and the kids went outside to meet them. Two paramedics appeared first, and I directed them to Perenelle. She insisted on walking on her own and going outside with them, but she accepted Nicolas's steady hand.

"I only wanted to bring her back," Adam whispered. "It all got out of hand."

Max wound the tape around Adam's wrists one more time, then leaned back and steadied himself against the wall. Pulling ourselves out of the painting had taken so much of our energy. Max looked as if he'd used the last of his reserves securing Adam, who was lying face down on the floorboards.

I stepped between Max and Adam. "Why did you kill Betty Kubiak? That's the one thing I can't figure out."

"It wasn't supposed to happen," he said. The fight had gone out of him. He was no longer squirming, but he turned his head to the side to look up at me as he spoke. "Betty was never supposed to steal your painting. I only wanted a small sample. Willow's research into the history of science combined with April's recipe succeeding showed me the truth. There are special qualities in some pigments that modern science hasn't figured out yet."

"Pigments like the ones in *The Apothecary's Cabinet*."

His chin scraped the floor as he nodded. "Oberon is great at art history research. From his work, I had a list of paintings I thought had similar special colors. When I learned one of the paintings had been sold to the husband of a local artist, I thought it would be easy to see it and take a sample. But I wasn't even sure I had the right Nicolas Flamel. There was so much secrecy around the painting. I made a mistake when I offered to buy it."

"So you needed a new plan," I said.

"I knew Betty from the local art scene. I'd always thought she looked a bit like an art historian whose photo I'd seen on a few of my books. So the idea came to me that she could pretend to be a respectable art historian. Since money couldn't buy access to the painting, I thought whoever Nicolas had given it to would at least show it to a scholar, and she could take a small sample. But you were protective of it, so she had to follow you home. She acted recklessly. Someone surprised her, so instead of slicing out a tiny corner of the painting you'd never miss, she panicked and took the whole thing. I was so angry she'd messed up our plan! We fought. I didn't mean to hurt her. She hurt me, too."

"You knew the authorities would find your blood on her," I said. "So you made up the story about a theft."

"None of this was supposed to happen," Adam howled.

Detective Vega came through the door. She pulled Adam to his feet and arrested him.

"Wow." The detective gave a start as she took a proper look at her surroundings. "This cabin looks just like that *Apothecary's Cabinet* painting."

CHAPTER 60

I barely had time to catch my breath in the week that followed the arrest at the cabin.

Perenelle spent one night in the hospital, insisting the next morning that she was well enough to go home, even though she hadn't regained her sight. She wasn't in pain, she could see shapes and colors, and her emotional state was better than I had anticipated for an artist who'd been blinded.

Nicolas and I went with her for her follow-up appointment, and the doctor told her it was entirely possible she'd regain her eyesight, given time, but she'd have to wait and see.

As Perenelle waited for her body to heal, she had another project. Since I had saved her notebook before the painting was destroyed, the notebook and Gwendolyn's meticulous research provided us with enough proof to set the historical record straight. The two of them had already begun collaborating on a book that told the truth about Philippe Hayden's life, legacy, and recipes. A truth that spoke more broadly to the injustices in the world.

They'd already hired two research assistants to help them with the project. Veronica was the first. She'd be helping read things that Perenelle could no longer see. The second was a nontraditional college student from Gwendolyn's university. He was studying art history while working as a security guard, and he spoke several languages fluently from the time he'd spent in the military. His skills might come in handy.

Perenelle and Gwendolyn were also now official members of a new incarnation of the Brushstrokes and Brimstone Society.

Detective Vega got a formal confession from Adam White, so the case wouldn't go to trial. I was glad about that for many reasons, not least of which was the fact that he was convinced the police were secretly using a drone shaped like a gargoyle. He was also suffering from a rash caused by poison oak he'd disturbed while searching for his missing hostages. I can't say I wasted much time feeling bad for him, but it's my nature to be a healer, so I couldn't resist giving the detective a chickweed salve for his skin.

Special Agent Mitchell was helping Willow and Oberon navigate a voluntary product recall process, which involved working with a federal regulatory agency. The agent's colleagues were amazed once again at her sixth sense for sniffing out crimes. She'd been thinking about retiring, but now realized her continued value in both her careers: official and underground.

Renaissance White would be ceasing operations, but Willow and Oberon hoped to continue their initial vision of combining modern methods and true alchemical inspiration. As soon as they made sure the recall was complete and had shut down operations, they wanted to get back to working on a vibrant color similar to Scheele's Green, but without the toxic arsenic that had killed people with color in the 1800s. They planned to call their non-toxic pigment April's Green, in honor of Oberon's wife and Willow's best friend whose favorite color had been green.

Veronica, Brixton, and Ethan were initially threatened with disciplinary action by both the school and their parents. However, as soon as their actions were found to be directly connected to removing a potentially lethal paint from the hands of two dozen students at the school, they were hailed as heroes. Veronica was also getting involved with the broader local effort to track down every paint sample that had been given out in Portland. We still didn't know exactly what would happen when the paint finished breaking down, so it was best to contain it.

Nicolas and Dorian were discussing the possibility of collaborating on Dorian's *Culinary Alchemy* cookbook. Dorian would be the primary writer, but Nicolas wished to retain editorial privileges, since his name would be on the book. I was eager to watch the transformation of Dorian's idea into a fully formed book. *Culinary Alchemy: The Art of Transforming Simple Ingredients into a Feast of the Senses* might take a while to write, but I couldn't wait to read it.

As for me, it had taken no time at all for me to get used to the malachite stone on my finger. The ring from Max fit so perfectly that it seemed like it had been molded to the imperfections of my skin, and I felt like part of me was missing when I removed it to work in the garden or take a shower.

Yet I also woke each day with a vague sense that I was mourning a loss, though the source of my grief slipped away from me each time I reached for it. The portrait of Thomas was gone, but I didn't think that was it. When I'd been inside the painting with Max, I knew it wasn't really Thomas who was there. It was his memory. A young man who'd lived intensely and been loved by many. I didn't need the painting to remember him.

That's what Adam had gotten wrong about grieving for his sister. Nothing could replace his beloved little sister, Lily, but he filled the void striving for something that would never have mattered, even if he'd been able to recreate the colors he envisioned.

Adam was behind bars where he couldn't hurt my loved ones, the paint created with backward alchemy was being recalled so it wouldn't poison anyone, and I was at peace with losing the painting of Thomas. Why, then, did I still feel a vague sense of bereavement? It must have been the loss of Perenelle's vision I was grieving. Even though I'd been worried about how powerful her alchemical skills had grown, I hated that she'd lost her sight.

"Two cups of lemon ginger tea," Max said as he backed through the kitchen's swinging door holding two mugs.

The sweet aroma of the tea held a hint of spice. The invigorating scent grew stronger as Max joined me on the couch. It was a full week since we'd gotten engaged inside the painting, and in the aftermath of everything that needed to be wrapped up, we hadn't had much time to ourselves. We finally had a couple of hours together this morning. It was raining outside, or we would have been sitting on one of our back porches. But as long as I was with Max, it didn't matter where I was.

"I've been meaning to ask you something," he said as he handed me the mug. "Whatever your answer, it's okay."

"You know you can ask me anything." I hadn't thought it possible to fall more in love with Max, but feeling his essence on an alchemical level while inside the painting had magnified our connection.

"When I asked you to marry me," he said, his voice barely above a whisper, "I realize you might have felt pressured by the strange circumstances—"

I sat up straighter. "Don't you dare undo the most romantic proposal I could ever imagine."

"You didn't feel you had to say yes?"

"Of course I had to say yes, because I *wanted* to say yes."

"Even though our age difference will only grow greater?"

"We'll figure out the problems of the outside world together. I've lived through far more serious challenges and overcome them. As long as you don't want to take back your proposal—"

"*Never*. There's nothing I want more than to spend my life by your side."

I blew on my steaming tea. "Even if there's often a gargoyle at my side as well?"

Max laughed, and before he could reply, knuckles rapped on the front door.

"Expecting a guest this morning?" he asked.

I got up and peeked through the curtains. When I saw who it was, I ushered Nicolas and Perenelle inside. They were wet from the rain, and Nicolas wasn't wearing his coat. It was in his hands, shielding a canvas.

"Perenelle insisted this couldn't wait," Nicolas said with a grin. Perenelle was smiling as well.

"Your vision?" I asked her.

"Not quite," she said. She was looking in my direction, but not meeting my gaze. "I'm still only able to see shapes and color, not details."

"She hasn't been able to use her alchemical paint," said Nicolas, "but she's discovered something else. Is Dorian here? I'd hate for him to miss the unveiling."

"In the attic," said Max. "I'll get him."

They returned less than a minute later, as Nicolas was about to burst with excitement from whatever he was shielding with his coat.

"Want to do the honors, my dear?" Nicolas asked Perenelle. He handed her the canvas hidden by his coat, and she held it up in front of me.

Lush greens of all shades covered the canvas, with two lively, abstract figures in the center. The shapes were simultaneously indistinct and recognizable.

"It's me and Thomas," I whispered. We looked nothing like we had in the *Brother and Sister* painting, but there was no question about what I was looking at. The love and intent that had gone into the original painting that was now destroyed was every bit as present here. And more importantly, I didn't have to hide this one away.

"This is a work of beauty," Dorian said. "A true masterpiece. A contemporary update to abstract impressionism."

"It's amazing, Perenelle," Max echoed.

"I love it." I took it in my hands and set it on the mantle before wrapping my arms around her in a warm hug. I didn't need to grieve for what Perenelle had lost, because she hadn't lost the most important elements of her being.

"I hoped you'd like it," she said, squeezing me back.

"This calls for a celebratory feast," said Dorian. He scampered to the kitchen.

"I know you and Max must be eager to plan your wedding," Perenelle said to me, "but there's one more serious matter to attend to first."

"The backward alchemy book," I said. That book that had somehow made its way to the British Library didn't have power on its own, but it was still a potential danger. "It's a long flight to London, so we'll have plenty of time to plan the wedding on our way."

"I heard that!" Dorian called from the kitchen. "Do not forget to book passage for a steamer trunk with a gargoyle statue and snacks packed inside. I cannot wait to explore the intrigues and culinary delights of London."

THE END

The Accidental Alchemist Mysteries will continue in October 2025 with
A Gargoyle's Guide to Murder!

Never miss a release! Keep up with all Gigi's latest books and get a free novelette and more recipes by joining Gigi's newsletter. *Scan the code below, or go to www.gigipandian.com.*

Read on for recipes and more goodies!

Scan to subscribe to Gigi's newsletter!

RECIPES

SALTED CARAMEL SAUCE (VEGAN)

An easy homemade caramel sauce that doesn't use butter and takes under 10 minutes to make. This is a recipe where Dorian would note that it's important to pay attention and not leave the stove.

Ingredients

- 1 cup brown sugar
- 1/4 cup coconut oil
- 1/4 unsweetened oat milk creamer or coconut cream*
- 1/4 tsp salt

Directions

Whisk the sugar, coconut oil, and cream together in a heavy saucepan and bring to a boil, then reduce heat to medium low. Continue whisking roughly once a minute for 5 to 8 minutes, until the simmering mixture has slightly reduced and reached a temperature between 225 and 300°F. If you don't have a cooking thermometer, simply watch to make sure it doesn't burn, and remove from heat after 8 minutes.

Stir in the salt, then transfer to a glass container to cool at room temperature.

The caramel sauce will harden as it cools, so it's ideal to add it to recipes the same day you make it. But if you don't use it up that day, store it in a covered glass container in the fridge for up to two weeks. To soften enough to use the leftover caramel sauce (which will have become a block of caramel candy!), remove it from the fridge at least one hour before using.

*Coconut cream is sold separately in small cans, but it's also the hardened cream at the top of cans of full fat coconut milk. So if you don't have a creamer on hand for your coffee, coconut cream serves the same function in this recipe.

This isn't a true caramel, but is an easy way to get a caramel-like flavor without cooking. Add a dollop of this caramel-like sweetness to anything that could use a pop of creamy sweetness, like the cookies below.

Ingredients

- 1 cup pitted dates, soaked in hot water for 10 minutes
- 1/2 cup full fat coconut milk
- 1/2 tsp vanilla
- 1/4 tsp salt

Directions

Add the dates to a blender *without* soaking water, but don't toss the soaking water yet.

Add the rest of the ingredients and blend until smooth, roughly 1 minute in a high speed blender. If the mixture is too thick, add some of the date's soaking water little by little, until it blends well into a sauce.

Use immediately, or store in the fridge for up to two weeks.

ALMOND BUTTER OATMEAL COOKIES (VEGAN, PLUS A GLUTEN FREE OPTION)

This recipe works well either as breakfast or dessert—the only difference is whether you drizzle caramel sauce on top for added sweetness!

Dry Ingredients

- 1 cup rolled oats
- 1/3 cup all-purpose flour*
- 1 tsp cinnamon
- 1/2 tsp baking powder
- 1/2 tsp vanilla
- 1/8 tsp salt

Wet Ingredients

- 2 Tbsp coconut oil
- 1/4 cup almond butter
- 1/4 cup maple syrup

Directions

Preheat the oven to 350°F and line a large baking sheet with parchment paper.

Mix the dry ingredients in a medium bowl. Melt the coconut oil on the stovetop or in a microwave, then stir the three wet ingredients into the dry mixture.

Scoop spoonfuls of the mixture onto the lined baking sheet, 2 inches apart. You should end up with around 12 cookies.

Bake for 12 minutes, then let cool on the tray.

While the cookies are baking, if you're making dessert cookies, make one of the salted caramel sauces to drizzle on top after they come out of the oven.

*Variation: For gluten free cookies, simply omit the flour (there's not much in the recipe to start with) and bake for only 10 minutes. This version will be softer and doesn't travel as well, but it's every bit as tasty.

AUTHOR'S NOTE

Much of the history in *The Alchemist of Brushstrokes and Brimstone* is true.

Nicolas and Perenelle Flamel truly lived, though there's no conclusive evidence that they were successful alchemists, only people who gave to charity and whose graves were supposedly discovered to be empty. My depiction of them is entirely fictional.

All the artists mentioned from history were real people except for artist Philippe Hayden, who is fictional. References to women artists whose work was misattributed to men for centuries are all true stories, portrayed to the best of my ability. The guild system in Europe began in the early Middle Ages and was almost exclusively the domain of men. That system transitioned to the academy system around the Renaissance, but was not initially welcoming to women. Individuals and organizations have attempted to right historical wrongs, but there are still many misattributed paintings hanging in museums, and lost works of art gathering dust in unknown basements, waiting to be discovered...

The process of creating pigments from scratch is truly complicated and laborious—and often poisonous. Historically, it's also been quite treacherous and deceitful, with countries spying on each other for color secrets they didn't yet possess. There's enough intriguing history in this realm for another novel! Many recipes for creating colors were lost to history, even before modern chemistry found close approximations. Fine artists of the present day still miss some obsolete colors, and in my research, I came across many artisans making their own pigments with traditional methods.

Artists of the past couldn't visit their local art store to buy tubes of paint, so as apprentices, they learned the process of creating it from their masters. But not all pigments could be created by individuals and needed larger scale production. Apothecaries sold raw pigments before Colormen began to provide artists with prepared paints around 300 years ago. There's a renewed interest in creating pigments from scratch, and there are terrific online resources to learn how to make your own dyes and paints, including videos from The Alchemical Arts and Lost in Colours.

Alchemy, as it exists in the fantasy world of my novels, doesn't exist. Please don't play around with any of the alchemical ingredients my fictional alchemists use. But Alchemy was indeed a precursor to modern chemistry, and art and science were once much more closely linked. Though perhaps they're coming together again. The acronym STEM (Science, Technology, Engineering, and Math) in education is often now being referred to as STEAM—with "Art" added to the mix. Art fosters scientific curiosity, after all.

The British Library uses yellow slips to signify restricted documents that scholars aren't allowed to photograph, either because of copyright issues or because they're sensitive to light. Sadly, a cyberattack on the library occurred in October of 2023, wreaking havoc and bringing its vast wealth of online research to a halt. As I write this note in the spring of 2024, services are not fully restored, but much in-person research has resumed. I was fortunate to conduct some of the research for my debut novel, *Artifact*, with a Reader's pass to the British Library in London, so it holds a special place in my heart. If you ever find yourself in London, it's worth a visit. I'll be heading there once more this year, to research the *next* Accidental Alchemist novel.

You can sign up for my email newsletter for more behind-the-scenes content at gigipandian.com/subscribe.

ACKNOWLEDGMENTS

With each new book I write, I'm indebted to so many people. My Fearless Foursome writers' group keeps me inspired and on track. Ellen Byron, Lisa Q. Mathews, Diane Vallere, what would I do without out weekly meetups? Thank you to Emberly Nesbitt for our café writing meetups, and Rachael Herron and Sisters in Crime for your online write-ins (shoutout to Kim Keeline). And I so appreciate my early readers who looked at the book when it was the seed of a good idea but still a wild mess.

Thank you to my publishing team, especially my editors Amy Glaser and Trish Long, my agent Jill Marsal, the team at Audible, and brilliant narrator Julia Motyka. Julia, I don't know how you breathe such life into each character in the audiobooks, but it's magic!

My amazing family, I'll never forget that you supported my writing from the start, long before my books were successful. I'm so lucky to have you. I didn't inherit the poetry gene from my mom, so thank you to my multitalented mom, Sue Parman, for writing the poem in Max's storefront typewriter.

I'm also grateful for the broader community of book people. There are far too many organizations, conventions, festivals, librarians, and booksellers to mention here, but if you're a book person, thank you!

And my readers, you're the best! An especially big thank you if you've recommended my books to a friend. It makes such a difference. I love hearing from you—and seeing your gargoyle photos! You can contact me through my website, gigipandian.com.

SELECTED BIBLIOGRAPHY

Brushed Aside: The Untold Story of Women in Art by Noah Charney

Invisible Women: Forgotten Artists of Florence by Jane Fortune

The Brilliant History of Color in Art by Victoria Finlay

The Alchemist's Kitchen by Guy Ogilvy

The Craftsman's Handbook by Cennino d'Andrea Cennini (written circa 1400)

The Lives of the Artists by Giorgio Vasari (first published in 1550)

Don't miss *A Gargoyle's Guide to Murder*, the page-turning ninth book in the award-winning Accidental Alchemist Mystery Series!

A vanished body. A deadly bookshop. A country house party full of suspects. Can a living gargoyle and an alchemist decipher the clues before poisoned pages claim another victim?

Dorian Robert-Houdin is used to living his life in the shadows, his existence only known to a few trusted friends. When a dangerous book from his past resurfaces, he follows his closest confidante, alchemist Zoe Faust, from Oregon to England to investigate.

Before he can examine the magical book, Dorian witnesses a murder amidst the foggy lanes of Oxford. But when he takes Zoe to the scene, there's no body—and no evidence a crime has taken place. Using his unique skills as a gargoyle, Dorian sets out to solve the baffling crime nobody else believes occurred.

When Dorian and Zoe discover a dead man in a bookshop filled with arsenic-laced books, the victim isn't a stranger—he's connected to the vanishing crime scene. The trail leads to a country house party where a group of bibliophile suspects have gathered and a storm is brewing. Could the killer be the mercurial Agatha Christie scholar? The prickly literature professor? The secretive rare books expert? With an unscrupulous book thief lurking, can sleuths Dorian and Zoe unmask a murderer before the next page brings them to a perilous end?

Get your copy now!

BOOKS BY GIGI PANDIAN

The Accidental Alchemist Mysteries

The Accidental Alchemist (Book 1)

The Masquerading Magician (Book 2)

The Elusive Elixir (Book 3)

The Alchemist's Illusion (Book 4)

The Lost Gargoyle of Paris (Book 4.5, a novella)

The Alchemist of Fire and Fortune (Book 5)

The Alchemist of Riddle and Ruin (Book 6)

The Alchemist of Monsters and Mayhem (Book 7)

The Alchemist of Brushstrokes and Brimstone (Book 8)

A Gargoyle's Guide to Murder (Book 9)

Jaya Jones Treasure Hunt Mysteries

Artifact (Book 1)

Pirate Vishnu (Book 2)

Quicksand (Book 3)

Michelangelo's Ghost (Book 4)

The Ninja's Illusion (Book 5)

The Glass Thief (Book 6)

The Cambodian Curse & Other Stories (Locked Room Mystery Collection)

The Secret Staircase Mysteries

Under Lock & Skeleton Key (Book 1)

The Raven Thief (Book 2)

A Midnight Puzzle (Book 3)

The Library Game (Book 4)

NEW SERIES FROM GIGI: THE SECRET STAIRCASE
MYSTERIES

An ode to classic locked-room mysteries, this series blends traditional and cozy, with a dash of romance and gothic undertones.

Book 4, *The Library Game*, is available now! **There's a body in the library—and everyone is a suspect.**

PRAISE FOR THE SECRET STAIRCASE MYSTERIES

"**Wildly entertaining.**" —*The New York Times Book Review*

"An enchanting new series . . . **a must-read.**" —Deanna Raybourn

"Pandian is **this generation's queen of the locked-room mystery!** A whimsical confection." —Naomi Hirahara

"**Excellent... a fresh and magical locked-room mystery** filled with fascinating and likable characters, incredible settings, and Tempest's grandfather's home-cooked Indian meals." —*Library Journal*

"**Pandian is in top form** in this thoroughly enjoyable series launch. . . Lovers of traditional mysteries with quirky characters will be well rewarded." —*Publishers Weekly* (starred review)

ABOUT THE AUTHOR

Gigi Pandian is a *USA Today* bestselling and award-winning mystery author, breast cancer survivor, and accidental almost-vegan. The child of cultural anthropologists from New Mexico and the southern tip of India, she spent her childhood traveling around the world on their research trips. She now lives in the San Francisco Bay Area with her husband and a gargoyle who watches over the backyard vegetable garden. A cancer diagnosis in her thirties taught her that life's too short to waste a single moment, so she's having fun writing quirky novels and cooking recipes from around the world. Her debut novel, *Artifact*, was awarded the Malice Domestic Grant, and she's won Anthony, Agatha, Lefty, and Derringer awards, and was a finalist for the Edgar Award. Her books include the Accidental Alchemist Mysteries, the Jaya Jones Treasure Hunt Mysteries, and the Secret Staircase Mysteries. Read more and sign up for Gigi's email newsletter at www.gigipandian.com.

bookbub.com/profile/gigi-pandian
facebook.com/GigiPandian
instagram.com/GigiPandian